NEMESIS

SERAYA

Published by SeRaya

Edited by Emily A. Lawrence (Lawrence Editing)

Cover by Cat (TRC Designs)

Interior Formatting by Sam Lynn

To those who are constantly pushed to fit into the mold of expectations and responsibilities put on them. It's okay to put yourself first and do something that brings you happiness.

AUTHOR'S NOTE

Readers discretion advised. *Nemesis* is a dark, contemporary romance and contains strong language, sexually explicit scenes, and other dark themes that may be triggering to some. It is my hope that I've handled these with the care they deserve.

Although I believe it's best to go in blind, it is important for me to make sure you have all the information you need before diving in. You can find a list of detailed triggers on authorseraya.com

PLAYLIST

Track 1: Déjà Vu by James Arthur
Track 2: Slowly by JON VINYL
Track 3: Face Down by Vedo, OG Parker
Track 4: The Beginning by WAR*HALL
Track 5*:* Carry Me by Tayc
Track 6: Butter by Devon Culture
Track 7: Blood in the Water by Joanna Jones as The Dame
Track 8: Belong to You by Sabrina Claudio (ft. 6LACK)
Track 9: Bghit W Ga3ma 7assit by Zouhair Bahaoui
Track 10: Mount Everest by Labrinth
Track 11: Play with Fire by Sam Tinnesz (ft. Yacht Money)
Track 12: That's How It Goes by Zoe Wees (ft. 6LACK)
Track 13: Hrs & Hrs by Muni Long
Track 14: You Put A Spell On Me by Austin Giorgio
Track 15: Vigilante Shit by Taylor Swift

Track 16: you should see in me in a crown by Billie Eilish
Track 17: Waiting Game by BANKS
Track 18: Addicted by JON VINYL
Track 19: Put On Repeat by Sabrina Claudio
Track 20: Love You Like Me by William Singe

PROLOGUE
SOFIA

I'd always found it fascinating that life could lead you one way and then turn on its axis the next, completely changing its trajectory.

Like here I was, just shy of my twentieth birthday, visiting my parents after a year abroad for college, when, just like that, my life changed completely. Fragments of bullets shaping where it went next.

They say there are five stages of grief. Denial, anger, bargaining, depression, and finally acceptance. Mine only encompassed one.

Revenge.

He stripped me of everything I had and I would be back to end him.

Patience was a virtue and I'd waited seven years to avenge their deaths. The promise of blood, chaos, and revenge filled the air, wrapping around my body in a tight grip while I watched him from afar.

CLICK.

CLICK.

CLICK.

CHAPTER 1
SOFIA

Gasping for air, I jolted awake, bolting upright. Terror seized my veins as I frantically pressed my palms over *that* side as though it would somehow prevent what happened next. But of course it didn't. The end result never changed.

A gunshot. Followed by piercing pain.

Blood.

So much fucking blood coating my front and pooling underneath my body, life seeping through the veil separating me from reality.

Utter stillness warping my senses before everything went dark.

Seven years.

Eighty-four months.

Two thousand five hundred and fifty-six days.

And yet, I could still clearly see the gun pressed to my father's head.

My mother *begging* for mercy as a bullet shredded my father's skull.

My mother *pleading* for him to spare us.

But none of it mattered. *He* certainly didn't give a shit. He just shut her up, gifting her the same fate my father faced.

You would expect the person executing your family to look like a movie villain, a sneer decorating their scarred face. But the man who stared me right in the eyes before pulling the trigger looked as normal as they came.

He didn't even bother to shield his identity because he wasn't expecting anyone to survive him.

My body was drenched in sweat, the thin material of my shirt matted to my heaving chest, my breathing ragged. I threw my legs off the side of the couch and ran a hand through my tangled curls.

"*Fuck*," I breathed out, allowing my eyes to adjust to my surroundings. My eyes roamed around me, the dim glow from the TV unveiling that I was in a different living room.

Relief washed over me when I realized I was in my run-down apartment and not where I once called home.

He even ruined the word home for me because now, every time I thought of home, all I could picture was crimson painting the floor, fragments of brain decorating the family photos hanging on the wall.

Shaking my head from the memory, I reached over and grabbed my phone, glancing at the time: 4:00 a.m.

These nightmares were a regular occurrence, and you would think that after seven years, I'd be used to them, but they never stopped plaguing my mind ever since that fatal night.

Knowing they wouldn't let me rest any further, I tossed the phone back onto the coffee table and leaned forward, resting my forearms on my knees, pushing the disturbing images to a deep corner of my mind as I attempted to regulate my heaving breaths.

In and out.

In and out.

In and out.

I kept going until my heart slowed, my muscles relaxing. I closed my eyes, taking in one last deep breath before standing from the couch and heading toward the bathroom at the end of the hall. The apartment was mostly submerged in darkness, the only light coming from the TV screen flickering.

My apartment wasn't anything special, but it was enough for what I needed it to be. The dark-brown couch I slept on sat in the center of the living room, while tables with files scattered onto them were set up throughout the space, the computer monitors I used for surveillance sitting on them.

There were empty paper coffee cups strewn across the countertops, and white to-go containers filled the room with the smell of takeout from the hole-in-the-wall across the street, leaving the nostalgic feeling of *mama's* cooking in their wake.

Groaning, I shuffled down the hallway and rounded into the small bathroom, flicking the switch on, the yellow bulb above the sink cabinet fluttering before it buzzed alive. I sighed and braced a hand on the side of the sink as I flipped on the faucet and glanced up in the mirror. A stranger's reflection stared back at me.

I watched as it lifted my fingers to probe against the ridges of my cheekbones, so sharp they cast deep shadows over the sunken skin.

My face looked drawn. Tired. Not that I'd had much sleep in the last few years.

I placed my hands under the running water and cupped a handful, bringing it over my face. I used the rest to swish around my mouth in an attempt to erase the metallic taste that seemed to linger when I relived the shooting.

After turning off the faucet, I flipped the knob in the shower behind me, the spray stuttering before the stream evened out. I waited for the steam to rise before stepping under, hoping the scalding water would wash over the sore muscles wounding my body and everything else that stuck to me.

I willed the punishing stream to replace the festering nightmares, allowing peace to douse over me, but the events from that night kept replaying endlessly in my mind. Every time I closed my eyes, I saw their faces and reviled myself for not being able to save my parents.

I wished I'd died that night alongside them.

I tried enjoying the sensation of the water pelting my skin, letting it cascade over my shoulders and down my body. I even tried to close my eyes and breathe deeply, attempting to shake off the anxiety clogging my pores. But all of my efforts were to no avail.

Instead, my breathing picked up, my head dropping as I braced myself on the wall.

Gunshots. Pleading. Screams.

Deafening silence.

I scrubbed roughly at my cheeks, trying to pull myself back from the brink of an attack. I stumbled back and pressed my back against the cold tile wall, sliding until I was seated, knees clutched to my chest.

I tilted my head back and let out a heavy sigh, the water scorching me with its heat and steam. I closed my eyes in defeat, angry with myself for letting my emotions rise.

Just for a little while, I promised myself.

That's how long I'd allow myself to mourn. How long I'd allow myself to *feel* the loss.

I sank even deeper into the tub and let the water trickle over my skin, focusing on the warmth it provided. My mouth parted on a muffled cry, capturing the taste of my salty tears mixed with the water trailing down my face.

Once the water ran cold, I stood and grabbed the shower gel, quickly washing myself before stepping out. Wrapped in a thick robe, I padded over to grab my pills, popping one into my mouth before sliding the medicine cabinet's door shut.

I swiped a hand over the fogged mirror, granting myself one more minute before I left the helplessness behind and let my anger push back the tattered edges of my grief. If I allowed the ache in my chest to grow, I would end up drowning in it.

My body slowly settled back into the only emotion that had been fueling me for the last seven years.

Revenge.

Back in the living room, I pulled my suitcase out from under the couch and changed into a pair of sweats, an oversized T-shirt, and a pair of unmatched fuzzy socks to warm my feet. I was still living out of a suitcase even after all these years, ready to move if the need arose.

I walked over to the kitchen to start a batch of coffee, when the mention of a familiar name filtered out from the TV, stopping me in my tracks.

Morales.

Heart pounding, I marched back to the couch and

reached for the remote lying where I'd been sleeping, then turned the volume up.

"Sources are confirming that Elena Morales, wife of Victor Morales, CEO of Morales Industries, has unexpectedly passed away in a fire that ravaged their summer home in Adrar," the reporter said. "As of now, authorities haven't released any information surrounding the events of her death. While we wait for more information, let's take a look at the live footage from the Moraleses' residence."

The scenery shifted to an English style country home before the camera frame zoomed in on a black town car making its way up the driveway. As soon as it pulled to a stop, a swarm of men in black suits walked out of the house and stalked toward the car.

They barricaded the car door while one of them opened it, allowing its occupant to come out. The camera panned slightly past them to land on the individual they were shielding and my throat tightened once it finally focused on them.

It's really him.

His black hair was slicked back, the salt-and-pepper scruff of his unshaven face emphasizing the sharpness of his features.

It was one thing to see him in pictures or when he haunted my dreams, but I was never prepared to see him *being*. Living his life carelessly, without regard for the lives he stole.

Reporters rushed toward them en masse, shouting questions and attempting to get a word from the newly widowed CEO, but one of his men pushed the cameras away as they advanced to the front door.

Another man, probably his attorney, stayed behind and turned to face the cameras.

"Mr. Morales is deeply affected by this news and needs time to process. We kindly ask for your discretion and privacy during this very difficult time."

As he finished, one of the reports tried to follow up his statement with another question, but the attorney quickly shut him down. "No further comments," he said before stepping away from the camera and heading toward the house.

It took a second for the information to sink in as the puzzle pieces slowly shifted, locking into their designated places.

The anchor's voice cut through my thoughts and when I looked up, the frame was back on her. I grabbed the remote again and flipped through the channels until I landed on a *Lalla Fatima* re-airing, needing, *craving* any sound as a welcomed distraction.

After the *incident*, noises in any form had become the only solace I sought. The deafening quiet was too much to bear, an incessant ringing combined with the shattering of flesh and bone always replacing it. So anything, literally *anything* else was better to drone it out.

Stalking to the other side of the room, I lowered on the

stiff plastic chair behind my desk and tucked my foot under me while I waited for my devices to power up.

Several worn notebooks were stacked beside the monitors and I sorted through them until I found the one I was looking for. The pages were colored with various shades of ink, filled with cramped writing.

The notebook contained everything I'd learned about Victor Morales. Every little detail, no matter how minute. From the moment his pathetic self was born, down to what he liked for breakfast.

I'd spent the last seven years becoming an expert on Victor Morales and everyone in his surroundings, each one of them with a dedicated notebook. I'd taken all my anger against the man and boiled down all my elaborate revenge daydreams into a single plan.

Once powered up, I connected my external hard drive and opened the news channel's website, scrolling to find the broadcasted footage, and made a copy of it. While the video downloaded, I reached for the manila envelope on the far left and opened one side to retrieve the recent pictures I'd taken.

Studying them, I peered into her gaze, into the haunted look ghosting her eyes. The average onlooker wouldn't notice the shadowed bruise under her eyes, the strategic distance she put between her and her husband, the slight wince when she moved. The average onlooker might not have seen the signs, but I did.

The video automatically started playing after it

finished downloading. I only glanced up when I heard his name called. When he came into the frame, I paused it and zoomed onto his face.

Smirking, I reached for last night's leftovers, tossed a broken piece of the cold meat-filled *briouats* into my mouth, then washed it down with black coffee.

This is my way in.

The loss of his wife was my perfect opportunity.

CHAPTER 2
SOFIA

I was always told that *everything heals with time*, but what people really meant to say was that time just gave more space for anger to well inside until it spread, infecting every single cell in your body.

More space for the wounds to fester and rot. Ironically enough, just like what was under this cemetery.

I had never been to a funeral before. The only one I'd ever wanted to attend, I wasn't able to because someone had put a bullet in me and left me fighting for my life. That someone being the catalyst for my presence here today, two weeks after his wife's death.

The graveyard was at the back of the church and was filled with rows upon rows of headstones etched with inscriptions. While everyone was inside for the service, I waited behind the thick trunk of a tree in the middle of the forest behind the burial site to watch him put his wife to rest.

At least he was given the opportunity to do so. I hadn't even been able to bury my own parents.

Having to bury someone you love was painful, but not being able to bury them was even worse. I had no place to mourn, no grave to tend.

The sky slowly grew dimmer, the clouds creating shadows above us right as the swirling wind picked up. Shivering, I pulled my jacket tighter against my body in an attempt to warm myself up as I continued to wait for the first half of the service to end.

It was another twenty minutes before a large group of mourners gathered around the empty grave pit. They moved to sit on the black chairs lined to the right while they waited for Elena's casket to be transported to its designated spot.

Victor Morales was amongst the crowd, leading them at the front.

The official ME report claimed that Elena Morales died of smoke inhalation at their summer house in Adrar where she was vacationing for the summer. The fire was ruled as an accident by the fire department, where they'd claimed a faulty wire had jumped and initiated what led to her death.

Elena's body had been so severely burned—making her beyond recognition—that they'd decided to proceed with a closed casket. Once it was in place, the priest's voice boomed across the lot, "Elena Morales was a beloved wife and friend. Now, her husband, Victor, would like to say a few words."

Victor Morales rose from his seat and made his way to the small stage where the priest was standing, stepping in front of the microphone. "Thank you, Pastor Hernandez," he said, giving a small nod of gratitude in his direction.

After all these years, you would think that the effect of his voice would have faded, but the sharp reminder remained.

Grief permeated the air, coating my lungs, but it was quickly replaced by the familiar bitter taste of anger. My heart squeezed tight at the memory of the last time I'd heard him, my eyes fluttering shut as the memory crashed into me like a tidal wave against my will.

THE SCREAMS. The gunshots.

My mother's lifeless body on the floor of our living room, her once vibrant brown skin now dull, tendrils of blood writhing like venomous snakes across the front of her robe.

Her eyes wide, fixated on me as shadows of terror clouded her expression when she realized that it was over.

And I was next in line.

THE MECHANICAL THRUM of the casket lowering into the earth brought my attention back to the present. I shook the flashbacks away before my eyes landed back on the man who took everything from me.

When the casket descended and disappeared from view, the priest gestured the cross sign over his chest, then closed his Bible and called to God by proclaiming an "amen," which was quickly followed by the echo of everyone else's "amens."

Morales bent down and grasped a handful of soil before tossing it onto the casket right as droplets of rain started to batter against my skin.

After paying their respects one last time, guests drifted away, a sea of black and umbrellas leaving the cemetery. I huddled closer to the tree, making sure to remain out of everyone's sight.

A few people stayed behind, chatting on one side, while his men motioned for Morales to move to his car, but he lifted a hand, stopping them as if he needed more time before leaving her.

Then, he just stood there, looming over his wife's dead body. As if he ever truly cared.

My hands trembled with the need to end this charade, but I shoved them in my coat's pockets instead, gripping the gun tucked inside, the cold metal stinging the urge away.

My longshot had improved over the years and I could easily end this with a bullet to his head. But a quick death would never be a satisfying enough end for him.

Revenge was so much sweeter when you could savor it.

Death was only one moment in time, but I wanted him to live in misery. I wanted to hurt him in the worst possible ways, wanted him to see the thing he loved the most seep from his fingers.

Control.

Since one of his most prized possessions was already underground, there was only one thing left for him to lose. One day soon enough, I would take joy in making sure he witnessed everything he'd *worked* for go down in flames.

Despite the storm picking up, he remained still. He was wearing a three-piece black suit, with polished black wingtips, the rain sluicing over his frame. His ebony hair was plastered to his face, a mask of grief etching his features.

From the outside looking in, people saw a heartbroken husband mourning his wife, which gave the opportunity to the few hidden cameras to snap a picture.

The man *loved* himself a good photo op.

Victor Morales loved to play the role of the poor widower in mourning as if that might garner enough sympathy to hide his rotten core. However, if you paid closer attention, you'd be able to discern his true colors.

The picture of a man more successful at painting his wife with his anger than honoring his marital vows of protecting her.

I unglued myself from the wet bark, pulling the hood

of my coat over my head before walking back to my car, the fallen leaves crunching beneath my shoes. Once in, I flipped the key in the ignition, my car rumbling to life as the sound of the rain pelting against the windows filled the stillness inside.

I waited for my car to warm up, the windows slowly fogging, before I shifted the gear in reverse. Right before I pulled out of my parking spot, my gaze wandered over his figure through the rearview mirror, knowing this wouldn't be the last time I would see him.

This was just the beginning.

Even if I had to make *'til death do us part* a reality.

CHAPTER 3
SOFIA - FIFTEEN MONTHS LATER

After the candles were blown, I peered up. The smoke vanished and unveiled the people seated around me. We were all settled around a large table covered with white linen, crystal flutes, and white china adorning it, the cling of cutleries scraping against each other echoing around us.

I carefully studied their laughing faces illuminated by the soft lights hanging down from the ceiling of the restaurant where this celebration was taking place.

The man of the hour must've said something funny, something I hadn't caught while lost in thoughts, since more shrieks of laughter filled the otherwise empty restaurant, which had been specifically rented for this event.

Most of the guests present tonight were either non-family members or from Bemes's most elite. He most likely invited them for the sake of publicity since Victor Morales was an opportunist, taking advantage of any occasion to show he was an exemplary family man.

But in reality, he was a fraud, a man hiding behind a curtain of violence and corruption while portraying the image of a loving husband and morally upstanding citizen.

The princess cut diamond of my new ring glinted off the dim lighting, and I glanced down, my heart squeezing at the sight of wearing someone else's ring.

A ring that isn't his.

A champagne flute appeared in my peripheral vision, tearing my eyes away from my hand to look at him as he handed me the glass.

I plastered a smile on my face before taking a small sip of champagne and glancing around the room. Everyone seemed at ease, laughing and smiling as they honored the union of two people joined by commitment, love, and loyalty.

All of them *completely* clueless that they were celebrating a shimmering illusion that had been carefully curated to present the image of a perfect and loving marriage.

But the most clueless of all was the one standing right next to me. Wearing a perfectly tailored gray suit and his signature deceiving smile for our audience, salt-and-pepper hair impeccably combed back, was *my dear and beloved husband.*

The man who vowed to protect and cherish me was the same man who executed my parents and pulled the trigger on me a little over eight years ago.

He was almost attractive, but I guessed it was fitting for the devil to be in a perfectly suited disguise, lavishing enough to lure away souls.

How could I marry such a man, you ask? Well, the answer was quite easy. I wanted him to feel betrayed by the one person he was supposed to trust the most.

Morales kept his inner circle quite tight, not extending it further than his immediate family and a few close associates. He was a God-fearing man who would only give his trust if a contract was bound by blood or faith.

And since blood wasn't on my side, I needed his downfall to be crafted around blinded faith.

Bringing down Morales was the only way to bring my family peace. To bring *me* peace. So I inserted myself in his life and seduced him into matrimony. Although that part didn't require much convincing.

You see, men weren't that difficult to discern. They were actually quite simple creatures. Their eyes immediately sparked with interest when they spotted vulnerability.

Show them the possibility of control and they would get down on their knees and beg to be granted an ounce of power.

After the funeral, I'd spent the next few days distancing myself from being *Sofia Maria Herrera* and becoming *Olivia Kane,* a twenty-six-year-old widow who had recently lost her husband to a tragic car accident and who had decided to move to the city for a fresh start, giving herself a chance to heal and rediscover herself.

Since I'd been put into protective custody, a lot of my personal information had been manipulated. But I still had gone through all the databases, combing through every possible record where my name had been mentioned—hospital stays, schools frequented, events attended.

Herrera had vanished within a few keystrokes and Kane had been born. Since most medical institutions had gone digital, Kane had been crafted after I'd hacked into the local hospital's patient records and had replaced a Jane Doe's file with her information.

My body and face had changed a lot over the years, so all I needed was a good pair of scissors and a box of black hair dye to become this new version.

After the loss of his wife, Victor had a habit of visiting the Mogador, a hotel a few blocks into downtown, like clockwork. Two weeks into following him there and learning his routine, I'd found myself sitting at the same bar, at the exact same moment he had been nursing his fifth whiskey, his nose and cheeks flushed from the alcohol.

The rest had been quite easy. Our conversation eventually had led to me opening up and sharing that I was newly widowed and new to town. He'd offered to show me around the city and a few weeks later, he'd proposed.

See, easy. It was a shame for him that he thought he was getting a sweet, innocent wife to keep at his side.

A smug smile tugged at my lips, but my attention snapped back when *my husband* splayed his hand on my lower back, pulling me closer to his side. He cleared his throat and gestured over our guests to silence them so he could recite his scripted speech.

After grabbing his glass with his free hand, he started spewing how grateful he was to have found a second chance at love with me.

I forced the hatred I had for this man away and shoved any hint of repulsion from his touch back down as I put my hand over his chest and plastered a well-practiced smile on my face while I waited for him to finish.

"To you, *mi amor*," he finally said, raising his glass in a toast before planting a chaste kiss on my cheek.

Everyone lifted their glasses in response and drank. I turned to whisper a "thank you" in his ear, then took another sip of my own drink, letting the bubbles distract me from the resuming chatter.

When our guests looked at me, they saw a devoted wife gleaming at her husband with love in her eyes, when I was actually fighting the urge to pick up my dinner knife and drive it into his neck, just so I could watch his blood decorate the white cake made in honor of our union.

The soiree was dragging on for longer than I expected,

slowly draining my social battery. I wasn't much of a people person and I would much rather be at home, on my couch, doing nothing, than dealing with people. But I had to change my habits and learn to become a social and caring wife to execute this role perfectly.

It wasn't always an easy task.

Being the wife of Victor Morales was an infuriating paradox. I was supposed to find my greatest happiness in giving and serving my *husband*, yet was also required to be independent. I was supposed to dress to impress, but not enough to attract attention. I was supposed to be successful and supportive, but not to the extent of over-shadowing him.

The only good thing about marrying him was that he was one step closer to his death and I was one step closer to my revenge.

When most of our guests started receiving messages from their babysitters to pick up their kids, my husband and I thanked everyone for coming and made non-committal promises to see each other soon.

After they all left, Victor's hand found my lower back once again, escorting us out of the dining room and into the lobby for us to wait for our driver.

The drive home was quiet. Victor spent it going

through his emails and notes his assistant left him regarding the meetings scheduled for this upcoming week and I was more than happy to not have to entertain him with idle conversation.

Our driver put the blinkers on before turning down the gravel road, slowing to a stop to enter the codes at the entry gates, which were installed a few months ago, courtesy of the paparazzi that kept harassing us ever since the announcement of our prompt engagement.

As soon as Omar parked behind the line of vehicles in our circular driveway, Jaxon, our head of security, emerged from the front door of the house and walked down to greet us.

Tall, with broad shoulders, his dark hair was shaved close to his scalp, emphasizing his strong brows-and-hazel eyes that complemented his dark brown skin. Jaxon had been working for Victor for the past five years, taking over after his father's retirement.

There were six other guards working under him, only two staying overnight while the others only came every now and then when Victor needed reinforced security on the premises. When they weren't at the house, they fulfilled whatever tasks Victor sent them to do.

"Anything to report?" Victor asked after climbing out of the car.

He glanced back at me and offered his hand to help me get out of the car. *What a gentleman.* I accepted it regardless since I was wearing these insufferable six-inch red bottom heels all because he'd thought they would match perfectly with the dress he'd bought me specifically for this occasion.

I wished Omar a good night and closed the door behind me.

Jaxon bowed his head in deference. "Nothing out of the ordinary, sir. Just a gift delivery for your anniversary. Rosa left it on top of the table in the entryway."

Linking our fingers together, Victor dropped his free hand on Jaxon's shoulder. "Thank you, Jaxon. If that's all, you and the others can take it easy for the rest of the night."

"Thank you, sir. Señora Olivia."

Jaxon bowed his head once more, then left to join the rest of the team in the back where their offices were.

We moved toward the front door, when my eye caught the blinking red dot signaling one of the security cameras around the property. There were five cameras in total covering the house. Three faced the front at different angles while one was in the back, covering the security team's wing, the last one covering the front gates.

A beautified prison where nobody could come in and nobody could get out. Well, unless you were me.

We walked up the stairs and through the large double black doors, stepping inside the house. Victor flipped the lights open and the crystal chandelier hanging on the high ceiling instantly lit up the space, the glossy wood floors gleaming under it.

As I looked up, I noticed the package on the large, black round table in the foyer that sat in front of a split white carpeted staircase. Victor approached the anniversary gift awaiting us while I removed my coat and hung it in the entry closet.

"I wonder who sent this," he mused.

Yeah, me too.

I glanced at him over my shoulder and watched him reach for the box, untying the ribbon around it before removing the lid. A startled expression marred his features.

"*¿Qué diablos?*"

"What is it, Victor?" I asked, worried.

My heels clicked on the wooden floors as I stepped closer to him. I scrunched my nose when the faint smell of gasoline filled the air. Standing behind him, I peeked over his shoulder just as he retrieved the object inside.

It was a small, identical replica of the summer house that had burned with his wife inside. A matchbox was leaning against the structure with a letter with his name written on the outside tucked underneath it.

He peered back at me over his shoulder and I returned what I hoped was a worried look.

As if I had no idea what is going on.

In another life, I could have been an actress with the amount of faking I'd had to do around this man.

He reached for the envelope, inspecting it. It was postmarked August 21, the date of the fire, and the return address was the address of their summer house.

"Victor." I paused. "What is this and why does it smell like someone doused it in fuel?" I asked again since he had ignored my previous question.

He ripped the top of the envelope open with his house keys, retrieved the note inside, and flicked it open before he started reading.

His shoulders tensed as he kept reading, his face paling, the blood slowly draining from it by the second.

As he finished reading, he looked straight ahead, his mouth tense as his expression changed again. But this time, rage settled over his features.

His jaw clenched and his knuckles whitened with how hard he was fisting the piece of paper. I whispered his name over and over, but he just kept staring at the note.

I attempted to soothe him with my touch, but he jerked his arm away, tossed the paper on the floor, and stalked toward the back of the house. He threw one of the sliding glass doors open and marched into the backyard, yelling Jaxon's name.

I crouched down and picked up the crumpled piece of paper to read its content.

A lit match starts with a flicker
Before it meets the air and arrogantly becomes
a flaming torch
Leaving the ashes of a beloved behind

Will you let history repeat itself?

I left my scribbled note behind, my knees cracking as I stood. From the kitchen, I stepped outside and followed Victor's strained voice chewing Jaxon's head off for not being more careful.

"How could you let this happen again?" he snapped, anger dousing off him. Jaxon apologized and relayed that they had seen no harm in the package since it was a gift for our anniversary.

"Victor, what's happening? What do you mean by *again?*" I interrupted, letting a fake tear slide down my cheek as I forced my bottom lip to tremble.

Victor quickly zeroed his attention on me. He gave a dismissing nod to Jaxon before marching toward me and pulling me against him, wrapping his arms around me.

When the security's office door closed, his hand was in my hair and he pulled me tighter into his chest, my arms limp at my sides. I closed my eyes and did what I thought would be appropriate in this situation by burying my face in his shoulder.

"It's nothing, *mi amor.* Trust me, I won't let anything happen to you," he murmured just above my right ear, trying to reassure me.

I shuddered in his arms, not from fear, but from the disgust that washed over me every time he touched me. I finally wrapped my arms around his middle and caught our reflection in the window from the door behind him.

My eyes locked on my reflection and a small smirk pulled at my features while I let another tear escape. Becoming the catalyst for Victor Morales's downfall felt like glorious retribution. Making him anticipate and fear the moment his world came crashing down would be exhilarating.

Let the games begin.

CHAPTER 4
THEO

My phone buzzed with a new message as I pulled into my driveway. I parked and turned off the ignition, then picked it up to find a message from Noah.

> Noah: Call you when I get out of the office. I got a job for you.

Noah and I had met when I'd suggested recruiting him for the academy. I had been sifting through applications and scores when I stumbled upon his. He had still been in college when he'd taken the test and managed an almost perfect score, without his knowledge, which was a rarity at the bureau.

When I'd first showed up on his dorm's doorstep with an offer, he'd initially slammed the door in my face. But after showing up every day like clockwork, he'd finally caved and accepted it.

After graduating, he'd started working for the DEA, while I went to work in organized crime. A few months into his new position, he'd been assigned to a high-profile case and had to move to Sardenya, a small island coasting the shores of Bemes.

He'd disappeared for a few years after his partner's death before coming back to become a training officer at the academy in Blackwell, which was two towns east of here. Rumors had been that he'd accepted the position to protect his late partner's kid, who'd survived the fire that killed his parents.

I hadn't heard from him ever since I'd left the bureau.

Until now.

I put my phone away and walked inside my house. Everything was quiet, felt empty. No personal possessions decorated it, no trace of the man I used to be. For years, I'd moved around every few months because whenever I stayed somewhere for too long, memories of what I used to have and lost crept in.

It hadn't been until last year that I decided to build this house and finally settle somewhere.

I laughed coldly under my breath at my pathetic reality. Pulling my mind from the unwelcome thoughts that tried to trickle in, I scanned the premises to look for anything out of place, a habit that stuck from my days at the bureau.

Once I was confident that nothing had been disturbed, I tossed my keys on the table beside the door and removed my gun from its holster, placing it into the drawer. I headed for the bathroom, stripped off my clothes, and stepped under the boiling water to wash today's case off.

After I'd spent the weeks following my resignation basking in loneliness at my place, I'd started dabbling in private investigation to quiet the thoughts that plagued my mind. If my brain wasn't constantly in working mode, it would crawl into a space where the voices would take over and I couldn't let that happen.

I didn't leave the bureau because I hated my job. I actually used to love it.

It was thrilling, *fulfilling*.

But it was never the same after she left. Nothing had felt real anymore.

It still didn't.

Showing up for work, even getting out of bed, became daunting. I was barely hanging on by a thread trying to find her until I was forced to move on. The bureau thought I had developed an unhealthy obsession and threatened to dismiss me if I didn't stop looking for her.

But how could someone move on from having the only person they ever fell in love with leave them? My work had always been my escape, but I had found solace in her.

That was until she vanished, taking a piece of my soul with her.

I washed the thoughts away with the last remnants of

soap and reached for a towel that I wrapped around my waist.

My phone rang as I walked toward my closet to get dressed. I almost ignored it, leaving it to go to voicemail, when I saw Noah's name flashing on the screen.

"You realize what time it is?" I hissed into the phone before setting it on speaker and placing it on the bed. I dried myself off, reached for a pair of black boxers, and pulled them on.

"I have a job for you," he said, completely ignoring my comment. I returned to my phone and sat at the edge of the bed, rubbing the damp towel over my head to dry off my hair.

Before I could ask him what he meant, the sound of heavy pounding against my door echoed through the house. I stood from the bed, grabbed my phone, and pressed it to my ear.

"Hold on a sec," I said to him while I headed into the living room.

My eyes darted out the window, but no cars were in sight. I made my way to the entryway and tossed the phone on the console table to pick up my gun. Clicking the safety off, I slowly approached the door and swung it open with one hand, drawing my gun up.

I was met with a completely unfazed Noah as he hung up on our call and placed his phone into the back pocket of his pants.

I gave him a quick once-over. He really looked like

shit. His dark brown hair was unkempt, his eyes blood-shot, with dark bags beneath them. Telling signs that he probably hadn't slept in days, something I was unfortunately quite familiar with.

He scowled at me and I lowered my gun, tucking it back into the drawer.

"You look like shit, my friend," I said, cocking a brow at him.

He offered me an annoyed glare before marching in, forcing me to step aside. "We need to talk and I don't have a lot of time," he stated irritably, holding up a file as he headed straight for the kitchen.

"Please." I waved my arm before shutting the door behind him. "Do come in and make yourself at home."

He stood behind the kitchen island and did a once-over, frowning when he noticed my state of undress. "Why are you only in your underwear?"

"I just stepped out of the shower. Didn't think I'd have company at *one* in the morning." I huffed, annoyed at his tone, as I went to my bedroom to put some clothes on.

I grabbed a shirt that was lying around and brought it to my nose to make sure it didn't smell before pulling it on, then stepped into a pair of sweatpants. I reemerged a moment later and took a seat in one of the island chairs across from him.

Leaning back in my chair, I started drumming my fingers against the marble countertops. "What's this all about?"

"I have a job for you," he stated, his whiskey eyes drilling into my dark ones.

I raised a brow, waiting for him to elaborate, when he thrust the folder he had in his hand in my direction and I reached out to grab it. Flipping it open, I retrieved the thick stack of papers inside and dispersed the contents out onto the counter.

There were a dozen black-and-white pictures of the same woman in different settings.

I tilted my head up. "Who's this?" I asked, confused as to why he was giving me countless snapshots of this woman.

He leaned against the stove and crossed his arms over his chest. "Olivia Morales. Your new assignment."

*Morales...*I played with the name around in my head a few times. The name seemed familiar, but I couldn't quite place it.

I reached for one of the pictures, analyzing it before glancing back up at him. "Who is she?" I paused when the word assignment finally clicked in my mind. My drumming slowed to a stop, a hollow laugh escaping me. "Wait, what do you mean *my new assignment?*"

"Victor Morales owns Morales Industries, the textile company that's looking to expand globally. Last night, he and his wife came home from their wedding anniversary dinner to a threat on his wife's life." He pointed to a picture of a scanned note.

My eyes quickly scanned the writing but stayed focused on the last words.

Will history repeat itself?

"What does this even mean and how does this have anything to do with me?" I asked irritably, flipping through the rest of the grainy surveillance photos.

They were all taken from a distance and the subject seemed to always be wearing glasses that were hiding the majority of her face. I couldn't get a clear picture of what she really looked like, but that didn't stop my eyes from roaming over her curvy figure and her dark curly hair that grazed the middle of her back.

When I looked at her, only one word came to mind. *Beautiful.*

He cleared his throat, snapping me out of my trance. "He's looking for someone to protect his wife and I gave them your name."

My fingers tensed over the picture I was holding, my brows furrowing. "I'm not a fucking babysitter and I don't have time for this," I said through gritted teeth.

"Like you have anything more interesting to do."

He looked over my unkempt living room before his gaze landed back on me.

I decided to ignore his snide remark. "Besides, why do you want me for this job? I left the bureau months ago, remember?" I pointed out. "Can't you give this to one of your newbies?"

His shoulders tensed, while his body straightened, his

expression turning serious. He hesitated for a second before letting out a heavy sigh. "You're the only one I can trust for this job."

Confused, my brows pinched together. "To watch over the wife of a billionaire?"

He avoided my gaze before reluctantly adding, "It's more complicated than that."

"Please, do elaborate," I retorted sarcastically. Leaning forward, I rested my elbows on the cold granite while waiting for his explanation.

"I can't," he snapped.

What the fuck? He was asking me for a favor and getting mad when I requested more details.

I stood up, frustration flaring up my insides. My jaw clenched and I closed the file, then handed it back to him, preparing to walk away. "Then you can count me out. You know where the door is. You can see yourself out."

He went quiet for a moment. Running his hands through his disheveled hair, he blew out a deep breath. "Listen, Victor Morales isn't who people think he is. I can't have my people dig into it, so I'm asking you this as a favor," he confessed, sounding defeated.

I searched his gaze, his tone perplexing me. Noah had always been so assured, so seeing him this tired and defeated over something like this didn't make sense.

There was a pause. "And you owe me."

Groaning, I ran my hands over my face and down my beard. I'd always been loyal to a fault, and Noah had covered for me so many times while I was out looking for her, desperate to find her during the months following her disappearance.

Disappearance, the little voice in my head scoffed, mocking me.

The look on his face combined with our past was what made me finally accept. "Fine," I breathed out.

This wasn't how I thought this would go.

A week later, I was on my way to their estate. Noah hadn't told me much about this assignment, only that I would be spending the next few weeks watching over Morales's wife until they caught the perpetrator.

Apparently, everything had already been set up before Noah even brought the offer to my attention; he'd only stopped by my place as a mere formality since he'd already discussed my *interest* with Victor's head of security, Jaxon Valdez. Someone who also happened to be one of his informants.

Noah had mentioned to him that I used to work for a private security company with the government before I branched out to work independently as a private investigator.

That was my story. No one really knew what I did for

a living, not even my family, which was what happened when you worked in organized crime.

Before leaving that night, Noah had ended up revealing that he was in the middle of investigating a drug cartel and had found out that Morales might be one of their close associates.

He'd kept his explanations vague and I wasn't sure what Noah was up to or why he didn't want his team at the bureau involved, but I knew Noah better than anyone. If he was being secretive, then he was probably trying to protect them.

A few hours after he'd left, I'd received an encrypted link with more information on the Moraleses. I'd then spent the remainder of the week learning about Victor's work and most importantly, his wife. Her digital footprint was practically nonexistent and there was barely any information about her life prior to marrying Morales, only that she'd been involved in an accident and had lost her husband.

Almost like she was a ghost.

What did I get myself into? Me and my stupid sense of loyalty.

I clenched my fingers around the steering wheel, pushing the notion aside right as I turned onto their street. As their house came into view, my eyes caught a glimpse of it.

The memento permanently etched on my skin, weighing heavily against my ring finger.

CHAPTER 5
SOFIA

I t had been exactly a week since the *package* was delivered and I had Morales exactly where I wanted him.

Suspicious of everyone and slowly losing his control and sanity.

Over the last week, he'd fired almost the entirety of his security team, hiring a completely new one, except for Jax, his most trusted advisor. He'd briefly mentioned wanting to hire someone specifically for my own safety, and we'd argued on the subject more than once, but he hadn't brought it up again.

He must have simply let the idea go, which wouldn't be surprising. He usually gave me everything I wanted, so this shouldn't be any different. Besides, I definitely didn't need another person to worry about.

I was finishing up a call with one of the caterers for the

company's annual charity event that was four weeks from now when I heard someone knocking on my office's door.

"Come in," I called out.

Jaxon stepped inside, placing his hands behind his back before nodding in greeting. Jaxon wasn't a man of many words. He tended to only speak when he deemed it necessary. Apparently, verbal greetings weren't part of that category.

"Yes, Mr. Valdez?" I prompted him.

He slightly pursed his lips at my use of the formality, especially after he'd been constantly asking me to simply call him Jax ever since we met. But formalities guaranteed that no connection or attachment would be created. I did like Jaxon, but if I ever found him to be a threat to my revenge, I'd have no other choice but to take him out.

"*Por favor, señora*, just Jax is fine," he pleaded before adding, "*Señor* Victor would like to see you in his office."

"About?" I asked, my brows pulling together in question.

Discomfort flickered in his eyes before he sealed his reaction and continued in his usual composed tone. "I believe it's better if he explains it himself."

Explain? What would my husband have to explain?

With a groan, I clicked out of the spreadsheet that contained the list of confirmed vendors for the gala and rose from my seat before following closely behind Jaxon.

My heels clicked against the hardwood floor as we made our way to Victor's office. Jaxon's knuckles softly rasped against the door, announcing our presence. He waited for the faint sound of a confirmation before opening the door and gesturing me inside.

Victor finished typing on his computer, then closed it and rose from his chair. Rounding his desk, he sat against the corner and reached for my hand, pulling me between the V of his thighs.

He glanced over my shoulder toward Jaxon, who'd stayed near the door, and gave him a dismissive "thank you." The door closed behind him with a soft click, leaving me alone with *my beloved*.

"You wanted to see me, *mi amor*?" I asked, swallowing the rising bile from the term of endearment.

God, I fucking hated calling him that, but I was supposed to play his loving wife after all.

He hummed. "Yes, *cariño*. We're about to meet your new bodyguard."

"My what?" I blinked up at him, my brows drawn together. My insides coiled at his announcement and my fingers twitched in his hands. The urge to ball them into fists boiled to the surface, but I regained composure, swallowing down my frustration.

I sifted through my repertoire that I'd spent years mastering and transformed my expression into a disappointed one instead.

"Victor, I thought we'd already talked about this? I don't need a personal bodyguard. We already have a team and I told you I was fine. I just got a little scared when we got the letter. I'm sure this was just an untasteful prank from one of your competitors to unsettle you, especially since you announced wanting to expand the company." I gave him a small smile in an attempt to ease his worries about last week's situation.

Victor's hands roamed over my sides and I had to wrestle my disgust under my carefully curated mask. My stomach clenched as he trailed them down to my hips, where he tightened his grip.

Here we go.

"This isn't your decision to make, Olivia," he said coldly. "Never—"

The soft click of the doorknob twisting interrupted his next words.

"Sorry for the interruption, Mr. Morales," said a deep, velvety voice from behind me, diverting *my husband's* wrath from me.

A familiar shiver ran down my spine, recognition flooding my body before my mind could register it. Because somehow I *knew*, I just *knew*, even though the probability of him being here was nearly impossible. Because there was no way it was him.

My mind was obviously playing tricks on me. It was the only plausible explanation.

I turned to discredit my hypothesis, when my gaze finally focused on the man who walked in.

No… It couldn't be.

The blood drained from my face and my mask faltered

when I came face-to-face with the one person I never thought I'd see again, the only man I'd ever loved.

The man I spent seven years trying to forget.

The man I left behind to kill another.

He stepped across the threshold, and the room instantly felt smaller. The air shifted, Victor's greetings fading into the background as everything seemed to come to a stop. As if he could hear my thoughts, he lifted his head and familiar dark eyes settled on mine, holding me in place.

I couldn't look away even if I wanted to.

It can't be. There is no possible way for him to be here. This has to be a dream.

The air pressure in the room dropped, leaving something heavy sitting on my chest, crushing it under its weight, stalling the breath in my lungs. My heart hammered against my ribs as blood roared in my ears.

How is this even possible?

I was prepared for every obstacle that would come my way, but I had never prepared for this.

Never prepared for him.

He is even more beautiful than I remember.

In front of me, dressed in an all-black suit, stood the only man who had ever haunted my darkest desires. The only person who showed me that I wasn't alone in this life after the murders.

The man I left to protect. And now he was back to protect *me*.

My chest ached at the thought, pain searing through my middle as if the bullet that had lodged inside years ago was resurfacing, leaving a firing trail as it crept up without warning, threatening to take me out at the knees.

He seemed to occupy more space than what I remembered. Everything about him just seemed *bigger*.

Despite the blaring alarm in my head warning me to break the connection, I couldn't resist taking him in. My gaze moved over his form. He was taller, had broader shoulders, and thicker thighs filled his suit. My eyes trailed over his face, taking in this older, more… ruthless version of him.

Tanned skin, dark brown eyes with a small speck of hazel in the left bottom corner of the right one, and full lips with a full beard decorating his jaw.

Even after all these years spent apart, he was still quite possibly the most beautiful man my eyes had ever landed on, and despite all the slight changes, he still was, still *felt* like my Theo.

Everything about him still felt so familiar, all the way down to the ache in my chest that had never left.

Fuck, is this why this hurts so bad?

Knowing how good he felt in my arms but not being able to run up to him. Knowing he'd been mine once and I'd forfeited the rights.

As he approached, a single tendril of his dark wavy hair fell down his forehead, brushing against his harsh brows, grays gracing his temples.

My mouth went dry and a tingle of awareness spread across the pads of my fingertips. A flush enveloped my entire body as the memory of my fingers running through that same hair, tugging, pulling him closer flooded my mind.

It'd been seven years, yet my body still reacted to him as if I'd only left yesterday.

The memory quickly dissipated when I realized he stopped in his tracks, a slight frown pinching the skin between his brows. His strong bearded jaw shifted as he took me in, his deep brown eyes roaming over my body in a slow, calculated assessment.

His eyes traced the shape of my face, sending a rush of warmth through my body. For a slight moment, we both shared the same stunned expression, an unspoken connection coursing between us. The longer I stared, the more I was convinced I was imagining him.

Until my name escaped his lips on a breath, confirming that this really was him, that he was really here.

"Sofia...?"

My name on his lips triggered something inside me, something I hadn't felt since the night we'd spent together.

A memory from that pivotal moment rose unbidden and I closed my eyes from the force of it, completely forgetting where we were.

Stolen glances and touches yielding under a burning

passion. Lips mere inches apart after an argument. Fingers tracing lines of a body as if they'd spent hours memorizing it.

A strong hold at the nape of a neck, a forehead dropping to another before a whispered, "I need to kiss you," was brushed against lips. And without waiting for an answer, they crashed together.

I JOLTED out of my daydream and the previously stuck air escaped in a *whoosh*, my chest compressing with the weight of shared memories.

Cold seeped into my skin as I noticed him studying me closely, the oxygen getting trapped on its way out. I almost averted my gaze, but I needed him to believe in the disguise I spent months, *years* crafting.

I had to act as if we were strangers, but this time while carrying the memories of him, of us. I had imagined seeing him again, imagined our reunion countless times.

But not now, not before all of this is over.

Panic swelled in my chest and it took everything in me to keep a neutral expression when everything inside me was strung tight, threatening to snap. I wanted to take a moment to recover from his presence, but none of that was a possibility. So I steadied myself, straightening my spine and standing a little taller than before.

He opened his mouth to continue, but whatever he was about to say was lost to the sound of *my husband* loudly clearing his throat. That's when I realized I had moved farther away from him, my hands now limp at my sides.

"Sofia?" Victor repeated, a hint of irritation in his tone.

As if in a trance, my soon-to-be bodyguard ignored his question, keeping his eyes fixed on me, the weight of his stare feathering a light touch against my skin.

Everything around us buzzed with a dangerous hum. As if *my husband* finally sensed the change in the air, I felt him move from the edge of his desk before he snaked an arm around my waist, fitting me back against him.

This might come across as a loving gesture, but Victor was an expert at that, *loving and attentive illusions*, when in reality his fingers were digging into my hip, reminding me of who I supposedly belonged to. But I didn't care that his fingers were making the scar on my hip itch with the promise of revenge because my eyes were still glued to our guest.

Victor tried to interject once again after failing to break our connection the first time.

"Mr. Alvarez, this is my *wife*, Olivia," my husband said, putting an emphasis on the word wife. Just another reminder to everyone in the room that I was his property.

But all I could think of was that he'd just confirmed once again that this was really Theo.

My Theo.

For a split second, something flickered in Theo's gaze. It was fleeting, *barely there*, but I didn't miss the stiffness in his shoulders and the clench of his jaw at the word *wife*. It quickly disappeared, leaving a controlled tightness in its wake.

Once he slipped back into his rehearsed stature, he stepped closer with his hand extended.

Victor's mouth flattened for the briefest second, then he schooled his expression into a politically correct one and plastered a wide smile in return. Victor shifted slightly as Theo approached us, placing his body in front of mine as if to block me from Theo's view.

He then grasped his hand, giving it a firm shake. *Men.*

Unfazed by the subtle show of possessiveness *my husband* showcased, Theo removed his hand from Victor's and turned his attention back to me. He moved his hand in my direction, and I instinctively leaned in to take it, feeling a strong gravitational pull to him.

My breath hitched alongside my heartbeat when the warmth of his skin connected with mine. His familiar fresh and heady scent washed over me, sending an intoxicating thrill down my spine.

Our gazes locked and lingered for a moment longer than necessary. His body was slightly angled toward mine, his chest rising and falling in a rhythm that matched my own.

The clearing of a throat pierced through our daze, our connection slowly dissipating. I blinked twice, trying to force my attention back to the man I'd married.

I was reeling my emotions back in while Theo slightly loosened his hold on my hand.

"Olivia, this is Theodore Alvarez, your new body-guard." Victor's voice boomed in his office, cutting through the tension roaring around us.

Beneath his calm tone lay a razored edge, sharp enough to cut. His grip tightened once more around my hip, sending sparks of pain reverberating down the length of my leg.

Right when our hands disconnected, Theo's thumb lightly brushed against my bare wrist, a whispered touch I thought I'd imagined.

Until our eyes briefly met again and I watched his pupils dilate ever so slightly before he averted his gaze and settled it back on *my husband*.

"It's a pleasure to meet you both," he said in an easy voice, attempting to dissipate the taunting strain humming in the room.

Slipping my mask back on, I cleared my throat and turned my attention back to Victor. "I told you I didn't need a bodyguard," I said, challenge dripping in my tone.

Something I knew I would later come to regret.

From the corner of my eye, I glimpsed a flash of hurt flickering across Theo's face at the sound of my dismissal, causing a pang of guilt to ripple through my gut. I pushed it down, forcing myself to ignore it before it bled through.

"This isn't up for discussion, Olivia." Victor snarled through gritted teeth, leveling me with his stare as his jaw clenched at my small defiance. He turned his attention back on my new bodyguard, his arm leaving my side to step closer and grip Theo's shoulder.

"Mr. Alvarez, please excuse my wife," he apologized. "It's probably that time of the month. Now, let me show you where you'll be staying for the length of your contract."

My head whipped around once the fact that he would be living here registered.

"What?" I asked louder than I'd intended to, thinking I'd misheard.

"What is it this time, Olivia?" He frowned, visibly annoyed by my outburst.

Knowing the outburst would probably cost me later, I scolded my tone back to the sweet, innocent one I'd perfected. "He's staying here?"

"Mr. Alvarez took a full-time position. I don't think you realize the gravity of the threat on your life, *mi amor*. I promised you nothing would happen to you," he answered with finality, the expression on his face indicating he was now expecting me to stay quiet.

I stared between the two of them, my nails digging into my palms to dampen the urge to argue further. I nodded like the obedient wife I was supposed to portray.

There was no point. I'd have to adapt.

"I'm glad we've managed to reach an understanding." He nodded to himself, appeased. As if he hadn't just reached the *understanding* on his own.

"My staff is currently prepping the guest pool house,

which should be ready by tomorrow. You can take the rest of the day to coordinate with Jaxon, my head of security, and come back in the morning."

Theo nodded, extending his arm. "Lead the way, sir."

With that, Victor moved to the door and stepped out into the hallway, Theo following closely behind. I watched his back, waiting for him to leave, but he looked over his shoulder, meeting my gaze one more time, a hand resting on the doorknob.

My heart slowed and crackles of electricity hummed beneath the weight of his gaze.

"Mrs. Morales."

"Mr. Alvarez," I replied, nodding in his direction.

When the door of the office clicked shut, dread sank deep in my stomach as their footsteps slowly faded away.

¿Qué diablos acaba de pasar?

Being the only person I ever let get close, he'd always been a threat. He was a dangerous distraction, one I couldn't afford. Which was why I'd left without saying goodbye.

Theo's presence would complicate things, making this little game of mine a bit more difficult, but when did I ever back down from a challenge?

I'd done my best to keep tabs on his whereabouts throughout the years, convincing myself it was to make sure he would never come too close to finding me. He'd spent months on end on unsuccessful solo party searches before the bureau reassigned him to another case and he was forced to let me go.

But had he moved on or did he still care for the girl he'd protected all those years ago?

I need to keep my distance in case he's still looking for her.

CHAPTER 6
THEO

S he was fucking beautiful. The pictures barely did her justice.

I didn't know what overtook me, but before I was able to stop, I found myself reaching out, the sudden urge to touch her swarming my senses.

But that hadn't been the strangest part of our interaction. An ominous feeling had sparked when my fingertips had grazed against the pulse point on her delicate wrist.

A simple touch, the light graze of my thumb on her bare skin had set a flurry of goose bumps skittering up my arm, a shiver moving through *both* of our bodies.

I hadn't had a similar reaction to someone in a very long time, not since *her*.

I couldn't even bring myself to say her name because it would make every memory I'd pushed away to the farthest part of my brain resurface. Not that that had ever worked.

Reminders of her had always been present in every confine of my mind, haunting me like a living ghost.

But Olivia looked so much like her, *felt* so much like her.

The delicate features of her face, the slope of her nose, and a mouth you couldn't take your eyes away from.

The last time I'd touched her was still crystal clear in my mind, reminders of her soft lips and how perfectly they'd molded against mine taking up permanent residency.

Olivia reminded me so much of my Sofia.

Your Sofia, the voice in my head tsked. *She was never truly yours.* It continued, taunting me.

But it wasn't her.

It couldn't be her because that would've meant I'd spent the last seven years looking for someone who was right here all along, right within reach. It would've meant I'd spent the last seven fucking years looking for someone who didn't want to be found.

Because she'd never reached out. Never looked for me.

I'd messed up that night by kissing her, *wanting* her. But if she'd stayed, I would have given her anything she wanted. Even if that had been a life without me.

I only wanted her to be safe, *happy.*

I was at the warehouse that night, working on our

latest assignment, when I received the call about the shooting at *Señor* Herrera's house.

The bureau had been keeping an eye on his family ever since his office had announced that he'd wanted to enforce a new legislation that would restrict deliveries through the ports. Something we'd known the cartels wouldn't be too happy about since the new restrictive measures would be a hindrance to their primary mode of trading.

We'd busted a few smaller groups over the years, but the bureau had always struggled to find the leading cartel. We'd eventually figured out that the Amoretti and the Valente families weren't the only players in the drug and gun trade between the countries. They'd only been sourcing whoever was monopolizing the business here.

However, during my last years at the bureau, I'd become more suspicious of the Barreras, a highly influential family down south, but it had been difficult to concretely tie them to the disappearance and bodies we'd suspected they left in their wake.

Whoever was in charge had always gone after rival families or people who might become a problem later, but they had never aimed their target on high-stakes figures.

At least not until that day.

I'd seen a lot of crime scenes throughout the years, but the Herreras' murders had probably been the worst. When I'd arrived at the scene that night, I'd been met with a deafening echo of silence.

57

And *so* much fucking blood, you couldn't even tell who it was originating from.

That had been when I'd found her, thready pulse and barely breathing. The moment I'd laid eyes on her face, my heart had stuttered inside my chest, my throat growing impossibly tight.

Despite all the blood she'd lost, she had been by far the most beautiful person I had ever seen. Crimson strokes painted her tanned skin, dark brown curls framing her like a halo, her beauty shining through the macabre sight.

I'd rushed to her side and tried to contain the blood that was seeping out of her side while we'd waited for the medics that had been on their way. When they'd arrived, we'd rushed her to the hospital where they'd spent hours in the operating room, trying to control the internal bleeding the bullet had caused.

If I'd arrived a minute later or the shooter had aimed his shot a millimeter up, she wouldn't have made it.

And I would have been robbed of the best year of my life. Robbed of meeting the love of my life, no matter how brief my time with her was.

It was all worth it.

Following the surgery, they'd transferred her to the ICU for monitoring until she would be deemed stable enough for us to move her into a more secure location where our own medical staff would be able to keep an eye on her through her recovery.

When the anesthesia had worn off, she'd been in such a

panicked state that she wouldn't settle down unless, surprisingly, I had been in the room with her.

A few days following the surgery, our deputy director had paid her a visit to introduce the assigned agent who would've become her guardian in the witness protection program, but she'd refused to go under protective custody unless I was the one to do it.

Despite being the lead on another case, the bureau had tasked me with protecting her since I'd be able to continue my surveillance remotely.

I hadn't been thrilled with the idea of my field work being paused, but something about needing her to be safe made me accept.

We'd spent months in isolation to make sure they were still convinced that she'd died during the hit, just like her parents. To make sure they wouldn't come back and finish what they'd started.

When I hadn't been helping with her recovery, I'd drowned myself in finding who had done this to her. I'd made it my personal mission to find the bastard who'd harmed her.

But to this day, we still had no idea who'd ordered and executed the hit.

When you'd worked cases like the ones I'd been tasked with for years, it rewired your heart. I'd been hired to keep an eye on her, but the natural instinct to protect her eventually became more visceral than duty-driven.

It didn't take long for her to revive my soul and bring it back to life, and I fell for her.

Hard.

Yes, she had been beautiful—you'd be blind not to see it—but what had really drawn me in was her resilience. Despite everything she'd gone through, from witnessing her parents' murders to being shot, she had been stronger than most of the guys I'd worked with.

I'd tried limiting my interactions with her and avoiding any situations that would have the potential to veer me away from professionalism because I had a job to do. I'd needed to keep a clear head to protect her.

But she was fascinating. *Intoxicating.* I shouldn't have wanted her. I *couldn't* want her.

Or at least I'd thought so until that night when everything had changed.

Of all the people in this world, I'd ended up falling for a heart that didn't beat in synchrony with mine.

My stomach flipped, twisting my gut as I thought about the day I'd woken up without her by my side. It took a conscious effort to keep my hackles from rising. I shoved my hands in my pockets, so I could clench my fists without anyone noticing, attempting to prevent the anger from taking over.

I hadn't seen or heard from Sofia. That didn't mean I'd stopped looking for her. Because trust me, I hadn't.

For seven fucking years I looked for her.

I honestly didn't know why I kept searching when

she'd left me without a single word. But something deep in my gut had always told me to continue.

The sound of the sliding glass doors opening pulled me back from my thoughts. The pads of my fingertips were still tingling from touching her, so I swiped them along the side of my thigh and trailed behind her husband out onto the terrace.

He led us to a marbled patio table, where he took a seat in one of the chairs. "There's something we need to discuss. It's about Olivia," he said, gesturing at one of the free seats in front of him. "Sit."

My brows shot up in confusion, wondering if he'd bring up my reaction to seeing his wife. "What about Mrs. Morales, sir?"

I sat across from him, leaned back in the metal chair, threw my arm over the back of the one next to me, and propped the heel of my black Oxford on my other knee.

Morales exhaled, reaching slowly inside his suit jacket. He pulled out a small stack of crinkled notes, then laid them flat on the table. I reached for them, reading the one on top, quickly realizing it was the same threat note from Noah's file.

My eyes drifted to that last line again where *"will history repeat itself"* was scribbled in black ink. The image of his wife filtered in my mind and a violent flame burned in my chest at the thought of her suffering the same fate as his late wife.

This was ridiculous. I had just met her.

She reminds you of Sofia, the part of me that was still holding onto her said. I inwardly cursed it, silencing it for the time being.

"Mr. Morales, what did they mean by history repeating itself?" I asked, my mind unable to piece it together. I knew I was hired to protect his wife, but any information I'd been given was hazy.

I needed to know more.

He didn't respond. Something haunting lined his expression. Silence stretched between us, but I decided not to press him further. I needed him to hand me the information willingly, something I believed he wasn't accustomed to from the look on his face. While I waited for him to answer, I scanned through the other notes— more threats with the same scribbling.

Wait, I thought it was just one note, but there are at least a dozen here.

I met his gaze again and he blew out a breath, surveying our surroundings. "The fire that killed my wife wasn't accidental," he confessed. "She was murdered."

There was a pause. "It started out the same with just the letters until it escalated one night and they came after her. The other letters you have in your hands are all the ones I got before they took my Elena from me."

They? Who's they?

Perplexed by his revelation, I glanced back and forth between him and the papers I was holding. Putting them down, my brows creased in the middle before I relayed the information I'd gathered from his wife's autopsy report. "The police report showed that your wife had died in her sleep from smoke inhalation and dehydration from her severe burns. The fire department claimed the fire had been an extremely unlucky occurrence where a faulty wire jumped, causing the electrical fire."

Morales hesitated, quickly glancing around us once more before shifting in his seat.

"Because my men made it look that way. After we received the first note threatening Elena's life, I asked them not to alert the police because I was certain it was simply from a competitor using it as a distraction since we were working on expanding."

This wasn't surprising since corrupt men like him always had at least one person in the police department working for them. But despite his transparency, I didn't trust him.

There had to be more to the story, because why would he lie about his wife's death? Why would he cover it up, only to have to deal with this all over again with his latest wife?

He breathed out a dark chuckle, running a hand through his hair. "It wasn't like that had never happened before, but they'd always been empty threats."

After a pause, he swallowed. "At least they were, until I got a call from the chief of police informing me of my wife's death."

He rose to his feet and looked in the direction of his

house. "Olivia doesn't know the truth about Elena's death and the other letters." He turned his attention back to me, picking up the notes from the table to put them back inside his pocket.

Looming over me in what I assumed was a threatening stance, he clasped a firm hand on my shoulder. "I would like to keep it that way."

We locked eyes, annoyance churning my insides at his challenging command. This wasn't a suggestion. It was an order.

I swallowed down my annoyance. "Very well, sir," I finally said, pushing my chair back to get up, its legs grating against the stoned slabs.

"Good. Now, I'll have Jaxon show you around."

I started following behind him when a silhouette caught my eye, appearing behind the curtains of a window that overlooked the garden.

I hadn't been able to protect Sofia, but I would protect *her*.

CHAPTER 7
SOFIA

Cold rain lashed my face as I sprinted away from the house, pulling my hoodie tighter over my head. My feet seeped through the wet ground, but I kept pushing through, running faster.

Every once in a while, I looked over my shoulder, making sure I wasn't being followed. Although I knew Victor was fast asleep and the night team wouldn't do another round until morning came, one could never be too careful.

If there was one thing I'd learned, it was that anyone could be hiding in the shadows.

The lights from the house slowly faded away, plunging me into the thick darkness of the woods lining the back of the house. The ground was barely visible and its uneven-ness, combined with the gnarled roots sprouting out, made running in these woods a fucking hassle.

But since I'd spent hours exploring them and memorizing the satellite pictures of the property and the lands surrounding it, I already knew the way out.

With only shadows of moonlight seeping through the thick canopy of trees, I made my way to the other side of the land.

Sneaking a sleeping pill in *my husband's* drink had been a bit of a challenge since his paranoia surfaced after the little delivery we got last week, but I had to make sure he wouldn't startle when I left in the middle of the night.

Once he had been sound asleep, I'd sneaked out the bedroom's window, using the vines down the side of the house. I'd crept along the wall of the premises, staying out of the security cameras' scope, blending in with the shadows to keep me out of sight.

When I'd hit the corner, I'd peered around it to look for any movement in the garden before making my way to the only blind spot on the property and had taken off sprinting into the woods.

Before I'd moved in, I'd hacked into the property's security system and discovered the cameras didn't cover the west side of the garden, right where the guest house was.

Hence why this couldn't wait.

I had to do this tonight because, starting tomorrow, my new *bodyguard* would be watching over my every move. Sneaking out would be a bit of a challenge since he would be living in the said blind spot and I couldn't afford getting caught, not after all these years of waiting to strike.

Tonight was my only chance to set the rest of the plan in motion.

As I made my way through the thick of these woods, I tried to keep my focus on getting to my destination. Keeping my focus on what I'd worked eight years for, but fragments of my old life kept tugging me back.

Carajo.

A vision of the past followed every step I took away from the house. Memories came flooding back, jabbing me square in the sternum. Memories of *him*.

Mi luz en la oscuridad, mi cielito, mi Theo.

Despite the branches scraping my ankles, the dirty rain pouring over my eyes, both attempting to bring me back to the present, his face was all I could see.

Memories of us etched in my brain.

The confusion he'd experienced seeing me, followed by the subtle recognition that had morphed into hope right before it had been annihilated by two simple words. *My wife.*

I felt the volume of my beating heart expand, compressing my lungs, squeezing out the air and leaving my throat constricted from the lump it created.

Seeing him after all these years was seriously fucking with my mind. And I couldn't have that. I couldn't risk it.

There was more than me at stake.

My heart twitched violently inside my rib cage as the

muddy dirt shifted into concrete and I lifted my gaze toward the building ahead of me. Filling my lungs with the wet air to fight the tightness in my chest, I took a step forward, clawing my way out of the darkness toward the run-down abandoned barn where I hoped my *Rosalina* was still waiting for me.

The barn door was slightly ajar, and I slowly pushed on the old, weathered wood. The door opened with a creak and I slipped inside. It was mostly dark, but slivers of moonlight seeped through the cracked roof, allowing me to see her form.

I breathed a sigh of relief and made my way toward her. I bent down and removed the tarp covering her.

"Here you are," I said when my eyes settled on Rosalina, uncovered. My ride or die, where I spent countless nights in her back seat until I found a decent paying job that allowed me to rent a place.

I reached for the latch to pop the hood open and grabbed the keys taped under the lining of the hood.

The rain was coming down much harder, thunder rumbling in the distance. I walked to the side of the barn to open the side door. After sliding behind the wheel and clicking the seat belt in place across my damp chest, I started the car. She stuttered for a beat before her familiar rumbling sound filled the air.

I shut off the headlights and pulled out of the barn, turning onto the small driveway.

Once I was on the main road, I turned them back on to avoid any suspicions from patrolling cars. I drove through the streets, taking different turns whenever I felt another car trailing behind me.

My mind was on autopilot and half an hour later, I drove through Bemes until I passed the city's limit, heading into my old neighborhood.

I hadn't seen this place in almost a year.

I pulled around to the back of the apartment complex and parked my car, but I didn't get out right away. Instead, I turned off the ignition, waiting to see if anyone had tailed me.

Leaning back into my seat, I fought back the emotions clogging up my throat from being cornered into lying to Theo.

Everything about me, about this charade of a marriage —even my name—was a lie. I didn't want to lie to him, but I also wouldn't be able to live with myself if anything happened to him because of me.

I could live with breaking his heart, but I would never be able to forgive myself if I was the reason it stopped beating. Deep down, I knew this was what I had to do.

When I was confident enough that I hadn't been

followed, I reached over the console to grab my gun and gear tucked in the glove compartment. I slipped out of my car and headed toward the last door on the right, sliding the set into my back pocket and holstering my gun in my waistband.

A dark breeze whistled past me, making my nose tingle and my skin prickle with goose bumps.

The sound of a car interrupted the steady silence and my stomach flipped. *Fuck*. I whipped my gaze behind me and watched a car whiz down the street.

Cálmate. Nobody's following you. You made sure of it.

When I reached the front door, I glanced behind me one more time and got to my knees, taking my kit out of my back pocket. Unfolding it at my side, I retrieved a paperclip and unbent one side. With a deep breath, I grabbed the small wrench and inserted it into the lower edge of the keyhole, applying a slight pressure.

Turning the lock slightly to the right, I gently pushed the small crook of the paperclip and lifted it back and upward. Increasing slightly the pressure of the wrench, I repeated the circular motion with the paperclip until the sound I was waiting for resonated into the quiet night.

Click. Glad to know I hadn't lost my touch.

I fully turned the knob this time, and the door creaked open. I walked into the dark space, a cold, musty scent invading my senses. I scrunched up my nose and spun around to close the door behind me, locking it.

The dim yellow bulbs from the flickering streetlights of the parking lot filtered through a slight gap from the heavily draped windows. Dust coated every surface and the stale air was overpowering, but it looked exactly how I left it.

Before leaving this apartment when Victor had proposed and asked me to move in, I'd given the owner a generous advance to keep the place untouched. Cash in hand, he'd left without uttering another word.

My boots squeaked against the floor as I ventured into each room, gun in hand, making sure the place was empty. Once every room was cleared, I walked to the only place that truly quieted the raging anger.

This was where it all started. Where I'd spent countless hours gathering intel on Victor Morales and had found a team to help carry out his end.

I sat at my desk, laid my gun down next to me, and powered up my monitors. The familiar humming sound spread warmth through my limbs as I shrugged out of my damp hoodie, a resounding thunk echoing when it landed on the back of the plastic chair.

I breathed a sigh of relief. Computers were the one constant piece in my life. I'd always felt more at peace surrounded by their soft hum than anywhere else. They took me into a different dimension, where problems didn't exist. They would never disappoint and I could always count on them for the truth.

After I'd left the bureau's protection, the only way I'd felt like I could survive was through arrays of algorithms. Theo had taught me the basics and I'd found comfort in

71

the clicks of a keyboard, but after leaving, I had no other way of learning.

So, a month after trying to survive on my own, I'd snuck into a computer programming class one evening. When my professor had found out I didn't have the materials necessary for the assignments, she'd lent me a used laptop for the semester and it became my most trusted companion ever since.

In a few short weeks and countless sleepless nights, thanks to the nightmares, I'd opened a bank account and secured it by bypassing the bank's firewall and creating my own unique one within theirs, making sure it was untraceable.

Then, I'd started transferring small amounts from different accounts of rich people who wouldn't notice a few hundreds missing from their accounts.

After that, all that had been left was to create an alias, building a second line of defense for myself in case my coding was tracked. After setting myself up for a few years, I'd started what would end up being seven years of waiting patiently for the right moment to strike.

My eyes flickered to pictures of my parents filling my home screen, nostalgia engulfing me like a tidal wave, making my heart squeeze. I shoved it down as I let my fingers fly over the keys to access the encrypted server and started typing.

NEMESIS: CHANGE OF PLANS.

CHAPTER 8

THEO

After getting acquainted with Jaxon and what little remained of his team, following Morales's firing spree because of what happened last week, I made my way home right after grabbing food from one of the street vendors on the way.

I cut off my engine, grabbed the takeout bags from the passenger seat after tucking my phone in my pocket, and stepped out of the car.

With every step I took closer to my condo, reminders of *her* tugged at me. Reminders that I was walking into an empty house and not one with her in it.

A bitter laugh singed my throat. You would think that after all these years, I would have forgotten her, but everything that surrounded me was just a constant reminder of what I no longer had.

Seeing Olivia Morales today added itself to that

lengthy list, her unannounced appearance in my life throwing a severe wrench in my routine.

What the fuck was I thinking saying yes in the first place? Especially now after seeing what my new client looked like.

When I reluctantly accepted Noah's offer, I didn't know I would have to look at someone who would constantly remind me of what I'd lost.

El destino era un puta perra.

Eventually, I dragged myself inside my house, loosening my tie, the self-loathing flaming hotter within my chest. After finishing my checks, I tore a small piece of *batbout* and grabbed a bit of *zaalouk* with it before stuffing it in my mouth to satiate my grumbling stomach, leaving the rest on the counter, planning to come back to it later.

Walking past the living room, I headed toward the side floating staircase, taking the steps two at a time. A few doors peppered the walls at the top of the stairs, and I headed for the one at the very end, slipping into my bedroom.

I stripped off my clothes and dropped them onto my bed, then walked farther into the en suite and turned the shower on.

Stepping into the gray-tiled stall, I let the icy water from the rainfall faucet spray my skin, but nothing seemed to quell the flaming bitterness raging inside of me.

Propping one hand on the wall next to the handle, I

rested my forehead against the cold tile, droplets of water running down my nose, blurring my vision.

Suddenly, wide chocolate-brown eyes and dark curls framing her face replaced the cloudy image, while invisible tendrils of coconut and warm honey swarmed the shower. The sensation of her soft skin prickled my fingertips, making me ache to touch her again.

Despite all these years, Sofia remained seared so deep into my consciousness that I could still smell her. Still *feel* her. Memories of her body beneath mine, nails digging into my back, echoes of my name escaping her lips in a breathy moan.

My need for her pulsed harder, making my cock twitch at the memory of how good it felt to finally have her in my arms, even if it was just for one night.

Groaning, I shook my head to dispel the visions of her, pushing down my hard length, trying to temper my arousal at the thought of her, but more images forced themselves through.

Muttering a curse under my breath, I caved, fisting my angry swollen cock, the tip already dripping pre-cum. I leaned my weight into the wall, squeezing my eyes shut, letting my mind drift as I pumped slowly.

Flashes of soft lips parting for me, the tip of her tongue prodding my slit, teasing and tasting before wrapping them around my crown, sucking.

Oh. Fuck.

Any ounce of self-control I had evaporated instantly.

My fingers curled against the cold tile as I picked up speed, moving faster, harsher, tugging while I imagined my length feeding into her. My movements were rough, angry, almost resentful that I still wanted her so much as I worked myself toward release.

I got lost in the fantasy that she was still mine.

Heat bloomed within my spine, coiling at the base, and my blood soared, rushing through my ears as it drowned out the sound of the cold water pelting my back.

I came into my fist with an illicit, deep groan, the sound vibrating through my chest, bouncing against the walls. My eyes popped open, and my body slumped from the exertion, waiting for my hammering heart to slow back to its normal pace.

All that was left when I came down from the high was the echo of my release mocking me.

When I finally stepped out of the bathroom with a towel wrapped around my waist, I walked into my closet and dried myself off. I changed into a pair of sweatpants and grabbed my glasses before I headed back into the kitchen.

I grabbed a soda and carried the rest of the food from the counter to the living room, where files about my new assignment were waiting for me.

My hair was still damp as I sat on the couch to look over the files splayed in front of me. I studied the pictures Noah gave me last week as well as some information I'd gathered on my own.

I was probably fishing for more than there was, but something deep down told me there was more to this story. More to Olivia Morales.

Condensation dripped from the glass bottle onto one of the manila folders underneath. I grabbed it and took a sip before biting into one of the now cold meat-filled *batbout*.

I was reviewing information about Victor's businesses when my phone rang, breaking the silence I was working in. I ignored it, grabbing another file.

It rang again and I rummaged through the folders, looking for it. I flipped it to see who was calling, only to see Noah's name on the screen.

Groaning, I swiped right to answer and put him on speaker, then placed my phone back on the glass table.

"What is it this time?" I huffed.

"Well, hello to you too, dear friend," he replied, mocking me.

Ignoring the annoyance that bubbled right beneath the surface of my skin, I ran a hand through my hair, pushing the fallen wet stands out of my face, and leaned back onto the couch.

"Noah," I replied through gritted teeth. "Last time you

called, I ended up becoming a babysitter. Should I also be expecting another nightly visit from you?"

"Not tonight." He chuckled. "How was it?"

"Fine," I grumbled.

"I'm gonna need you to give me more than that."

Irritation clawed inside my chest, and I leaned forward, propping my elbows on my knees and shoving my glasses up my forehead.

"Noah, it was the first day," I muttered, driving the heels of my hands into my eyes.

He remained quiet for a moment, then cleared his throat, a shuffling sound filling the line.

I'd be willing to bet good money he was still at the office. Noah Brown was the definition of married to the job. He barely even dated, but that might have more to do with the five-foot-four green-eyed DEA agent he still, to this day, refused to acknowledge he had a crush on than the lack of offers.

He sighed. "Just keep me posted if you notice anything out of the ordinary."

Click.

I glanced down at my phone, bewildered. This was weird. I really didn't have anything to report, but it wasn't like Noah to give up so easily. He was the type to grill you until he got exactly the answer he was looking for.

His voice sounded strained, almost on edge, but he'd hung up before I got to ask him to clarify.

I pushed down the uncertainties about his behavior

and stared at the documents, resuming sorting through the information as I looked for a clue indicating what Morales might have been mixed into.

My phone buzzed this time, and I leaned over to pick it up, thinking Noah had texted me.

But it wasn't him.

I swiped on the notification, unlocking my phone. I waited a beat for it to direct me to the app that was now showcasing a live video feed of outside the Moraleses' house, my screen splitting into six squares.

Earlier today, while Jaxon was distracted explaining how everything worked, I planted a small chip into their security system to make sure I'd be alerted if there was any movement around the premises during the window periods when the team was either asleep or not actively surveilling the property.

They had a solid system, but I never trusted anything if I hadn't had a hand in it.

I brought up the security footage and clicked through the different slides, looking for the source that alerted my system.

I was about to put my phone back down, thinking an animal might have triggered it, when I noticed a flicker on the screen, but it disappeared as fast as it appeared.

What the...

Knowing I hadn't imagined it, I rewound the footage and paused when the shadow of something flickered again at the corner of the screen. A barely visible figure was plastered against the wall before it disappeared into a blind spot.

There seemed to be a blind spot on the property, right where the pool house was. Right where I would be staying.

I zoomed in closer on the intruder and even though their face was barely visible underneath the hood, I recognized it immediately.

The side of Morales's wife came into view.

What is she doing out at this time? More importantly, why is she avoiding the cameras?

I stared down at the documents in front of me, skimming each page again and landing on a picture of Olivia to make sure my eyes weren't playing tricks on me, only to confirm my initial guess.

Maybe I'd have to keep a closer eye on her for other reasons than her security.

Olivia Morales would become a problem I'd enjoy solving.

CHAPTER 9
SOFIA

I finished writing the last code into the system as the sun peeked through the horizon, slivers of it sneaking through the edges of the curtains, illuminating the wooden floors. A shiver ran through me, the cold sweat coating my body from the remnants of the rain.

I brought one hand up to my temple, massaging the small throb pounding in my skull before stretching my back to work out the kinks that had built throughout the night from staring at the monitor for too long.

Once satisfied with my work, I pressed enter, and the screen turned blank before rows of numbers rolled down, destroying all the evidence from the hard drive, right before it shut down.

Swiping my phone off the desk, I shrugged into my now-dry hoodie, the smell of rain engulfing me until my head was out. The outside air was still cold, but thankfully no rain was in sight.

The breeze picked up as I headed to the car, gun in hand. I climbed behind the wheel, threw my gun back into the glove compartment, and drove off, making my way to the drop spot.

Once I made it back into town, I parked on the off-road pathway, leaving the car with the keys under the seat, and moved to the third tree trunk on the left where a burner phone was waiting for me. After grabbing the plastic bag hidden inside the old animal den, I started hiking back toward the main road.

Relying on the fact that it was still too early for anyone else to be out, I jogged back the last five miles separating me from the house.

Half an hour later, my head was incessantly throbbing with each fall of my feet against the pavement. Despite all the forced training Theo had put me through, I still fucking hated running. But I couldn't drive back to the old barn. It would be too risky and I couldn't afford to get caught.

When I made it back to our neighborhood, I pulled my phone out and looked at the time.

Fuck.

The guys were gonna start their rounds soon, and I needed to be there before the morning crew arrived. I picked up my pace, rounding our street's corner, making sure I reached the house before someone saw me and started asking questions.

I punched in the code to the gate, quickly closing it behind me before jogging up the driveway and halting midway. Beads of perspiration dripped down my forehead, and my legs were burning. A brutal cramp seized my left side, sending my hands to my knees. I squeezed my eyes shut, trying to breathe through it.

"Mrs. Morales," a gruff voice said, startling me. "May I ask what you are doing out this early?"

I jumped back, whipping my head toward the source, a hand flying to my throat. I slowly lifted my head, peeling my lids back to meet the voice's gaze. Panic flooded through me, and I swallowed hard over the dryness in my throat when I came face-to-face with none other than Theo.

Debes estar bromeando. What is he doing here this early?

He was wearing a black sweater that clung to his chest, dark gray slacks molding the outline of his thighs. His thick dark curls were messy like he'd been incessantly running his fingers through it.

Dios mío. Why did he have to look like that?

Scrubbing my hands over my face, I exhaled forcefully. "I was just out for a run. What are *you* doing here?"

"I work here. You shouldn't be out on your own," he said accusingly.

"I'm fine," I replied drily.

"Mrs. Morales, you should take your security more seriously."

I leveled him with my gaze. "Who said I wasn't?" I answered, the beginning of exasperation licking around the edges of my patience as I passed him, making my way to the front door.

I walked in the house, Theo following right behind me. I passed the archway and stalked across the hallway that led to the back of the house. Relief coursed through me when I entered the kitchen, finding it empty.

I peered at the clock above the stove. There was still time before Jaxon and the rest of the staff came in to debrief over breakfast.

With one hand massaging my lower back, I crossed the room to the cabinet next to the stove, standing on my tiptoes to reach for the ibuprofen on the top shelf.

Before I could grab it, the warmth of his chest seeped against my back as he loomed over my head. "Here," he said, bringing the bottle down for me.

His proximity sent my heart thudding against my chest. I bit my lip to prevent the hitch in my breath from escaping. Our fingers brushed against one another as I grabbed it from his hand, gripping it tight, willing my racing heart to calm down.

He barely stayed for a second longer and backed away, but the presence of his body lingered against my own.

Shaking the feeling off, I closed the cabinet door and

turned around to find him now leaning against the refrigerator, a water bottle in hand.

"I could have done it myself." My voice came out raspier than usual, revealing just how much his presence affected me.

He pushed off the steel door, walking to lean his elbows against the quartz countertop, and pushed the bottle in my direction. "A simple thank you would suffice."

I stayed quiet, leaving the water he'd handed me on the counter. I shook four ibuprofen from the bottle and swallowed them dry while maintaining his gaze.

He chuckled, his eyes slightly crinkling up at the corners as he scrubbed his free hand over his beard. "Noted."

His expression turned serious and for a few moments, we simply stared at each other. My mind drifted to the reminiscence of us in the same position when we first started living together after I was discharged from the hospital.

The injuries I'd sustained hadn't allowed much mobility for the first few weeks post-surgery and Theo had to pretty much help me with everything, which wasn't something I particularly liked.

I'd never been good at handing over control and fought him over every little thing. I didn't need help. I didn't *want* help. Rationally, I knew he was just trying to make it easier for me, but I didn't deserve to be helped.

Not when both my parents weren't granted the same opportunity.

With the small glimmer in his eyes, I wondered if he was thinking about the same thing. But then I remembered that even if he was, *I* was someone else.

The longer I stared at him, the more I felt the jagged scar in my chest slowly tear open.

The clearing of a throat pulled us from our thoughts and we both turned toward the source, only to find Victor leaning against the frame of the door that connected the hall to the kitchen. The ingrained response to his presence engaged my mask to slide firmly back into place.

I straightened my back and approached him, painting a smile on my face. "*Buenos días, mi amor.* How did you sleep?"

I let him wrap his arm around me, his fingers gripping my shoulder tightly as he pulled me closer. I turned to face him and tilted my head back as he placed a small kiss on my lips. I barely masked a scowl at the contact before pulling away.

"I'm okay, *mi amor*, although I did feel a bit groggy when I first woke up." He paused. "Wait, why weren't you in bed this morning and why are you so damp?" he asked, slightly pushing me back in disgust when he realized I was sweaty.

Knowing Theo was watching our interaction, I placed a hand on his chest and giggled. I fucking giggled, because that's what women in love with their husbands did, right?

"I went out for a run." I kept my voice sweet and innocent.

"And since when do you run?" Victor asked, a skeptical look on his face.

"The girls at the country club thought it would be a good idea."

"I agree, you need it."

And you need a bullet in that head of yours.

I ignored his statement, keeping the smile on my face. "I'm going to take a shower."

"You do that," he said before finally turning his attention to Theo, as if he had just noticed he was in the room.

I headed toward the hallway, their chatter fading into the background once I reached the stairs and made my way to the shower.

CHAPTER 10
THEO

I'd been her bodyguard for only three days. Just three fucking days and she was already driving me insane.

Since the job entailed being with her almost twenty-four seven, she had spared no minute in making my life a living hell, trying to evade my protection any chance she got.

Going against everything I said seemed to be her new favorite pastime. It was like anything else was against her nature. I would bet good money that she woke up every morning and plotted my demise as her meditation.

The mental exercises I found myself engaging in when we were alone were strenuous as I forced myself not to strangle her pretty neck and cuff her to my side to make sure she didn't wander anywhere without me.

I would never hurt a woman, but one glance at Olivia

and I swear she made me want to forget about my principles and teach her a lesson or two on how to behave.

Not that the idea to take her over my knee wasn't appealing.

The thought washed away when I heard the front door slam shut, the garage door whirring open.

Not again.

I made my way outside and stood in the driveway in front of the garage door. Our eyes clashed through the rearview mirror once she noticed me, but instead of coming out of the car, she engaged the gear and reversed the car.

Two could play that game.

I stayed put, maintaining eye contact, until the back end of the car grazed my knees.

After putting the car in park and turning off the engine, she pried the car door open and exited.

"Move," she ordered.

I took a deep breath, repeating to myself that murdering your client was never a good idea, no matter how appealing the thought might be.

"Where are we going?"

"*We* are going nowhere. *I* have to go pick a gown for the gala."

"Keys, Mrs. Morales," I insisted.

"You don't need to go with me. I'm sure you have better things to do than go dress shopping. It's rather boring, I assure you."

"I find dress shopping quite riveting actually. Now, the keys. I don't like repeating myself."

She stood there, glaring at me. After a beat, her face morphed into realization, knowing I wouldn't budge, and she threw the pair of keys in my direction.

"Good girl," I whispered under my breath, my lips tugging at the corner once she brushed behind me, making her way to the passenger's side.

I followed suit, getting behind the wheel. Once inside, I turned to her, while her nose was buried in her phone, her fingers typing away.

"Where to?"

We drove in silence, the only sound coming from the tapping of fingers on her phone. Twenty minutes later, we parked across the street, climbed out of the car, and made our way toward Anaya, a small boutique located in central Bemes.

The moment we walked through the door, two saleswomen greeted us with their best customer service smiles.

"Good afternoon, Mrs. Morales. It's so nice to see you again," the taller of the two said, greeting Olivia by giving her a side-kiss to her cheek.

Olivia placed a lazy smile on her face, greeting her back. "You too, Maria."

Maria then turned her attention to me, granting me the same smile. "You must be her husband," she said, extending her hand toward me.

"No," both Olivia and I responded firmly.

I cleared my throat, enveloping her hand in a firm handshake. "I'm her bodyguard."

She laughed shyly, a blush creeping up her neck as she apologized. "I'm so sorry, I just thought—"

Her assistant inserted herself by cutting her off, interrupting the tense moment. "Care for any refreshments?" she asked, and we both shook our heads in response.

"Then, let's go look at what we put aside for you," Maria said, placing her hand on Olivia's upper back, guiding her to where the preselected dresses were hanging from a rack next to the fitting rooms.

I locked the front door behind me, casting my gaze around the store. It was empty apart from us, most likely a courtesy from Morales. He'd probably rented the space for the day so his wife could shop in peace.

As their chatter faded away in the background, I took in the space. Despite the boutique looking rather small from the outside, it was actually quite spacious inside.

Long black curtains were hanging from a black steel structure, framing the changing rooms. There was a large vintage mirror leaning on the wall next to them, and a small platform placed right in front of it, a crystal chandelier dangling from above.

A blue velvet couch was sitting in the middle of the

room, with a dark wooden table placed in front of it, a pile of various magazines stacked on top.

The building had two exits. One at the front and the other at the back, which I'd noticed when we'd walked in. Only one security camera covered the store. Despite having large windows adorning the front, the displays were hiding the majority of the front street, which was useful to keep prying eyes away.

We stayed in for what felt like hours while she tried on dress after dress. The shop's assistant, Sarah, I'd learned later on, kept asking me if I wanted to sit and I politely declined every time. I knew if I sat on that plush couch, I would most likely fall asleep and no way in hell was I giving Olivia any ammunition to use against me.

Besides, the couch wouldn't allow me to properly see Olivia.

Although I tried convincing myself that the decision was stemming from a purely professional standpoint, that it was my duty to keep an eye on her at all times, deep down I couldn't deny that part of my motives were purely selfish.

Because from where I was standing, I had the perfect view of her every single time she came out of the changing room in those *fucking* dresses.

It probably went against all the rules I'd established when it came to clients, but there was just something *different* about Olivia Morales. I just couldn't help myself.

I wasn't sure why this was taking so long. Everything

she tried on looked beautiful on her. Every time she would come out, it was a struggle not to stare. I tried forcing my gaze away but couldn't seem to stop myself from admiring her, my attention ensnared by her presence.

More time passed before I heard Maria say, "I think this might be the one. What do you think?"

My head snapped up to see what they'd decided on, but I wasn't prepared for what my eyes laid on. I never thought I'd be this *mesmerized* by the sight.

I watched in fascination as she pulled the curtain open and came out of the dressing room, a black gown fitting her body like it was made for her, clinging to every curve on her figure.

Fuck me, she was beautiful.

She was the most exquisite human I'd seen in a long time, her beauty almost ethereal.

Her hair draped against her bare back in soft, loose curls, brushing her lower back, the ghost of two dimples slightly peeking out from under the fabric, begging for my tongue to explore them.

She grabbed her hair in her hand, swept it off her back, and turned around to get a better look. The fabric draped in the back, swooping right above the curvature of her ass.

My eyes couldn't settle on where to look while they roamed over every inch of her. I kept taking her in, until the feel of her stare burned against my skin.

I finally looked up, our eyes locking, and for a

moment, there was just us in the room. The expression on her face sent electricity zinging directly through my chest and it took everything in me not to physically react. She watched me with such familiarity that it sent my mind into a frenzy of questions.

But any thoughts I had halted when she skimmed her hands down her sides and over her waist at a torturous pace. My breath stuttered, a lump lodging in my throat.

Her eyelids fluttered shut as her mouth parted slightly. My gaze bounced from her eyes to zone in on her mouth. My mind conjured images of the same expression painting her face, but under completely different circumstances and I was suddenly met with the desperate urge to know what she tasted like.

She slowly opened her eyes and I tore my own eyes away from her, running a hand through my hair.

"I think it's perfect," I heard Olivia say as she moved back to the changing room to change back into her clothes.

No matter how tempting the idea of her was, I couldn't.

I'd never allowed myself to cross that line.

Throughout the years, I tried drowning my emotions and resentment in alcohol and sex, but I could never bring myself to be tempted by the offers. Every time a woman touched me, the ink etched in my skin burned stronger, making it impossible to erase Sofia from my mind. Not even for a single second.

Once they had arranged for the dress to be picked the day before the event, we made our way out. We both reached for the door before she took a step back, letting me do it for her.

We walked to the parking garage on the other side of the street, tension and silence humming in the air. Once we made it to the car, she turned to say something, but my eyes focused on a white envelope stuck to the windshield, underneath one of the wipers.

I scanned the surroundings, finding nothing, the space utterly quiet. I pushed her behind me before dropping to the floor, looking for any signs of alterations to the car.

Getting back up, I turned my attention to her. "Inside, Mrs. Morales," I ordered her, gesturing for her to get in the car. Knowing she wouldn't listen, I added, "Now."

I waited for the passenger door to slam shut before making my way to retrieve the envelope.

I retrieved the note from inside and read its content. Only one sentence, four words, were scribbled on the cream paper.

Time is running out.

CHAPTER 11
SOFIA

It's been a few days since the last threat. Or should I say my last threat.

After reading the note, Theo had run to the driver's seat and had driven off. As soon as we'd arrived at the house, he'd gone straight to Victor's office, where he'd debriefed him about today's event, Jaxon joining them shortly after since he'd already been debriefed while we were making our way to the house.

They'd spent the rest of the day and night, as well as the days following, running the paper for prints and analyses on the writing, comparing it to the other notes.

Unfortunately for them, there hadn't been any fingerprints on either the envelope or the small note that was inside. They had, however, found similarities in the handwriting, but despite that small win in their eyes, I knew it was handwriting they'd never be able to compare to anything in any of the databases they'd run it through.

I was fucking good at what I did, so of course they wouldn't find anything.

"I'm really looking forward to next month's gala. I heard through the grapevine that you were doing an amazing job so far."

I stopped twirling the champagne in my flute and glanced up.

I'd been chatting with one of my husband's business associates for what felt like an eternity. He and his wife had invited a few of us over to celebrate the latest addition to their family and he'd been going on and on about his newborn daughter, showing me the countless pictures he'd taken on his phone.

Theo was off tonight since it was just a casual dinner and Jaxon was staked outside as a precaution. They didn't deem it necessary to have both of them here tonight. Besides, it would only raise suspicions amongst everyone and Victor couldn't have that.

He had an image to preserve. No one was to know about the special deliveries we'd been getting.

I was still stuck with whatever his name was, when Victor got interrupted by a call from one of his overseas contacts. He moved into a secluded corner of the room, away from curious ears, but close enough for me to hear whispers of his conversation.

I half paid attention to the man next to me as I watched *my husband* from my periphery.

His shoulders instantly tensed, his face scrunching when he received the news. I then heard Victor mutter something about a missed shipment that was supposed to arrive at the port last week, which I may or may not have had a hand in.

"Olivia?" our host prompted.

"Yes, I'm looking forward to seeing it all come together," I finally replied, a polite smile tugging at the corner of my mouth. He resumed talking about his daughter and I let the rest of his rambling drone out.

Then, I felt him before I heard him. I forced myself not to recoil at his approaching presence.

"Here you are," Victor announced, cutting off the rest of the ensuing conversation as he wrapped his arm around my waist. "Thank you for having us tonight, Brian. But we unfortunately have to get going."

"Really, already?" Brian's bushy eyebrows snapped together.

"Yes, duty calls," Victor pressured, his arm tightening around my waist.

Yeah, he really wasn't happy about the unfortunate mishap with the shipments.

"Well, it was nice seeing you two tonight," Brian finished.

He gave me a warm smile before moving his gaze to Victor. "You are a very lucky man," he said, winking at him. Victor may appear relaxed to anyone looking, but I'd spent so many years studying him that I was attuned to the slight changes in demeanor.

Which was how I knew there was nothing relaxed about him right now. He was tense at my side, and the innocent praise sent my husband's fingers digging into the side of my hip in response.

"I don't know what I would do without her." He chuckled, planting a kiss on the side of my head.

What probably looked like a display of affection was simply a reminder, a warning of what was to come. Despite his bruising grips that were born out of jealousy and possessiveness, Victor hadn't laid a hand on me so far, a fate I knew his wife hadn't been as privy to.

But my gut told me that tonight might not end well for me and I had to prepare myself to brace for impact.

After saying our goodbyes to the rest of the guests, we headed to the house, Victor's tension-filled silence taunting me during the entirety of the car ride.

Omar dropped us off in the driveway, and we both climbed up the small steps, walking through the front door. Once the door shut behind me, I reached down, removing my heels one by one.

Heels would definitely be one of the many things I wouldn't miss after this charade was over.

"Well, tonight was great. I'm going to head upstairs to shower," I said as I started up the stairs, a hand on the banister.

Victor's voice stopped me in my tracks. "You looked rather cozy with my associate. What were you guys talking about?"

Here we go.

I peered down at him. He was still standing by the door, his hands shoved in his pockets.

"Nothing important, *mi amor.*" I kept my voice sweet, attempting to fend off his questioning that I knew would lead to anything but a good outcome.

"Didn't look like *nothing* to me," he said with a slight edge to his voice, his shoulders now tense beneath the fabric of his suit.

"Victor," I started.

"Olivia, I asked you a question." His tone was harsher this time, the expression on his face darkening as he stepped forward. I instinctively stepped back, trying to escape the anger vibrating off his body.

Stay calm, Sofia.

"Victor, we were just talking about the upcoming charity gala that I'm planning and his new baby."

His disbelieving laugh filled the room. "Just talking? I saw the way he was looking at you." He paused. "I saw how *you* were looking at him."

Is this man fucking serious?

I knew Theo was probably already sleeping, but I needed to deescalate this situation before he heard the commotion and decided to barge into it.

I climbed back down and walked to stand in front of

him, placing a hand on his bicep. I felt the uprising rage trembling through his body. I wanted to tell him he was reading too much into it, but anything close to an accusation would only fuel the already tense atmosphere.

Instead, I let out a soft laugh, smiling up at him "*Mi amor,* he's happily married and so am I. Let's just go to bed, yeah?"

Something shifted in his gaze, but I decided to ignore it.

I walked back toward the staircase, but before I could even make it, he grabbed my wrist and whirled me around, slamming my back against the wall, sending spikes of pain through my shoulders.

His bulk crowded over me, his fingers tightening around my bones, sending pain lancing up my arm. "This conversation isn't over." He gritted through his teeth.

I looked down at his punishing grip on my wrist, my arm trapped between our bodies. Snapping my eyes back to him, I calmly said, "Victor, let me go."

Instead of letting me go, he spun me around and twisted my arm behind my back, slamming me into the wall as punishment. My face collided against the plastered wall, a loud thud resonating across the room, sending the edges of my sight blurring.

Fuck. This is going to leave a bruise.

The sound snapped him out of his angered trance, and his hand dropped immediately.

"Ugh, look at what you made me do," he said, annoyed.

Was this man serious? He hit me, and now it was my fault. God, I couldn't wait to put a bullet through his skull.

I swallowed the urge to retaliate and ignored the throbbing pain in my face before I turned to him. He stayed quiet while I just stared at him, his eyes roaming over my injured face, contempt filling his.

"Next time, remember your place," he finally said, his words heavy with warning. He turned on his heels, storming down the hallway and into his office.

When the door slammed shut behind him, I brought my hand to my cheek, hoping it would dull the pain as I made my way upstairs. I walked into the bedroom, heading straight toward the bathroom.

I switched the light on, locking the door behind me before turning the shower on. I grabbed a few painkillers from the cabinet and bent to wash them down with water from the sink.

I swiped my hand across my mouth and glanced up, catching the first glimpse of myself in the mirror. I brought my hand up, gently touching the swollen area, and winced at the contact.

I leaned against the bathroom counter, reminding myself I was doing this for a reason.

You'll get what's coming for you, Victor Morales.

CHAPTER 12
SOFIA

Today had been another dreadful day filled with jarring meetings for the upcoming fundraiser, from budgeting to securing pieces for the auction.

I was currently sitting in on my last meeting of the day with one of Bemes's most elite to secure their endorsement, eagerly counting down the minutes until it ended.

Selene Fares had recently been elected as governor and she was proving to be more selective when it came to budgeting than her predecessor was.

She'd been fighting a private war with the illegal drugs and guns trade, which made her very hesitant to invest in anything that she was remotely suspicious of. She mercilessly aimed to erase the corruption in our city, especially after her son was caught in the crossfire of a deal gone wrong.

Although it was a rather honorable mission, I didn't

believe anything could erase the disease that'd sprouted so deep and taken seed over the past two decades.

The Barrera cartel had gained monopoly when I was still young, ruling the majority of the country with an iron fist. Over the years, they built strong ties overseas with the Spanish and the Italians, erasing most of their competition by doing so.

They built up their legal business side to a point that it was extremely difficult to catch them. Everything the authorities had on them now was barely circumstantial and they tended to stay low in Bab El Mansour, where their headquarters were located.

And ironically where I am from.

The only reason I knew all of this, despite being from there, was because I'd done my research on Victor Morales, and he just so happened to be in relations with them. He'd been tasked to do their biddings at the Bemes port, monitoring what came in and out of it, illegal or otherwise.

My assistant Mariam, who'd joined me for this last meeting, and I had been going back and forth with Governor Fares for the past hour, attempting to draw out a potential investment from her, when the ringing of a phone cut through the room. Everyone around the table looked at their phones, but it didn't seem to be coming from any of us.

The ringtone blared again and I glanced over my shoulder at where Theo was standing.

He pulled out his phone from his pocket and looked down at the caller, his stoic expression changing quickly.

"I'm so sorry, Mrs. Morales, but I really have to take this," Theo announced, worry etching his features. He quickly apologized to the rest of the room for the interruption before leaving in a hurry, the door clicking shut behind him.

Mariam took over the conversation, discussing numbers and logistics while I tuned their voices out, my mind drifting back to Theo's sudden shift in demeanor, which was a rare occurrence.

Theo had never left my side before, let alone for a phone call. I was grateful the meeting was wrapping up because the curiosity to know what was so important that he'd answered a personal call on the job was rearing its head.

"My assistant will be in touch with yours," Selene said, drawing me out of my thoughts.

After setting a date for our next meeting, we shook hands and I made my way out of her office, parting ways with Mariam once we finished discussing tomorrow's agenda.

Theo was at the other end of the hall, his body tense as he paced back and forth. I watched from afar, hearing him curtly reply a "fine" to whoever was at the end of the call before hanging up and dialing another number.

Once the new number he dialed answered, he visibly

relaxed, his shoulders slumping with relief as a shadow of a smile formed at the corner of his lips.

"Hi, *mijita*," he greeted the person at the other end of the line and my stomach sank at his use of the endearment.

I clamped my jaw shut as I let the drone of his voice wash over me, jealousy slowly slithering through my veins, coiling around my muscles, and pulling them tight.

Even though I had no right in having monopoly on Theo, the mere thought of another woman having him infuriated me.

I knew I'd been the one who'd left, but I'd never meant to stay away forever. I knew I couldn't have expected him to wait forever, but deep down, I'd wished he'd never moved on, that he'd waited for me.

It was selfish, but I couldn't help it.

After finishing his conversation with whoever she was, he strolled back to where I was standing, an apologetic look on his face. "I'm very sorry for the interruption earlier. It won't happen again."

He paused, mulling over his next words. "There was a slight family emergency. Would it be okay if we made a quick stop on the way back? It shouldn't take long."

I swallowed the knot around my throat that'd formed when he uttered the word family.

"Of course," I replied forcefully.

Twenty minutes later, we were parked in front of an old building that read Bemes Valley in blue-tainted metal letters on its front. A little girl was sitting outside on a bench a few feet away from the front door, an older woman standing right next to her.

This explained why he rushed to the store on the way here to grab a car seat.

I couldn't see her face clearly, but she didn't seem to be older than five years old. She was wearing what seemed like a school uniform, a yellow backpack strapped to her back. She was dangling her short legs on the edge of the bench, her eyes roaming around as she patiently waited for someone.

Is that...? No, it can't be.

"Stay inside. I won't be long," he said, breaking the heady silence that had surrounded us on the drive over. He quickly got out of the car, slamming the door shut behind him before rounding the hood and jogging toward her.

Despite his warning, I slipped out, compelled to get a closer look.

As soon as she spotted him, the young girl jumped down the bench and started running up to him, her excited squeals filling the air. Her dark hair billowed behind her as she raced his way, a beaming smile lighting up her tanned face.

Once Theo reached her, she launched herself at his long legs since it was the only part of his body she could really reach from her height.

I strolled closer, following the strong urge to watch their interaction. My steps slowed to a stop when I was close enough to hear them, but not close enough to be noticed right away since their attention was fully focused on each other.

I couldn't fully see her face yet, but I could see Theo's reactions from the side. He wore the softest smile on his face, one I hadn't seen in a long time.

"You're here," she said loudly, wrapping her little arms tighter around his legs before jumping up and down, buzzing with excitement. He placed a hand over her head, prompting her to stop and look up at him.

"I'm so sorry I'm late, Maya," he said softly, kneeling until they were at eye level.

She pointed behind her at who I assumed was her teacher. "It's okay. Miss Meena told me Mama is stuck at work and can't pick me up," she answered.

He gave her a small smile as he picked her up in his arms, tucking a loose curl that fell on her face behind her ear before placing a small kiss to her temple.

"Yes, they gave Mommy another few hours to work at the hospital," he whispered against her head.

"I missed you," she exclaimed, clinging to his neck, nuzzling her face in the crook of it.

When she pulled away, placing her hands on his cheeks, I froze in place, unable to move from the revelation that materialized in my mind when she finally came into full view.

She was absolutely beautiful. Her tight brown curls loose around her frame, cascading down her back as two small clips pinned the front pieces away from her round face.

What had taken me aback was that not only was she beautiful, she looked exactly like him, with her big brown eyes and high cheekbones. Tears flooded my eyes as the remnants of their conversation faded into the background.

A daughter. My Theo had a family.

Without me.

I felt my carefully constructed armor faintly crack under witnessing him be so at ease with her.

A soft laugh bubbled out of his throat and he kissed her temple. "Easy, baby." He chuckled. "I missed you too, *mijita.*"

The whispers of his laugh carried through the frigid air and washed over me, the sound squeezing my chest tight.

God, I missed that sound.

Once upon a time, I'd thought I'd always have all of his chuckles to myself, that I'd know what they sounded like under each circumstance. But at that exact moment, I was reminded of how long seven years really was, of how I'd missed so much of his life.

That the life we'd planned on having together was vanishing like quicksand.

Watching Theo hold her sent a hammer to my chest, the cold metal pummeling into my heart until I felt another notch add itself to the dozens already present.

I put my hand over my heart, pressing hard to ease the pain.

I thought of the possibility of him moving on with someone else, but witnessing it and seeing how happy he looked holding her made me realize I might not have a home at the end of this. That my biggest fear when I started all of this had come to reality.

I guess that is the consequence of seeking revenge.

Having my heart being collateral damage.

As if he'd heard my thoughts, Theo turned around and made his way to me. I schooled my features, placing my mask firmly back in its place.

Maya's smile grew brighter as they drew closer to where I was still standing, jolting me out of my lament.

"Who's this?" she asked, her eyes roaming over my face curiously.

Theo gave me a small smile and my heart jumped. "Maya, this is Olivia."

"Hi," I said shyly, giving her my hand to shake.

She ignored my hand and her little fingers reached for my cheek. "You're so pretty."

I blushed at her compliment, placing my hand over where she'd laid hers. "I could say the same about you."

She giggled.

"All right, let's head home," Theo said, walking back to the car, and I followed behind them.

After buckling her in the car seat for kids he'd picked up earlier, he drove away and I sat there, dwelling on the new situation unfolding around me.

I didn't know how much time passed before we reached our destination, pulling into the driveway of a one-story house. Theo barely had time to park before Maya unbuckled herself from the back seat and rushed to his side, then grabbed his hand and pulled him toward the house.

"Come on, let's go see *Mi*," she yelled in a happy voice.

His laughter boomed in the air as he followed behind her. "Slow down, Maya. I'm coming."

She peered back, noticing I was still in the car. "Are you coming, Olivia?" she asked.

I smiled at her. "Okay."

It was a quiet area, with family houses lining the street. As soon as we walked in, she ran to the kitchen into the arms of a woman who I assumed was the grandmother she was referring to earlier.

"*Mi, Mi,* look, we have a special guest," Maya exclaimed, beaming.

Her grandmother bent down to pick her up, throwing her a loving smile before planting an affectionate kiss on top of her head.

She glanced up, her eyes now trained on me as she offered me a welcoming smile. "I can see that, *tesoro*."

"Hi, it's nice to meet you," I greeted her shyly. I never thought I'd be this nervous meeting someone new, but I'd never met his mother before since we were in hiding when we were together.

I was meeting the love of my life's mother as a lie. Lying to him was hard enough, but now I had to pretend to be someone else to his family as well.

"It's nice to meet you too…" She paused, waiting for me to introduce myself.

"Olivia," I finished for her.

"It's nice to meet you, Olivia," she said with a smirk.

She put Maya back down and looked over my shoulder toward Theo, switching fully into Spanish, asking him who the pretty girl he just brought home was and that it was long overdue for him to bring someone home.

He placed a hand on the small of my back, sending a shiver down my spine as he walked past me to greet his mother. He wrapped his arms around her shoulders, pulling her into a side hug and kissing her forehead.

"Mama, she's my new client. And, she can understand you."

"Oh."

He chuckled softly, shaking his head. "Yeah, *oh*."

"Are you staying for dinner, *mijo?*"

"Sorry, I can't. We have to head back."

"Nooo, Uncle Theo," Maya whined as she hugged his legs. She looked up at him, pouting. "Stay, please."

Uncle? Wait, she wasn't his daughter.

"I can't, *mijita*. I have to go back to work," he admitted reluctantly.

"Tell you what." He crouched to her level, gripping her chin so she would look at him. "When Mommy comes home tonight, have her call me and I'll read your favorite bedtime story until you fall asleep."

She nodded, wrapping her arms around his neck tightly. "Okay."

"I love you," he said, planting a kiss on her forehead.

She smiled, giving a loud kiss on his cheek. "I love you more."

His mother came up behind him and rubbed his back. "Don't stay away too long."

"Promise," he replied, planting another kiss on her forehead.

He headed for the door and I took one last look at the kitchen where his mother and niece were laughing while cooking, my heart squeezing at the reminders of the countless times my mother tried teaching me how to cook growing up.

As soon as we were in the car, I turned to Theo and blurted out the question that had been burning my tongue since Maya called him uncle. "She's not your daughter?"

"No, she's my younger sister's daughter. Camila's an ER nurse and one of her colleagues called off at the last minute, so she had to stay for a few extra hours to cover until they could find a replacement. My mother hasn't driven in over ten years and my younger brother is away for college."

There was a pause. "Besides, I'm usually the first person my family calls when something's wrong or needs to be done."

He started the car, pulling away from the driveway.

"I didn't know you had siblings."

We'd shared a lot during the year we'd spent together, but we never really talked much about his life outside of the bureau.

He turned his attention to me. "Yeah. I'm the oldest."

His eyes drifted back to the road and we drove home in complete silence, with only one thought at the forefront of my mind.

Maybe not everything is lost.

CHAPTER 13
SOFIA

I'd been sitting in my office all day, waiting for Victor to leave the house for his late meeting with the suppliers after the delayed shipment incident. It was almost eleven at night and Victor still hadn't left the house, leading me to think it had been postponed.

I was almost done getting ready for bed when the headlights of his Maybach filtered through the bedroom's window, streaking the wall opposite in shades of white before they disappeared.

I walked to the window and watched it pull away from the driveway, Jaxon in the driver's seat. The gates closed right behind them as they drove off into the night, three black SUVs following closely behind, leaving us security-free for at least the next hour.

I had to act fast. This was my only window of opportunity to find out more about Theo's real reason for being here.

As the days went by, I'd caught flashes of uncertainty in his expression and I needed to find out why he was here, doing a babysitter's job instead of working for the bureau. I'd tried hacking through his call log, but whatever server he was using kept dodging my attempts at infiltrating his phone.

Theo would be coming back from his run any minute now and would head straight to the shower like he did every night, his routine like clockwork.

Not sure who goes for a run this late at night, but it is working in my favor right now.

My phone pinged with a notification, indicating the gates were opening again. Theo's showers usually lasted fifteen minutes, so despite the cold outside, I decided to forego grabbing a robe since it would only slow me down.

The house was quiet as I slipped out of the master bedroom and rounded the corner of the upstairs hallway. I strolled down the hall, and my breathing slowed, my heartbeat picking up as I tiptoed down the stairs in the dark, using the wall to guide me.

Rosa was staying over in our guest bedroom downstairs tonight since it would be an early morning tomorrow. I knew she was already sound asleep, but one could never be too careful.

Once in the kitchen, I stalked across it and pushed lightly against the sliding glass doors. Peeking my head outside, I did a quick scan of the backyard, confirming no one had stayed behind.

With no one in sight, I made my way outside, keeping low to the wall and dodging the scope of the cameras. I'd be able to alter the footage later, but it would be easier if minimal changes had to be done since I didn't have all of my equipment with me.

I'd been studying the pool house when an icy breeze sifted through my hair and sleeping gown, the waves in the pool rippling against it. I cursed under my breath, berating myself for not wearing something warmer.

I waited for the sound of the shower to filter through the slightly ajar window from the pool house before jogging across the yard.

My breathing grew louder, my heartbeat pounding in my ears as I looked through the curtained windows to see if he was still in the main living area. Then, I slowly turned the doorknob on the door and pushed it open just enough for my body to squeeze through.

Once inside, I gently closed the door behind me, a soft click echoing through the room. I turned my attention to the back of the house where the bathroom was, a soft yellow hue filtering beneath the door. I stayed silent. Watching. Listening.

No other sound came except for the shower spray. I took in the space around me. A dim pool of moonlight flowed across the hardwood floor, but it was still dark enough that it took a few minutes for my eyes to adjust.

Everything was still as it was. There was no personal touch. No pictures on the nightstand, no books lying around. You could barely tell someone was living here. You could barely tell *Theo* was staying here. Not that he'd ever been a messy person, but this looked almost clinical.

The large queen bed was made. A pile of clothes neatly folded sat in the corner. I walked over to the bed and kneeled down to look through the drawers at the base of it, opening each one.

Bedding. Towels. Clothing.

I rummaged through the layers, looking for any folders, computers, or burner phones. Nothing. I rose from the floor and drifted to the left side of the large room that served as his living space and into the small kitchen area. I opened each drawer and cabinet carefully, looking through each.

Again, nothing. I let out a frustrated sigh.

Think, Sofia. If you were Theo, where would you put anything of value?

And it clicked. In plain sight. First thing he'd taught me.

If you have anything to hide, do it in plain sight where the intruder wouldn't even think of looking.

I scanned the room once again and noticed the small drawer on the entryway table next to the door. I walked over and tried to pull it open, but it wouldn't budge. I muttered a curse under my breath, pulling harder until a small creak resonated.

That's when I saw it. A laptop with a phone resting on top of it. The shower was still running, but it wouldn't be enough time to go through both, so I went for the phone.

Right as I was picking it up, the clearing of a throat broke the silence in the room.

Fuck.

CHAPTER 14

THEO

I heard her mutter something under her breath, her hair tumbling around her delicate face, a scowl marring it. She carefully tried sliding the drawer open again, this time succeeding, triumph lighting her features.

She was completely oblivious to my presence, so I seized the opportunity to take her in. She was barefoot and wearing a silk nightgown that barely grazed her thighs, the fabric resting against the swell of her ass.

Jesus. *Fuck.*

I wanted to press my lips against that soft skin, to trail kisses up her thighs, feeling her body come alive under my tongue until I finally landed at my desired destination.

I wanted to part her legs and teach her a lesson about invading someone's privacy. I wanted my mouth filled with her cum as I watched her come apart, driving her to the same obsession she'd conjured in me.

The thought of touching another woman had never crossed my mind before, so what was it about her that made me want more? It was as if an unnatural force was preventing me from staying away.

Shaking the thought, I leaned against the bathroom's doorframe and cleared my throat, my arms crossing against my bare chest, still slick from the shower I just took.

"Can I help you with anything, Mrs. Morales?"

Her back stiffened, a sharp gasp escaping her. She slowly turned to face me, whatever words she was about to say coming up short.

Her face turned into a hue, the flush spreading across her tanned skin as her gaze swept across every inch of my body. Her eyes roamed down my length, stopping right where the towel sat around my hips, her eyes lingering there for a moment.

"Olivia." My voice was strained, the low hum of desire thrumming through my veins. I swallowed the lump forming in my throat, trying to tamp down the urge to walk over there and bend her over the wooden surface.

She dragged her gaze away from my groin and up to meet mine.

Unspoken need filtered through the space between us, the air standing still for a heartbeat, her perusal leaving warmth seeping into my skin.

A swallow worked through her, bobbing up and down her slender neck. My eyes dropped to her chest, the outline of her nipples searing through the material of her gown.

She schooled her expression about half a second late, but I caught it. I wouldn't believe whatever lie she was about to tell me.

"I was just looking for something I'd left here before you moved in," she lied, shutting the drawer behind her. "But it's not here, so I'll be heading back," she continued, pointing at the door.

I smirked before taking a step toward her. She stepped back, her back colliding with the wooden furniture, her hands coming up behind her to brace herself.

She moved to leave, but I closed the remaining distance between us and grabbed her by the nape of her neck, her body now flushed against mine. "Tsk, tsk, tsk. Not so fast."

I placed my other hand next to hers on the table and leaned down to murmur against her ear. Her eyes fluttered closed.

"I don't believe you."

I stayed a moment longer, her arousal overpowering my senses. When I pulled back, her eyes snapped wide-open to meet mine as if she'd just registered what I'd said.

"Excuse me?"

I leaned forward until the tip of my nose grazed hers, my breath fluttering against her skin. "I'd suggest you try a different answer, Mrs. Morales," I whispered, my words ghosting over her lips.

"I think you're overstepping your boundaries, Mr. Alvarez," she stated, a quiet defiance in her gaze.

"Your body is telling me a different story, Mrs. Morales."

Her chest expanded with every inhale, and my fingers involuntarily skimmed down her neck, her skin smooth as I glided over it. My thumb hooked under the strap of her sleepwear, and I toyed with it, daring it.

We both stared as the string of fabric fell from her shoulder, the thin material hanging limply against her skin, revealing more of the silhouette of her breasts. Her lips parted on a harsh breath as the silk brushed her skin, and my breathing stuttered.

My tongue thickened against the roof of my mouth as I watched her reactions to my touch, fascinated, her breasts rising and falling with each breath.

God, this woman is mesmerizing, enrapturing me in her orbit.

She blinked up at me, surprise coating her features as my fingers dared venture farther down of their own accord.

My fingers slowly trailed across her chest and a shiver raked through her body as I traced the swell of her breasts. Goose bumps prickled across my skin and an ache spread across my jaw as I grinded my teeth, resisting the urge to look down.

Resisting the urge to say "fuck it" and to do the same

on the other side until her dress pooled at her feet, giving me the pleasure of seeing her bend at my will.

Images of her on my lap, my palm resting against the curve of her ass as I spanked her for looking through what wasn't hers flashed through my mind. But those thoughts were dangerous.

My hand on her ass meant my fingers would be closer to her pussy, praying to find her dripping wet and ready to soak them even more once I was done with her.

The reactions this woman conjured within me were almost visceral and her resistance only made me want to fuck her into submission.

I continued exploring the lines of her body, waiting for her to stop me, yet she remained silent. I skimmed down her side, resting my fingers on the hem of her nightgown, taunting, but once again, she didn't move away from my touch.

Energy buzzed around us, sending my heart thudding violently against my chest, a fire erupting in the pit of my stomach, demanding more.

But I didn't dare move my fingers further. I was so fucking tempted to give in, but I wouldn't, not until she said something.

She tilted her head, intently watching me under her thick lashes, baiting me to continue. Something flashed in her brown eyes, but it was gone before I could decipher it.

Slivers of moonlight spilled through a gap in the drapes, highlighting her face. It was the first time I'd seen her without makeup. She was beautiful regardless, but there was a softness to her I hadn't seen before.

But with her tough shell scrubbed away, I also saw another truth she'd been hiding.

Traces of a fading bruise.

My body stiffened, fingertips clenching the fabric at the hem, my knuckles grazing her thigh in the process as a rage like I had never felt before washed over me.

Delicately, I brought a trembling hand to cup her face, the rough skin of my thumb swiping across the tender almost-faded bruising flesh.

She stilled.

"Who the fuck did this to you?" I asked, speaking through gritted teeth.

She winced from my touch, tearing her gaze away from mine. "I bumped into a table trying to grab something."

"You are a terrible liar." My thumb gently rested on her cheek, my index finger tilting her head back so she would look at me.

"Please." I paused. My eyes searched hers again until our gazes finally locked again. My heart skipped a beat as I asked, "Was it Victor?"

Confusion knitted her brows together, alarm flashing briefly across her face. The tense air suddenly dissipated as she jerked away from me at the mention of his name, my hand falling away from her as she shoved us apart, almost violently, putting distance between us.

"This never happened," she warned, storming out the door, slamming it behind her.

I didn't go after her.

I braced myself over the table she was previously pressed against, trying to calm my ragged breaths. I pushed the drapes aside, confirming she'd made it in safely, and after a few minutes, I saw her figure walk past the window in the master bedroom.

Ignoring the need to march into the house and murder Victor Morales, I untied the towel from my waist and dried myself before changing into the clothes I'd left on my bed earlier.

I didn't believe her lie, but I also didn't want to make it worse for her. It wasn't my place, but I'd be here if she needed me to be.

Once I was dressed, I lay in bed, staring at the ceiling and contemplating what this woman, this *married* woman, was doing to me.

I couldn't shake the feeling of how good she felt under my fingertips, how familiar her skin felt.

My thumb grazed over my lower lip, trying to commemorate the feel of her skin to my other senses.

Touching her was probably a mistake, but I let myself relish in the proximity she was giving me to the one person I'd been thinking of ever since I'd first met Olivia.

Sofia.

CHAPTER 15
SOFIA

"He's so hot," one of the ladies around the table said.

The women laughed, and I sported a tight smile, unaware of which *he* they were referring to, having zoned out of their conversation long ago.

These friendly weekly luncheons at Brownstone, our local country club, were usually short, but I always counted every second until they were over.

These women weren't my friends, and truthfully, they'd never be. They were who society dictated them to be. Status and wealth were what shaped these *friendships*. These were the people my *husband* wanted me to befriend since in this world, connections and the image you projected were everything.

And just like the dutiful *wife* I was, I'd done exactly what he asked of me.

"Tempting enough to contemplate cheating on my Mike," another added. More shrieks of laughter erupted. I just nodded, nursing the glass of champagne, sipping it every once in a while to avoid having to join the conversation.

I wished I had something stronger to make this more bearable.

Mila zeroed in her attention on me as she drained the rest of her glass of red wine, patronizingly lifting her hand to the waiter who was passing by for another one.

She was already on her third, and we were barely an hour in. Mila had never been a huge fan of mine, although she'd never come out right and said it. None of the ladies around the table were honest about anything—each hiding their own secrets behind closed doors.

Conversations were filled with pointed comments and backhanded compliments. As soon as one person had their back turned, whispers immediately started shortly after.

My *husband* was richer, more successful than their husbands ever would be and they were threatened by that.

If only they knew what made him so successful.

"I would pay to have a man look at me like that," Hailey said, her tone suggestive as she poked my side.

The table quieted, all of them waiting on bated breath, their attention now solely focused on me.

"I'm sorry, I was lost in thought," I responded, feigning ignorance to dismiss her suggestion.

"Come on, tell us," Hailey urged before continuing with a sly grin on her face. "He hasn't taken his eyes off you the entire time."

"He's a bodyguard. That's his job." I stopped myself from rolling my eyes at her, opting to take another sip from my flute.

"But he isn't watching you like it's *just* his job." She glanced at him quickly, returning her attention back to me, her eyes narrowing. "He's watching you l—"

"He's my bodyguard," I repeated, cutting her off.

She sighed dramatically. "Whatever." Hailey turned to Mila, sparking a conversation about the new family that had just moved into our neighborhood and how they didn't fit.

Realistically, who did?

Sighing with relief that their attention was no longer on me, I discreetly tried to steal a peek at Theo, but he was already watching me closely, that signature stoic expression on his face.

Memories of two nights ago were still plaguing my mind. His actions were so out of character, he'd caught me off guard, cementing me in place. His boldness was the opposite of what I'd expected.

Instead of keeping his distance, he'd stalked across the room and leaned closer, flushing our bodies together. There was so much of him all at once, that I hadn't been able to think straight.

His size loomed over me. His rich and familiar scent

wrapped around me, sending my stomach into a frenzy of somersaults. The water droplets slipping down his abdomen, cascading over every divot of his toned stomach made my mouth dry.

He'd barely touched me, barely any words were said, yet the desire was still just as palpable as ever, despite all the years apart.

But he wasn't aware of who I was. My heart tugged at the idea of him moving on with someone else. Despite Maya not being his daughter, what would stop him from having that with someone else other than me?

Seven years was a long time to wait for someone.

I'd been relieved when he hadn't further questioned me about the bruise on my face after that night. I didn't need another problem to be added to my plate.

I realized I had been staring at him this whole time when his expression morphed into a questioning one. I quickly diverted my gaze away from him and looked down at my watch, counting down the minutes until I could politely excuse myself from this charade.

The gathering continued, and I pretended to enjoy myself as I made an effort to chat with a few of the ladies near me, glancing at my watch here and there.

I hadn't realized he'd moved from his position, until I felt him looming over me.

"Sorry to interrupt, Mrs. Morales, but we have to go," he stated before leaning in next to my head.

My brows knitted in confusion. *Did something happen?*

"You seem bored. Let's go," he whispered in my ear, low enough for only me to hear.

I stood up, grabbing my purse. "Duty calls." I smiled tightly at the women, whose attention was now fully on Theo, hungry gazes roaming over his frame.

"We'll see you next week," they said in unison as Theo pulled my chair away, making way for me to exit. He followed closely behind and I muttered a thank you as we waited for the valet to bring the car around.

"Home?" he asked once we were both seated inside.

I shook my head slightly. "Could you take me to this address?"

He didn't ask questions, simply put the car in motion and drove to the destination.

Soon after I'd moved in with Victor and integrated into his world, I'd invested in this community center and taught computer programming here as often as I could, despite Victor's heavy reluctance toward it.

I hadn't been here in months since my dear *husband* forbade me from coming, but I obviously didn't listen. I needed this today.

These kids reminded me of myself. And in the world I'd created, where anger and vengeance suffocated everything else, I needed to find something that anchored the smallest amount of humanity I had left.

I couldn't let Victor take that away from me, not if I wanted to go after the missing piece of my soul after all of this was over.

Theo parked in front of the building and I peeled my suit jacket off and threw it in the back seat. Reaching for the small compartment under the floor of the back, I grabbed a pair of white sneakers, exchanging my black heels for them.

I felt him watching and turned to look at him. "What?" I asked, irritated.

He held both his hands up, a low chuckle escaping him. "Nothing."

"Good." I opened the door, shut it behind me, and walked into the glass building.

The staff was surprised to see me again after my long hiatus but put me to work immediately. I got lost in each kid's curiosity, the soft buzz of computers taking over my mind, calming my thoughts. A feeling of contentment replaced the incessant raging anger for just a few hours.

I heard one of the kids, Amina, huff under her breath as she furiously typed on her keyboard, trying different codes to solve the assignment I'd given them.

I walked over to her and dropped into the chair next to hers. "What's wrong?" I questioned her.

"Nothing's working." She turned, her brows bunched

into a severe frown. My thumb traced her forehead, smoothing it.

I spent the next few minutes guiding her. She was almost there but kept hitting a wall in the coding sequence. I chuckled under my breath when she finally cracked it and yelled a "gotcha."

I knew he'd been watching me intently since we'd walked in, surprise etching his features at seeing me so at ease here. I was tired of constantly playing a role. This was mine. I didn't want to be Olivia Morales for just a few hours.

I wanted to let Sofia out for a little while, even if that meant letting Theo see a small side of the real me.

The burn of his stare was becoming unbearable, so I glanced up at him. Our gazes collided. My breath caught in my throat. Hailey hadn't been wrong. Theo did have *something* glimmering in his eyes, the intensity in his gaze scaring me.

I could feel him getting too close, could feel my armor slowly crumbling.

Which was why I needed to create a distraction.

CHAPTER 16
THEO

When I bailed her out of her Wednesday weekly gathering with the wives of some of Morales's associates, I thought she'd want to go back home or spend the rest of the day shopping, but she did the complete opposite of what I would have expected her to, catching me off guard.

Volunteering her afternoon to teach these kids how to use computers was the last thing on my mind.

Not only did they all look like they'd known her well, but it seemed they'd even missed her and her lessons.

She was sporting an expression I'd never seen on her face before. She looked… content. Happy even. Her lips were drawn up in an effortless smile, her eyes crinkling in the corners.

There was a lightness to her features that had me entranced.

I felt my heart tug inside my rib cage at the sight. It wasn't just her beauty. She had that in spades. No, there was something about her, about her being in her element, that had my heart racing.

As I continued watching her smile, something inside me shifted. There was more to her than she wanted to let on. Her features were so serene. Gone were the annoyance and perpetual scowls she greeted me with.

It felt as if I was getting a glimpse of another Olivia unfolding in front of my eyes.

She sat with them for what felt like hours and I just couldn't stop staring. I could tell she knew I was, but, honestly, I couldn't care less. I wanted to bask in the glow she was radiating while she was with these kids.

A burning need to see her this way, this happy and carefree, in my presence took home inside me. This absurd need bloomed inside my chest as I realized I wanted her to smile *because* of me.

She eventually glanced up at me, our eyes caught in a silent exchange. Something had shifted between us two nights ago when I caught her looking through my things. She'd mostly kept her distance ever since, fighting me less and less, and I found myself missing it, missing our back and forth.

Despite how infuriating she was at times, I always loved feeling the fire she exuded when she wanted to be defiant. It only gave me more opportunities to dream of all the ways I could tame it.

She dismissed the class a few hours later, a blur of students chattering as they flitted toward the exit, but one of the students, a girl who seemed to be about the same age as Maya, stayed behind and took a hesitant step toward Olivia.

I couldn't quite hear their conversation from where I was standing, but Olivia crouched down to her level, tucking a loose dark curl behind her ear. A moment passed and then the girl wrapped her arms around her neck.

Olivia's face widened in shock, unsure what to do at first, but she eventually wrapped her arms around the girl's small frame, tugging her into a tight embrace. She said one last thing to her before the girl gave her a high five and ran toward the exit, leaving Olivia still on her knees.

She stayed still for a moment, then looked up and caught me staring at her. Looking away, she stood and retreated to the back of the room where the rest of the volunteers were gathering, chatting.

After saying her goodbyes to the remaining staff, she brushed past me and hurried to the car.

I had so many questions I wanted to ask her but decided against it and turned the radio on to fill the quiet space during our drive back to the house. Thirty minutes later, I parked in the garage and we both made our way inside.

We drifted past the living room as she made her way to

her office while I veered toward the kitchen, when a voice suddenly halted us.

"You're home," Victor noted. He might have sounded normal to anyone else, but I could hear an edge underlying it.

I'd never really paid attention to their interactions before, but ever since discovering the marks on her face that night, I started being more attentive to the way he spoke to her, the way she reacted to him when he was close, looking for any signs that he might have been the problem all along.

I was always alert when we stepped outside of these walls, but I'd never considered looking inside of them.

"Mr. Alvarez, would you please give us a moment?" he asked, more like ordered, with a tight smile. His eyes never leaving Olivia.

"Yes, sir." I wasn't going anywhere, but he didn't need to know that. I stepped down the hallway toward the kitchen but retreated back when I heard him start talking again.

I hid behind a wall, spying on their exchange. Although Morales had his back to me, I could clearly see Olivia's side profile.

Her arms were crossed over her chest and she stood straight, eye level with Victor, since she'd changed back into her heels before we walked in. He was tense, his fists clenched at his sides as he spewed muttered curses in Spanish under his breath.

Olivia stayed put, not moving an inch as he went on and on about how disrespectful she was being to him and how she was sabotaging his image by leaving the social gathering to spend time with those kids.

He spoke with such disdain that it took everything in me not to march over and put him back in his place for talking to her that way. But it would be overstepping boundaries and that wasn't my job.

I was here to protect her from outside threats, not to regulate marriage conflicts. But most importantly, I knew how men like Victor would react if they saw someone coming to their wife's defense, and I didn't want to create any problems for her.

Despite Olivia being a private person, I'd find a way to talk to her when it was just us, away from him, to try and gauge whether she needed me or not.

When he finished his ramble, she made a move to walk past him, but he wrapped his fingers around her wrist, gripping it and harshly pulling her back. The movement revealed a glimpse of his face and I saw red.

I saw his mask finally drop, showing the monster underneath.

Olivia curled around herself, bracing for impact as I watched Morales's arm outstretched in the air, ready to strike her.

But right before it connected, my hand grabbed his wrist forcefully, pushing it backward.

"I wouldn't do that if I were you," I said harshly, my grip tightening around him.

He stumbled a few steps back, his eyes glaring daggers at me. I met him with the same intensity, daring him to defy me. My body was vibrating with a murderous rage and I was two seconds away from disfiguring him with my fists. He should consider himself lucky that I wasn't murdering him right then and there.

His mask slid back in place, and he yanked his arm back. He walked toward his office, turning mid-way to glare at me.

"Never do that again, Mr. Alvarez," he said, displeasure coating his tone, then slammed the wooden door of his office behind him.

When the adrenaline faded, I spun around, only to find Olivia already gone.

I'd barely seen her these past few days. Five to be exact.

Yes, I'd counted, but I didn't want to think about that fact too much.

Since that afternoon, she'd spent most of her days locked in her office, only coming down to eat, then locking herself right back up.

Today was the first day we'd spent any time alone.

Earlier this morning, Victor had called me into his office, letting me know I was needed for the day. I'd been tasked with accompanying both him and Olivia to a brunch spot downtown for a last-minute emergency meeting with some of the board members from his company.

Victor had taken a car with Jaxon, while I drove with Olivia separately. I wanted to talk to her about what happened, but every time I went to open my mouth, she would shut me down with her gaze, not wanting to discuss Wednesday's incident.

The small café was located in a quiet neighborhood. Although Jaxon and I considered it was private enough that preliminary security clearance wasn't necessary, we thought it would be better if we were both here.

It'd been quiet for some time now. No other gifts or notes had shown up since the one from the parking garage. We'd found no fingerprints or anything really that could help us trace it back to its sender. I'd sent it to Noah, but I still hadn't heard back from him. I'd tried calling a few times, but it kept going straight to voicemail.

But quiet wasn't always a good sign. If anything, whoever was sending the threats might have stayed under the radar just to prepare for something bigger. We might just be on borrowed time.

I moved my attention back to where they were all seated at a round table in the middle of the shop, deep into an animated conversation.

Olivia was facing away from me, her back leaned

against a wooden chair. Her dark hair was tied in a pony-
tail, a few loose strands framing her face. She was
wearing some sort of navy pinstripe skirt suit, with an
oversized matching blazer, white lace hem peeking
through.

She looked beautiful. Well, she always looked
beautiful.

She leaned her elbows on the marbled surface of the
table, joining the conversation after one of the men asked
for her opinion about how to resolve the crisis they were
facing.

I took that opportunity to divert my attention from
her and actually do my job, evaluating the surroundings.

The room we were in was well lit, brightened mostly
by the daylight cast through the huge bay windows. A few
soft lights were hanging from the high inverted hull ceiling, wooden boat paddles used as fan blades. Old-looking
mirrors were lined behind the bar on the far right, plants
and dried flowers decorating its front.

Years in the field taught me to notice the unnoticeable,
see what others couldn't by recognizing the markings of a
guilty conscience. My gaze bounced from man to man,
searching for telltale signs of a gun protruding from a
waistline, a nervous hand twitch, a repeated glance
toward the exit.

One of the waiters brushed past the bench where I was
seated, a single drink on his tray. My gaze briefly flicked
it, noticing a small white paper next to the drink, but I

brushed it off and brought my attention back to Olivia, the waiter now approaching their table.

My eyes were still on her when an ominous feeling crawled on my skin. Instinctively, my back stiffened as every inch of me went on high alert.

Olivia turned to the waiter, nodding to whatever he was saying before she grabbed a piece of paper from him. Her eyes quickly scanned the content, then she got up, eyes wide as she glanced frantically around the room.

She eventually turned in my direction and the new position gave me a better view of her face, which was when I saw it.

A red dot was aimed right at her forehead—a sniper's dot.

My body went into motion before my brain registered it. I leapt from my chair and ran to her.

"Olivia, get down," I yelled frantically.

There was a moment of complete silence before chaos unfolded. My body slammed into hers as I grabbed and whirled her around, tackling her to the ground to shield her body with mine. A gunshot erupted through the window, the sound of fractured glass shattering across the ceramic floor echoing across the panicked room. Customers yelled and jumped from their seats, some crouching under tables for cover, while others stampeded toward the exit.

The shot was quick. The bullet slammed into my shoulder, the force of it blurring my vision.

"Fuck," I muttered under my breath. My bones groaned from the impact, and I felt hot liquid trickling under my shirt.

My eyes snapped shut as I tried to ignore the pain lancing down my arm, the ringing in my ears loud. This wasn't the first time I'd been shot, but it still hurt like hell.

I waited, quieting the shouts surrounding us, letting them fade into the background as I focused on trying to decipher if there were any more gunshots. None came.

A single bullet. And it was aimed right at her.

I was still trying to understand what was happening, why a sniper was targeting her, when I felt her squirm against me.

"Let me go," she hissed, trying to roll from underneath me.

I blinked twice, taken aback by her harsh tone. I was the one with a bullet potentially lodged in my shoulder and she was trying to get away, which did nothing else but infuriate me more. Did she always have to fight me even when I was trying to save her fucking life?

"Olivia Morales, stop being stubborn and stay low," I gritted in her face, pinning her in place with a hand around the nape of her neck.

She continued to squirm, but I leaned my face closer to hers. "I said stop fucking moving. Do not make me repeat myself." My grip was more firm, giving her no room to shift any further.

Every inch of my body was covering hers. Her eyes

went wide at our closeness, her breath hitching, turning shallower by the second.

I ignored the rapid effect her proximity had on me and looked around for Jaxon. I found him behind a turned table a few feet away, gun in hand, with Victor plastered against his back, a frightened look smeared on his face, like he'd just seen a ghost.

"Is the sniper gone?" I mouthed to him.

He shrugged, unsure.

I scanned the vicinity, looking through the shattered window for any signs of the sniper still being there. They probably retreated as soon as they missed their target. My guess was they'd probably be long gone by the time the authorities arrived.

"I'll count to three and we're gonna run toward the back hall there," I said close to her ear, turning my head to point to the back of the restaurant.

I pinned her with a glare before she could argue. My words finally got past the confines of her need to defy me. Relenting, she nodded in understanding.

When I deemed the coast clear, I drew my gun from the side holster at my hip. Then, I whispered "three" in her ear, tugging her up as I stood, and we both bolted to the back of the room, my body still shielding hers.

Finding the supply room I knew was on the left, I tugged on her arm, yanking us inside, and locked the door behind us. I knew Jaxon would get Victor home right away, and honestly I didn't really care about what happened to him.

My goal was solely focused on getting Olivia to safety.

My arm reached behind her to pull on the dangling string cord I'd noticed coming in, turning on the low watt bulb above our heads.

It flickered before dimming the room in a soft amber hue. My hand drifted to settle on the small of her back, pulling her to me. After slipping the gun underneath the waistband behind my back, I let my hands roam over her body, inspecting her for injuries.

She parted her lips as if she was about to say something, but no sound came out. Her eyes were wide as she focused her attention on me. She blinked rapidly, then shook her head, making a move toward the door behind me.

I caught her hand in mine, my fingers tightening around her wrist. I yanked her into me, her face now only inches away from mine. My other hand was quick to wrap around the back of her neck, bringing her even closer until our breaths mingled together. "Do you have a death wish?"

She lifted her chin up, defiance in her eyes, but she didn't utter a word.

Her frame tensed against mine and I willed my body not to shiver from how overwhelming her proximity was. I hadn't had this strong of a reaction to someone else in a long time.

It was probably the allure of the forbidden, but I couldn't deny the way my body was taken by her, by the sense of familiarity. The way she molded perfectly against me. The look in her eyes.

Fuck.

I pulled away from her, putting as much distance as I could between the two of us. I moved to take off my suit jacket.

"Wh-what are you doing?" she asked, perplexed.

Instead of responding, I unbuttoned my shirt, crimson soaking the left side, and shrugged it off my shoulder. I then undid the straps of my vest, wincing from the burning pressure.

I crooked a finger toward her. "Come here," I ordered.

"Theo…" she trailed off, her eyes now on my shoulder that was no doubt still leaking blood.

I sighed, closing the distance, and slipped the vest over her head. She watched me intently as I adjusted the straps to fit her properly.

Her hand reached my bare shoulder, her finger smoothing over my skin, smearing the blood in the process. "You're bleeding," she said breathlessly, concern lacing her tone.

I hazarded a glance down, to find her dark brown eyes alight with heat. The air became thick, as it always was whenever it was just the two of us in an enclosed space. This foreign yet familiar energy crackling between us.

I shrugged her hand off my shoulder, her touch too much to bear, and finished fixing the vest on her frame.

"I'll be fine. Keep this on."

She moved to step away, but I tugged her into me, lifting her chin with my forefinger.

Olivia opened her mouth to say something, but I cut her off, gripping her chin. "Listen, I don't care what you think right now. You need to learn how to follow instructions without arguing. Someone tried to kill you. If I say wear a bulletproof vest, you wear the fucking bulletproof vest. Is that clear?"

Her breath hitched and I could see the need to go against my decision unfurling in her eyes, but she simply nodded.

Olivia Morales might just be the death of me.

CHAPTER 17

SOFIA

Everything had gone according to plan. Everything except Theo's reaction to the *attempt* on my life.

I'd tried to get away from his hold, to see if anyone had been hurt since I'd planned to move slightly to the side, enough for Valentina to fire her shot. The goal was to have no casualties and do minimal damage to the place.

But of course he had to alter this plan as well by jumping on me. As in, he used his body to shield mine, ready to take a bullet for me.

Which he ironically did.

The realization only dawned on me when he pulled me into the supply closet. I couldn't tell to which extent his injury went, but I hoped it only grazed him.

My heart tugged at the thought of him risking his life to protect me, but I had to keep reminding myself that he was hired to do so, that he wasn't protecting *me*, Sofia Herrera. He'd jumped to protect Olivia Morales.

I tried engraving those words in my brain as I shook my head internally, reeling myself back to the supply closet we'd been in for the past few minutes.

"Wait here," he commanded, turning his back on me to pull his bloodied shirt back on.

I forced myself to tear my gaze from his muscular back bunching. "Where are you going?"

"To make sure it's safe for us," he said, looking over his shoulder.

"I'm coming with you."

"No, Olivia. You stay here."

"I'm coming," I said with finality.

He sighed heavily before reaching behind the back of his pants and retrieving his gun.

Gun drawn up, he cautiously opened the door, and we both slipped out. I followed closely behind, since I didn't have a gun with me. I would've asked if he had a second one concealed, but that might raise suspicion and the whole point of this distraction was to direct his skepticism elsewhere.

The main room was empty now. Everyone who had been here fled already. He did a quick sweep, and after deeming it safe, we headed toward the exit at the back of the coffee shop. We walked through the deserted kitchen, appliances scattered on the floor, and out the back door.

Once we stepped outside, he plastered me against the

concrete wall with one hand, hiding me behind a dumpster as he surveyed the back alley.

He picked up a door stop that was straying outside, next to the restaurant's back door, and rummaged through the back alley until he pulled out a long metal rod. He then headed straight for a run-down black Ford Explorer that was parked to the side.

I followed behind, watching him with curiosity as he rammed the door stop into the side of the door.

"What are you doing?"

"Trying to break into a car. If you let me," he stated with his back still facing me, continuing his task.

My expression morphed into confusion, my brows pulling into a frown.

He glanced at me over his shoulder. "They might still be after you. I'm not chancing them tracking the car we took here and coming after you again."

Flinging the door open, he dove into the driver's seat, ducking his head under the wheel for a beat before the roaring of the car echoed in the empty alley.

I stood there, unmoving. He rolled down his window and looked at me. "Are you coming?" he asked impatiently.

I rounded the car and headed for the passenger's side. I'd barely secured my seat belt when he slid the gear into first and slammed his foot on the accelerator, the sound of cop cars looming closer.

The car ride was tense once his adrenaline faded away, frustration radiating off his body in waves. He drove erratically, swerving across lines and speeding at least forty miles over the limit. He clearly didn't care whether or not we got pulled over.

We eventually crossed the security gates of the house and drove up the long driveway. We were barely parked when Theo jumped out of the car, leaving his door wide-open. I scrambled out after him.

He burst through the front, marching into the house, straight into the living room where a few men from the security team were gathered.

"What the fuck happened out there?" he yelled at no one in particular.

"Mr. Alvarez, we still aren't sure what—" Maddox, another one of Jaxon's men, started.

Theo turned so quickly, a blur followed his path. Maddox barely had the chance to finish his sentence before Theo had his right forearm against his throat, holding him against the wall.

Leaning threateningly close, he growled, "She could have died."

I'd never seen Theo this frustrated, this *angry*. Not since he'd learned what plagued my nightmares. Theo wasn't a violent man. Maddox just happened to be in his line of sight. In an attempt to calm him, and knowing he wouldn't hurt me, I walked up to him, putting a hand on his upper arm.

"Mr. Alvarez," I started, my voice soft. "Theo, look at me. I'm okay. Please let him go."

His muscles bunched up and he looked back at me. His eyes were angry, but they immediately softened once he realized who it was.

He eased his hold on Maddox's throat just as Victor charged into the living room, roaring over the commotion, Jaxon and the rest of his men following close behind.

He's called in everyone. Fuck.

"How did this happen?" Victor barked at the room.

Maddox slumped against the wall, falling to his knees, with a hand to his throat, coughing as he tried to regulate his breathing.

Knowing he hadn't noticed me standing behind Theo's large frame, I cleared my throat, pulling my features into a worried expression. "Victor?"

He rushed to my side in his still perfectly pressed three-piece suit and pulled me against his chest, raking his hands over my body, asking me repeatedly if I was okay.

I must be doing a good job of looking panicked.

I pulled away. "I'm okay, *mi amor*. What's going on?"

"Sir, I'd like a word," Theo said to Victor.

"What?" Victor snapped. When he noticed it was Theo who'd addressed him, he quickly regained his composure and nodded, urging Theo to go on.

"In private," Theo added.

Victor ran a frustrated hand over his face, then headed to his office. Theo followed him in, closing the door behind.

What the fuck could they be talking about that required privacy?

Everyone remained quiet. They came back out a few minutes later, with Victor looking angrier than he'd been earlier.

"You need to pack," he stated, leaving no room for discussion.

"I'm sorry?" I must have misheard. I was busy trying to understand what he'd just said when he spoke again. This time with more urgency.

"*Now.* You have five minutes while Theo gets the car ready."

My eyes narrowed at him, a mixture of confusion and impatience bubbling to the surface as I directed my attention to Theo.

Scowling, I crossed my arms. "I'm not going anywhere with him."

Victor shut his eyes, rubbing forcefully a palm down his face. "Olivia, don't start now. This isn't up for discussion. Go pack or you'll leave with nothing," he said, exasperation testing his patience.

Leave with nothing.

Like I fucking cared. I couldn't leave this house. I wouldn't have access to anything.

And being stuck with him. Alone.

For days.

Ay, carajo.

Theo chimed in, "There's been a compromise, Mrs. Morales. We need to get you to safety."

"And who the *fuck* gave you the power to make decisions?" I bit out, glaring at him.

"That's enough," Victor snapped, silencing both of us. "You now have four minutes before you both have to leave."

He turned to Theo, dismissing me. "I know this wasn't part of your contract, but I need you to keep her safe."

Their chatter faded as I marched up the stairs.

"I'll keep her safe, sir," I heard Theo say before I shut the door behind me.

Okay, Sofia, piensa. How the fuck are you going to keep this going if you don't have full access?

I stalked across the room, going straight for my dresser. I bent down, grabbing the nondescript, black phone taped underneath it, which had stayed there undisturbed for weeks, quiet and gathering dust. Powering it on, I sent a quick message to the only number on there.

Me: It's time.

Now, I just had to hope the person on the other end would understand and take over until I came back.

I ran back and forth, trying to fit as much as I could

into the large bag I'd found in the back of the closet. I was barely able to fit a few pieces of clothing when a knock came to the door. I reached for the doorknob as Theo opened it, hitting me square in the forehead.

Pendejo.

"We're leaving," he grumbled.

Obviously.

"That wasn't four minutes. I'm not do—" I started, rubbing a hand over my forehead to dissipate the headache that was looming.

"We don't have more time," he said, grabbing the bag from my hand and heading down the stairs before I had a chance to argue. I stalked after him and slammed into his back when he stopped abruptly at the bottom, where *my husband* was waiting.

This was off to a good start. First the door, and now this.

"Mrs. Morales, I'll wait for you in the car," he said without a glance back, leaving me alone with Victor as he headed outside toward a new SUV.

Over Victor's shoulder, I watched him chuck the bags into the back, muttering to himself. He then rounded to the driver's side, settled in, and started the car.

"I know you don't like this, but it's for your safety," he started. "I love you," he finished, bending down to press a kiss to my lips, and I suppressed a shudder as he pulled away.

"How long will this be for?"

155

His eyes narrowed. "For as long as it takes."

"Fine." I brushed past him, leaving him standing in place.

As soon as I got into the passenger's side, Theo quickly put the car in reverse and drove away, speeding down the road, wheels screeching from the speed.

"Where are we going?" I glanced at him, but his eyes remained on the road, one hand gripping the steering wheel, the other resting on his thigh.

"Somewhere safe," he replied.

I waited for him to offer more information, only to be met with silence.

I rested my forehead against the window, staring outside as time trickled by. The highway stretched as the trees got taller, cutting off more of the afternoon light. Every once in a while, he brought his attention to the rearview mirror, making sure no one was tailing us.

Slowly, the adrenaline from earlier washed over me and before I knew it, my eyelids drifted closed, the outside fading.

CHAPTER 18
SOFIA

A shift from the paved highway to a dirt road jolted me awake, the sound of gravel crunching beneath the tires.

I opened my eyes as Theo turned left and climbed up a steep gravel driveway. I stared through the windshield at the structure coming into view, tucked in the middle of a small clearing, the dark exterior blending with the surroundings.

The forest was dense, and I couldn't see much, but I assumed we'd arrived at our destination.

"We're here," he announced as he rolled to a stop in front of some sort of cabin. Or should I say a shed from the size of it. He reached forward and turned the car off, taking the keys out of the ignition.

Without another word, he reached for our bags in the

back seat, then stepped out of the car and slammed the door shut behind him while I sat still, gazing at the place.

We were literally in the middle of nowhere. I doubted I would get any signal on my burner phone. I'd check later, but my hopes weren't high.

Which meant I was fucked. Literally.

Not only was I stuck here, *alone*, with him, but I wouldn't even have remote access to anything back in Bemes.

I only waited another minute before opening my door. Cold air whipped at me and I wrapped my jacket tighter around my body, the chill biting at my bare legs.

Who could possibly, *voluntarily*, live in this temperature?

It was like stepping into a freezer. I shivered, my teeth chattering. I slid out of my seat and shut the door behind me, then stepped to the front of the car.

I wasn't able to tell exactly what time it was since I'd slept the majority of the car ride after Theo kept going in circles. I didn't know if it was meant to disorient me or lose anybody who would have trailed us.

The sun was casting down, the frigid cold searing into my skin. I shaded my eyes from the remnants of the sunlight casting through the thick woods and scanned the area.

The forest seemed to go on forever, nothing besides the secluded cabin we'd be staying in. I inhaled, the smell of earth drifting through my nose, the scent of water hanging in the air.

I closed my eyes to listen for the sound of running water but heard nothing.

It was utterly quiet. Too quiet for my liking and I hated silence.

What is this place?

I must have said it out loud because Theo's voice broke the static silence. "It belongs to someone I know. We thought it'd be best to take you somewhere that couldn't be traced back to your husband."

I looked away from the view and back at Theo.

Tossing our bags over his shoulder, he glanced back at me. His eyes held mine for a beat before he averted his gaze and made his way toward the cabin. I let out a breath, then followed a few steps behind him, up the wooden steps of the small porch.

Albeit small, the cabin had massive bay windows all-around that allowed anyone to peer inside. The interior reminded me of my old studio's setup, minus the mess and countless computer monitors.

He pushed the door open and turned to face me, waiting.

He'd changed into a black thin cable-knit sweater, the strip of a white bandage peeking through his collar. He most likely patched himself up and changed on the way here because last I remembered, he was still wearing his bloodied shirt when we left the house.

I cut past him, walking inside, and he followed, setting the bags down by the door after shutting it behind him.

It smelled exactly how you'd expect an old, uninhabited cabin in the middle of nowhere to smell like—musty wood and damp soot invaded my senses.

As I took in the space, he walked around, opening the windows. The interior was slightly bigger than I expected it to be, but everything just melted together, like one big room, with a narrow hallway to the side.

A rustic-looking leather sofa sat in the middle of the living room, a small worn down coffee table in front of it, with a woodstove in the far corner. A thick rug covered the front of the fireplace and the couch, but the rest was bare wide-plank beams.

The kitchenette had a black stove and a sink overlooking the field next to it. There was no dishwasher in sight, only a drying rack next to the sink. The fridge was on the far right, and a butcher block island sat in the middle of the area.

I guessed the bedrooms and bathroom were probably along the hallway.

I ventured down to the far right, a hand rubbing the back of my neck, massaging the kinks from sleeping funny in the car, as I moved toward the hallway. I opened the doors lining the hallway one by one, looking for where each of us would be sleeping for however long we stayed here.

I found a closet, a bathroom, but still no bedroom in

sight. I reached for the final door and unlocked it, then stepped inside.

A line instantly formed between my brows.

Esto tiene que ser una broma.

A single bed greeted me.

Like one bed. As in singular. Like there was just one. And a narrow one at that. The only way two people could ever fit in it was if they slept cuddled, one person on top of the other.

I turned to leave the room when I slammed into a solid frame. His steps were so quiet, I barely heard him approach. Startled by the heat of his body searing into mine, I took a step back, only for my back to slam into the doorframe.

A shiver ran down my spine at how close he was, my chest grazing his front with each inhale.

I dragged my gaze up his hard chest, and my breath hitched when our eyes collided, something I couldn't decipher flickering in them. My stomach tightened with anxiety, that this could be the moment he realized who I was. That the next thing out of his mouth would be my name, *my real name. Sofia.*

My gaze drifted to his full mouth, and I swallowed thickly.

He jolted back as if the thought of touching me any longer was physically excruciating and his gaze drifted above my head and into the bedroom.

"You can have the bed," we said simultaneously, meeting each other's gaze.

A muscle in his jaw flexed as he peered back over my shoulder, looking intently at the bed as if it would magically make another one appear. "Mrs. Morales, take the bed. I can sleep on the couch."

"Mr. Alvarez, I *insist*."

He shifted his glance back at me.

"*¿Te despiertas cada día pensando en maneras de fastidiarme?*" he gritted, frustration clear in his face.

"*Ay, Mr. Alvarez. Me voy a dormir pensando en eso también.*" I scoffed.

With how narrow the hallway was, none of us had realized that in the course of arguing about who gets the bed, we'd both stepped closer to each other until his harsh breath blew over my face, our wills clashing, emotion boiling in the air.

We stood there for a beat longer than appropriate before he took a step back, creating more distance between us.

Annoyance licked at my veins at him being the one to step back. I knew it shouldn't bother me as much as it did, but why did he always have to be the one stepping away first?

He cursed under his breath, a hand smoothing over his beard. "Mr. Alvarez was my father. Theo's just fine, Mrs. Morales. I—"

Groaning, I interrupted him before he had a chance to

continue. "And Morales is my husband's. Yet, you insist on calling me Mrs. Morales." I pushed past him and walked back into the living room. "I told you to take the bed, so do it. Besides, you work for me, not the other way around, remember?"

He let out a frustrated sigh. "*Olivia*, I was simply trying to be considerate."

I internally groaned at his use of the fabricated name, wishing deep down a different one would be called instead.

I halted, turning back to face him. "Don't be," I spat. My statement came out harsher than I intended, but I had to create a clear divide if I was to be stuck spending the next few days in his close proximity.

He rolled one of his sleeves and pushed it up past his elbows, revealing the sculpted muscles of his arms. My stomach flipped at the small action and I huffed a breath, annoyed that my body kept reacting so extremely to him, despite my best efforts at tamping it down to avoid giving myself away.

He went to work on his other sleeve when I realized the silence surrounding us was because I'd been staring. He quirked a brow, snapping me out of my trance.

"I'll go assess the surroundings to make sure we weren't followed."

Wind blew through the open window and I shivered, from the cold this time, and pulled my blazer closer. He moved across the room, shutting them closed.

"I'll also try to find some wood to get the fireplace started," he finished as he walked past me toward the front door. Without waiting for a reply, he left, closing the door behind him.

Once he was out of sight, I grabbed my bag by the door and settled on the couch, dropping the duffle on the table. I waited a beat to make sure he wouldn't come back and unzipped the bag, reaching into the inside pocket to retrieve the small black phone.

I checked for any reply to my previous text message, only to notice I had no service.

Mierda.

I walked around the room with the phone held up to see if it would start any connection, but nothing. I shoved the phone back into its place and grabbed a pair of sweatpants and a hoodie to change into.

I knew it was only for a few nights at most, but this was the first time we would be under the same roof in over seven years. I had to put as much distance between us, because based on our track record of being in proximity to each other, I wasn't convinced this getaway would go without a hitch.

As much as I tried to disregard it, I didn't trust myself around him.

CHAPTER 19
THEO

This was a mistake.

Why did I think that being completely alone with her for days would be a good idea?

But after reading the note she'd received before she was shot at, combined with what happened to Victor's late wife, my brain went into overdrive.

I was used to compartmentalizing—cases and personal life were usually always kept separate. Yet, when it came to Olivia, I had this visceral need to protect her.

I was trying to convince myself that my reasoning was solely based on the fact that it *was* my job to keep her safe, but I was failing miserably because I knew deep down I was lying to myself.

This unfettered access to her on a daily basis might get me in trouble.

On our way here, I had to keep my hands glued to the

steering wheel to stop myself from yielding to the need to touch her. She'd slept for most of the ride over here, but with every stir, her skirt kept hiking farther up, revealing more of her smooth legs. I eventually just grabbed my jacket from the back seat and covered her.

Something changed that night in the pool house when I caught her prying through my things, crossing a line I never should've.

I hadn't let myself want anyone besides *her*. Sofia was still all I could think about even after all these years. Looking at anyone else, *wanting* anyone else felt like a betrayal.

None of it made sense, but I couldn't help it.

She was etched in my skin, *quite literally even*, and I still had this stupid longing of one day finding her again. Of her coming back to me. *For me.*

What was happening between me and Olivia was different, yet so similar. She made me feel *something* I couldn't explain yet. Curiosity? Temptation? *Familiarity?*

Luckily, the benefit gala's planning kept her busy most days, which meant I barely saw her unless it was to take her to scout for venues, run errands, or through the screen of my computer when I spent my nights replaying the camera footage to study for any abnormalities during our outings.

At least, I convinced myself that's why I was doing it and not for the chance to stare at her for hours on end. Now, I was stuck with her for God knows how long in this tiny cabin, *my* tiny cabin. The same one I hadn't stayed at in years.

I walked the premises, making sure once again that nobody had followed us before I grabbed the spare phone from my back pocket and dialed Noah's number.

"Why haven't you been answering my calls?" he asked over the sound of a door clicking shut in the background.

"Was a little busy avoiding bullets."

"I heard. Anyone hurt?"

"The bullet grazed my shoulder, but Olivia's fine."

He cursed under his breath. "Where are you now? I haven't been able to track your location ever since you left the restaurant. Also, why are you calling me from your burner phone?"

"Can we stop with the drilling questions? We're somewhere safe. That's all you need to know for now."

I walked back to the car and opened the trunk, flicking the hatch open. I sandwiched the phone between my ear and shoulder as I retrieved the files.

"Listen, whoever's sending the notes knows how to cover their tracks," I said, examining the note. "Everything about the notes is generic. There are no identifying markers. I wasn't able to trace anything back to its source. The only thing I have is that they are from the same sender since the paper they're using and the calligraphy are all identical."

I paused, mulling over the information. "Whoever's after her isn't careless enough to leave fingerprints on it."

He stayed quiet for a minute before calling me by my name, something he rarely did. "Theo—"

Before he continued, I blurted, "I need you to do me a favor."

"A favor?" he asked, perplexed.

"I need you to find everything you can on Olivia Morales."

He mulled over my statement for a moment. "And why would I do that?"

"It's personal."

"I'm going to need more than 'it's personal' if I'm about to intrude on a civilian's privacy," he muttered, annoyance dripping in his tone.

"I have a feeling."

"A feeling?" His frustration was palpable even through the phone. "What's this really about?" He pushed, despite knowing he may or may not get an answer from me. Noah was intuitive and knew me better than most.

"You used to trust my *feelings*. Now, can you do this for me or not?"

"Please don't tell me this is about your ridiculous theory that she's Sofia. It's been seven years, Alvarez. Let it go."

Never. I would never be able to let her go.

Anger coursed through my veins. "Just get me what you have," I said through clenched teeth, hanging up. I threw the phone on the felted platform, mulling over the contents scattered out of the manila folder.

I wanted to know more. *Needed* to know more.

Something wasn't adding up. From Noah assigning me as the bodyguard of a billionaire's wife, to now someone trying to kill her.

If I found his reluctance to share more details about this case odd, knowing someone with the skillset to use a sniper was after her convinced me there was something amiss.

I grabbed the few remaining logs from the side of the cabin and made my way back inside, a heavy fog settling over the forest.

I was watching the surveillance footage of the shooting when I heard footsteps approaching. Before we left the house, Jaxon sent me a copy of whatever footage they'd been able to gather. I'd been watching it on a loop, trying to find any clues.

"What are you doing?" she asked.

I sneaked a glance sideways as she rounded the couch, taking a seat on the opposite end of where I was sitting. She'd changed out of her skirt and blazer into a matching set of a gray sweat suit. She pulled her legs up and curled further into the couch.

"I'm reviewing some of the footage from earlier," I said, clicking off the video.

"Any luck finding anything?"

Closing my eyes, I blew out a frustrated breath, pinching the bridge of my nose just beneath the bridge of my glasses. "Not yet," I replied tightly, dropping my hand to my side. "The restaurant only had a few sporadic cameras inside, but none on the alley where the shot came from."

I felt a massive headache blooming from the hours of footage I'd just watched, over and over again. I leaned back, pushing my glasses up above my head, then dragged a hand over my face.

I'd been through every bit of the security tapes. Main room. Elevators. Exit staircases.

Nothing.

Essentially, all it showed was the glass shattering and I still hadn't pinpointed the exact entry point or determined which building the shooter was stationed at when he took his shot.

I even hacked into the street security cams, but nothing covered enough grounds to show the alley behind the building and most of what I found only showed a screen of static footage.

I leaned forward and put my elbows on my knees, lacing my fingers together. I turned my head in her direction and stared at her, uncertain.

"Do you know *anything* about what happened today or why someone would be targeting you like this?"

She shifted nervously under my gaze, her jaw slightly

clenching at my line of questioning. I glanced down, only to find her clutching at the edges of the couch, her knuckles turning white.

She glared at me before she faced away from me. "How would I know anything?" she finally grumbled.

I tilted my head and studied her closely. I was quickly becoming an expert at reading Olivia Morales and her frustrated deflection wasn't fooling me.

Something was off.

I hesitated. "This was a last-minute meeting. How could someone have known we were there?" I muttered, more to myself than to her.

She just shrugged her shoulders. I got up and crossed the room. Crouching in front of the woodstove, I shoved another log into its mouth. The fire grew, the sound of the flames crackling filling the room as the rain battered against the windows.

We stayed quiet for a moment, while I finished adjusting the fire, when her stomach let out a deep grumble, loud enough to startle both of us.

I chuckled softly, turning my attention back to her, raising a brow. "Hungry?" I asked, standing back up.

"I'm fine."

Of course she is.

I strolled past her and headed toward the kitchen. "Olivia, you haven't eaten since this morning."

"I said I'm—"

"I swear if you say you're fine one more time. *Dios mío,*

Olivia, why do you always have to fight me over everything?"

I grabbed a few ingredients from the refrigerator and set them on the counter to quickly make her something. I'd stopped at a store on our way here, paying off a kid to grab a few things we'd need.

She padded to the kitchen and leaned her elbows against the island.

"Hand me a knife," I commanded softly.

She opened a drawer and pulled one from it, then handed it to me without a word.

That's a first.

I sliced pieces of bread, then did the same with some tomatoes and lettuce. Grabbing the cheese and turkey, I assembled two sandwiches, only pausing to ask her if she wanted to add anything to it.

I reached into one of the cabinets and pulled a plate down, then placed the sandwiches on it and handed it to her.

She crinkled her nose.

"What's wrong?"

"Hm, could you cut the crust?" She paused. "Please?"

Please. Another first.

I shook my head, a small chuckle rumbling in my chest at the memory of Sofia always asking me the same thing.

I obliged, pushing the thought of Sofia out of my head, and handed the plate back to Olivia, this time crust-free. I walked back to the couch and she trailed me, plopping down closer to me this time around.

She folded one of her legs under her before picking up a half and while she ate, I propped my reading glasses back on, diving back into reviewing the tapes.

Every once in a while, I glanced up at her and caught her staring at me. Her gaze wasn't hostile this time but rather appraising, as if she were attempting to solve me.

I noticed how close our thighs were to each other, barely an inch separating us.

I waited for her to say something, but she seemed content with the silence. I didn't know how long we sat there, her eating as I kept analyzing the screens, while the rain settled into a soft lull.

At one point throughout the evening, she got up and I heard her rummaging through the kitchen. A few minutes later, she came back and slid something in my direction. I glanced away from my laptop, only to realize she'd made another plate.

This time it was for me.

Inexplicably, my heart skipped a beat, and I looked up at her. We stared at each other before I eventually forced myself to look away, muttering a thank you.

It probably meant nothing, but no one had taken care of me in a very long time and her small gesture tugged at my heart strings. I tried to refocus my attention and concentrate on the task of finding something, *anything* in the footage Jaxon had given me, but every once in a while, I couldn't help but look over at her.

It was past midnight when sleep tugged at my consciousness. I turned my attention to Olivia, only to find her already fast asleep. I studied her in the dim light from the fire and the sight of her nestled against the corner of the couch constricted my airways, the air leaving my lungs in a whoosh.

I sighed, ruffling my hands through my strands.

God, she is breathtaking.

I gently shut my computer screen and moved off the couch. I wanted to pick her up and move her to the bedroom, knowing sleeping on the couch would be uncomfortable, but she seemed so at peace, which was such a rarity, that I didn't want to do anything to disturb it.

My eyes lingered on her form before they studied her face, noticing details I hadn't before. The slope of her nose, her thick lashes fanning her high cheekbones, the faint constellation of light brown freckles on her nose, the curve of her lush lip.

I'm fucked.

I tore my gaze away and my jaw clenched at the unwelcome images crowding my thoughts. I knew I shouldn't be thinking about her like this, but I couldn't help myself.

Her quiet snore snapped me out of my thoughts and I

slowly got up, making sure to move without waking her up.

I grabbed a blanket from the closet and draped it over her body. Her curls were pulled into a loose bun on top of her head. A stranded curl fell over her face and I got on one knee, hunching over to reach for it and tuck it behind her ear.

My thumb brushed over her cheekbone in the process and she stirred, releasing a peaceful sigh. My skin itched to touch her again and although I shouldn't, I brushed my thumb against her soft skin once more.

"*Dios, eres asombrosa,*" I whispered.

I finally got up, looking at her one last time before grabbing my bag that had stayed next to the front door and carrying it down back to my bedroom. I shrugged out of my clothes, leaving only my boxer briefs and grabbing a white shirt that I pulled on. I changed the soiled bandage on my shoulder in the bathroom and returned to the bedroom, flicking off the light before climbing into bed, my head dropping gently onto the stiff pillow.

I laced my hands behind my head and tried to ignore the pang that was settling in my chest. I closed my eyes, willing myself to sleep.

I eventually drifted off to sleep to the memory of her.

It wasn't until later in the night that a scream yanked me out of my dreams.

Olivia.

"No!" she cried out, terror lacing her voice.

I jolted out of bed, grabbed my Glock from under the pillow, and rushed to the living room, gun aimed and ready. I looked around to identify the intruder but didn't see anyone else in the room.

What the hell?

My eyes landed on Olivia's body, finding her writhing in distress, a hand clutched to her side. Her face was drained of any color, her eyes forcibly squeezed shut.

My heart tripped when her next words came out in a choked sound.

"*¡Mama! No me abandones.*"

CHAPTER 20
SOFIA

Click. Click. Click.

I heard screaming from afar and my throat strangely burned, but I couldn't tell where the piercing sound was originating from.

Am I the one making that sound?

Mama was on the floor and my lips parted on a gasp as I tried calling for her. Over and over again. But no sound would come out.

Her head lolled to the side, her lifeless eyes staring right at me. I tried reaching for her, but my hand was unable to move. My body wasn't answering any commands. No matter how desperately I demanded it to move, it wouldn't. I was completely frozen.

I felt an intense pressure in my middle, piercing and burning its way into every fiber of my insides. I looked down to figure out what was happening to me, only to be met with a gruesome sight, the smell of death hanging thick around the room.

Blood. So much fucking blood seeping through my shirt. I grasped at my side, trying to stop it from pouring out, but it was all in vain.

It never crossed my mind how many liters of blood a body contained up until then. Sure, we were taught in school, but the simple knowledge was nothing compared to watching it pour out of you, pooling underneath you.

My vision slowly faded, gaze unfocused, as my eyelids felt too heavy to remain open.

Darkness surrounded me, anchoring me deeper when I felt my body being shaken. A panicked voice screaming a name penetrated the deep fog my brain was slowly being submerged under.

The voice sneaked through once again, tugging at my consciousness, but a soft lull snaked throughout my body, tugging me further into the blackness that was threatening to take over.

Something heavy was grabbing my arm, roughly jostling me again. "Olivia, wake up," the voice said more urgently this time.

Visions danced behind my lids as something heavy dropped on my body.

I wonder who this Olivia is.

The voice screamed her name repeatedly and I tried latching onto the plea, letting it anchor me back as I attempted to crawl out of the darkness.

I know this voice, I thought to myself.

The familiar tone amplified, rousing me from my unconscious state. I was shaken once more, the harsh movement finally jolting me awake.

Sucking in a sharp gasp, my hands flew to my middle. My eyes snapped open, and my heart was beating furiously against my rib cage, the images of my parents burnt into my retinas.

That night I wasn't able to fight back against him. Now, I kicked and thrashed, trying to push myself up and save them, but the person above me shoved me back against the cushion, pinning my hands above my head.

The blurred vision's grip squeezed tight, their eyes wide. I felt them move on top of me, pressing their pelvis more firmly into me.

"Stop fighting and look at me," they commanded softly. They grabbed my chin, forcing me to look at them. "Look, it's just me."

I blinked rapidly, reality finally kicking in, as the memories of my fabricated life came crashing back to me, reminding me that *I* was the Olivia this person was calling for. My stomach twisted into knots, fear still coursing through my veins, setting all of my nerve endings fraught with panic.

A sliver of moonlight peeked through a small gap in the curtains, highlighting the man on top of me. My gaze slowly focused on him, studying him, taking in the thick, corded neck where an Adam's apple jumped up and down.

I moved my eyes upward until they clashed with his dark, worried gaze. Dark eyes I knew so well.

I spent years burying the memories in the back of my mind. They would still happen every once in a while when I met Victor, but they'd slowly dissipated when my subconscious realized I'd have to share a bed with the monster who'd created them.

I hadn't had a vivid nightmare like this one in such a long time that I truly thought they were gone. That I'd handled them, but I guess the shooting from earlier triggered something deep within me, letting the nightmares simmer to the surface and boil over.

His frantic gaze softened. "Olivia. *¿Estás bien?*"

I tried answering him, but my mouth was parched, my throat still burning from the effects of the dream. More unwanted images flooded my vision. Vivid images of shattered skulls and blood, so dark and thick, as it painted the room and sickly stuck to my dying body.

Phantom pain shot through my body, an iron fist squeezing my heart *hard*. I opened my mouth again to speak, but nothing came out, unexpected tears welling up. I tried to breathe, but no oxygen would bypass the knot in my throat.

Pinpricks of black swarmed across my sight, sending panic flooding my veins. My chest heaved as I squirmed under him, unwantedly giving us a tighter fit.

Freeing one of his hands, he grasped my chin with two fingers, yanking my head back.

"*Angel, mírame y respira,*" he spoke in a soft voice. Our gazes collided and his face softened as he moved his hand from my chin to cup the side of my face, his thumb sweeping over my cheek, drawing soothing circles.

"*Estás bien, ángel mío. Estás bien. Ahora, respira para mí,*" he said, his voice still soft but demanding.

My eyes fell shut and I took a few deep breaths, following his command and focusing on his gentle caress. My erratic breathing slowly became more regulated, my heartbeats slowing down from their battering thud, and I started to regain control of my body.

"*Bien.* Give me another one," he kept saying on a loop.

Once my breathing evened out, I peeled my eyes open. His face had come closer, his warm breath now skating across my skin.

That's when I realized he was straddling me, his knees on either side of me, the fabric of his boxers brushing against my exposed bare thighs.

Fuck. I didn't even remember removing my sweat suit.

My blood roared in my ear and his grip on my wrist turned punishing when I wiggled underneath him. Our eyes locked and the roaring intensified. The energy in the room shifted, a coiled tension crackling in the air between us.

His eyes darkened, hunger lingering beneath his irises, sending heat flooding straight to my core. The atmosphere grew heavy, suffocating me as heat buzzed between our flushed bodies, spreading all over my body. I reveled in his warmth, seeping and distracting me from the residual fear.

I wondered if he could feel how hard my heart was racing.

I felt him grow against my waist, and he shifted, but it only pinned me down even more. This new position pulled the oversized shirt I had on flush against my chest and I was convinced the outlines of my hardening nipples were now visible.

As if I'd conjured the thought in his head, his eyes dipped, and I could feel his stare roaming over my body.

My breathing grew heavy, waiting for what he would do next. All I could think of was how much I wanted him closer, how much I wanted his mouth on me.

After a beat, he drew his eyes back up, his heated gaze tangling back with mine.

A grunt escaped him, his ensuing swallow audible, echoing against the walls, joining the symphony of our heavy breathing. For a moment, I was convinced he would move off me and go back to his bedroom, but he didn't.

Instead, as if magnetized, his thumb skimmed down my cheek at a torturous pace until it brushed against the edge of my nipple, testing its shape.

My pulse was erratic, and my lips parted on a soft, audible exhale in response. His eyes followed the sound.

Slowly, his eyes swung back to mine, none of us daring to utter another word yet, afraid to interrupt whatever this was. Maybe as Olivia, I should be embarrassed about our position, but Sofia wanted to bask in this moment.

I wanted this. *I* wanted more.

As if I spoke the words out loud, he leaned forward another inch, releasing a deep, wanton sigh, mingling our breaths together.

My breathing stalled, my heart hammering even harder against my rib cage. Warmth spread through me, pooling between my thighs, and I arched into him.

Just *barely*.

But that was all it took for him to pull back, releasing his hold on my wrists. Our eyes were still connected, his eyes peering at me from his hooded gaze. I watched him intently, burning the image to memory.

He brought the thumb that was previously on my breasts to his parted lips, trailing it against the seam as if he were remembering the ghost of our mingled breaths, branding the feel of me on him.

Without any explanation, he pushed off me and settled next to me. Turning me on my side, he pulled me to him, his chest brushing against my back. I let out a small gasp from the sudden closeness, his heady, familiar scent suffocating me.

He shifted, snaking his arm underneath me, my head now resting against his bicep before it settled on my chest. He then dragged the blanket back up with his free arm, wrapping us beneath it.

My skin prickled with awareness at every inch of our

skin touching and I started to move, protesting against his touch, but his grip over my chest tightened. "Don't fight me on this. Go back to sleep."

Although I knew this was a bad idea, I craved his closeness, especially after what just happened. I usually didn't mind being alone after, but somehow, my body needed him.

I needed him, and it was as if he knew that I needed him close after the nightmare.

Of course he did. He used to comfort you all the time when you had these nightmares multiple times a night.

The strong desire to bask in his warmth combined with his authoritative tone made me concede.

"Okay," I whispered softly, deciding to concentrate on his fingers running through my curls, smoothing them behind my ears.

His other arm moved down to splay across my stomach, his finger drawing small circles on top of the thin fabric. My eyes shut at his touch, the feel of his hand on me after so long sending tingles down my spine.

A different tightness sprouted inside my chest, this time unlike the previous one left behind from the nightmare.

I'd missed him *so* much. I knew I shouldn't, since I was the one who left him, but I always wondered, what if I'd stayed? I had no right to go there, but I just hoped that when all of this was over, he would forgive me.

That he would give me a second chance.

As if he could hear the wheels of my mind working overtime, his hand left my hair to find mine under the blanket, clasping it in his own and giving it one gentle squeeze. I let myself relax into the warmth of his body, squeezing his hand back.

I felt my breathing shift into heavier breaths, my eyes growing heavy as I focused on the rise and fall of his chest brushing against my back. I tried to fight it, but, eventually, I slipped into darkness on a whispered echo.

What are you doing to me?

Theo

What the fuck just happened?

I moved to adjust myself, causing Olivia to stir beside me. Her head shifted on my arm as she tried to make herself more comfortable.

My body wanted to bring itself closer, to mold itself further into her, even though my mind knew that wasn't a good idea.

Mentally cursing myself for getting into this situation, I swallowed hard and decided *fuck it*. I shifted my body closer, pressing my chest flush against her back, every part of our bodies now touching.

The second I felt her cuddle against my body, everything in me settled, and calmness washed over me. An effect only one other person ever had on me.

She stiffened for a second at the intrusion but relaxed just as quickly, letting out a content sigh, and fuck if that didn't sound sweet coming out of her mouth.

Dirty thoughts crept in when her waist pushed back, her ass rubbing against my groin, making my breath hitch.

I'm utterly fucked.

I moved my hand from her waist to her hip, attempting to stop her from moving any farther, but it was like she took that as an invitation and rubbed herself against me even more.

"Olivia," I groaned under my breath despite knowing she couldn't hear me.

Holding her this close was making me crave more, but I had to stop myself. Having her this near to me wasn't supposed to make me feel like this.

I had to focus on protecting her, and I couldn't afford to get distracted, but I couldn't help but think that I hadn't felt anything like this since *her.*

Since Sofia.

A memory fluttered at the back of my mind, fragments of a similar situation flooding my brain. I didn't know if I could trust my memories, but the deep familiarity of her body cuddled against mine was spinning all my maybes further into certainties.

Frowning, I decided to test out my theory and gently squeezed her hand three times.

At first, nothing happened, but then I felt her stir.

Two squeezes.

I waited with bated breath. Seconds passed. Nothing.

She hadn't squeezed a third time.

I lay there, with her wrapped in my arms, listening to the sounds of her even breathing, counting every breath she took and the way her chest rose and fell beneath my palms.

Even though I desperately wished I'd been right, it wasn't her. I couldn't keep doing this to myself, thinking she was who I lost.

My lids fluttered close and I fell asleep too.

But as if willed by my silent plea, I felt a *barely there* third squeeze right before I stumbled into a deep slumber.

CHAPTER 21
SOFIA

I woke up to the sound of a faucet running, the rattle of dishes clinging against each other, and the smell of fresh coffee and eggs permeating the air. The early morning sun streamed through the windows, its rays warming my skin. I shivered, my body physically missing another kind of warmth.

I opened my eyes, squinting at the rays now shining right in my eyes. I rolled over onto my back, the images from last night still plaguing my mind, but a soft sigh escaped my lips as I remembered how it ended.

I slowly pushed myself into a sitting position, sending the blanket pooling over my bare thighs. I internally berated myself, forgetting I'd removed pretty much everything besides my oversized shirt last night.

Speaking of last night.

I quietly turned my attention to the small kitchen. My

pulse suddenly halted, swelling in my throat as I took in the sight in front of me.

Theo's broad shoulders stretched the thin fabric of his gray long-sleeved shirt, the sleeves rolled partway up. His forearms were on full display, flexing as he cleaned the dishes of what I assumed he used to make breakfast and the dark pants he had on were hugging his ass deliciously.

It wasn't the first time I'd seen him like this, but it had been so long ago that I couldn't help but keep gawking at him. I sat still, taking in the slope of his shoulder, and the curls grazing his neck that were just begging to be gripped.

I didn't know how long I stayed like that when his voice broke me from my trance.

"You're up."

Even though he wasn't looking in my direction, I looked down. Heat scalded my face, slowly blooming down my neck.

I swallowed tightly, clearing my throat before I could answer. "I am."

When I glanced back at him, he was now leaning against the counter, a coffee mug in hand, resting right below his lips. He took a sip and I used the opportunity to look at him again. I wondered how long he'd been awake since he'd already changed and had time to cook for both of us.

I grabbed my pants from where I'd tossed them on the floor and pulled them on before crossing the room, desperate for a cup myself. He turned, leaning his hip against the counter on the other side of the sink.

He studied me closely, his eyes skating over my body. My feet stalled in their tracks when he stalked over to me, closing the distance between us, his mug the only thing keeping our chests from touching.

I became acutely aware of his body, goose bumps sprouting across my skin after his gaze trailed it.

Those hands were on me last night, holding me, making me feel safe. He made me feel at home again for the length of a few hours.

My gaze dropped to his lower lip, a pinch forming in my chest.

God, I wish I could bite it.

He pulled me out of my thoughts by handing me his cup, and I took it from him, muttering a *thank you*.

Steam rose from the top and I slightly blew onto it before taking a small sip exactly where his lips were previously pressed. My lids fluttered closed at the faint taste of him.

I heard him suppress a groan, a headiness forming in its wake, tension suffocating us. I'd barely moved when his next question startled me.

"How often do you get those nightmares?"

I lifted a shoulder, avoiding his gaze. "Not as often anymore," I said, bringing the mug back to my lips.

I took another sip, the steaming liquid scalding my throat on the way down, distracting me from his attention. I could *feel* him watching me swallow, his gaze fixed on the slope of my neck.

When I looked back up, his brows pulled together. He was about to ask for more details when I shot him a look, silencing him.

He sighed, deciding to give up his line of questioning. "Food's in the oven. If you need anything, just call my name," he said, leaving me alone in the kitchen.

I made myself a plate and retreated back to the couch, then grabbed my computer from my bag. We didn't have cell service, so I couldn't make any calls, but Theo had brought an external modem to give us internet service.

I desperately wanted to message Valentina again, to see if she'd received my message, but I didn't have what I needed to cover my tracks. So instead, I plugged the ethernet cable into my computer and dove straight into work.

I spent the morning hunched over my computer, pouring myself into work as a distraction from everything else. I was in the middle of typing out an email when I heard a repetitive sound coming from outside.

Thump. Thump. Thump.

It stopped for a beat before resuming.

Thump. Thump. Thump.

Curiosity winning me over, I stood from the couch and grabbed one of Theo's sweaters that was lying around. I pulled it over my head, knowing it would bring me more warmth than what I currently had on.

Hugging it tightly against my body, I slid the screen door in the back open and stepped onto the wooden deck. It was midday, the clouds from the previous night breaking away, letting the sun come out. The air remained chill, but it was warmer than when we came in yesterday.

Trees towered overhead, but enough sunlight peeked through to see through the woods, the rays shimmering against the surface of the deep blue lake.

My gaze followed the sounds that had resumed, only to find Theo off to the side, his back to me. He swung the axe, bringing it down on the log of wood, splitting it in two. He bent down, grabbed another piece, and placed it on the tree stump.

He was still wearing his black slacks, but he'd removed his sweater, leaving him in a white sleeveless undershirt, his bandaged shoulder now visible.

I leaned against the doorframe and wrapped my arms around my body, fascinated by the way his muscles strained against the fabric with each swing.

He suddenly glanced over his shoulder, catching me off guard. His gaze stalled over my figure for a brief moment before he returned his focus onto his task without saying a word.

I debated for a moment, knowing I should probably

head back inside, but I was frozen in place. He was beautiful and I could watch his broad shoulders and tapered waist all day long.

Flashes of those powerful shoulders and arms tensing over me as he stroked deep inside, my nails leaving marks on his skin sprouted in my mind.

I was jolted out of the memory when a flash of movement caught my attention. I looked back to where Theo previously was, only to find him heading toward the lake, stopping at its edge.

He reached over his head, slowly peeling his shirt off, his back straining from the movement. He tossed the fabric on the rocks next to him before tugging his pants down, his shoes following suit shortly after.

I was too concentrated on him peeling off his clothes to actually realize he was now only in his underwear, his black briefs tightly hugging his backside and thighs.

My breath hitched as I watched him slowly tread through the water, waves rippling around his body as he swam farther in.

Once his body was halfway covered, he dove in, submerging himself completely before reemerging a few seconds later, running his hand through his soaked curls, smoothing them back.

An ache slowly formed low in my core. The desire to join him and run my hands all over him tingled the tips of my fingers.

He glanced over his shoulder once again, noting I

hadn't moved. His shoulders shook lightly with a chuckle before he dove his body down enough to tip his head back. His laughter boomed in the air, reaching my ears, the sound warming my heart.

I'd missed seeing him this carefree.

CHAPTER 22
SOFIA

God, I fucking hated cooking. Rosa also cooked for us at Victor's house and when I was living with Theo, he'd always insisted on being the one to do the cooking because I wasn't very good at listening to his instructions whenever he would try to teach me.

When it became just me, I only survived on takeout because it was either that or self-inflicted food poisoning.

Theo and I had barely talked since this morning and the last time I'd seen him was during our little encounter earlier this afternoon.

Frustrated with my lack of response regarding his questions about my nightmare, he'd waltzed out of the cabin and spent most of the day outside. It wasn't until later in the afternoon, after his little swimming session, that he waltzed back in, wood logs in hand, water droplets clinging to his shirt.

After showering, he locked himself in the bedroom for the rest of his day, the door firmly closed.

I eventually got hungry and nothing from the refrigerator could be eaten quickly. So here I was, standing at the counter beside the sink, haphazardly chopping vegetables, making the only dish I knew how to.

I was pretty sure that wasn't how vegetables should be cut, uneven sections and pieces flying all around, but they were still being cut, which was what mattered at this moment.

"Nobody ever taught you how to use a knife?" a voice said, its sound magnified by the previous silence.

I jumped, pointing the knife in its direction. A strong hand clamped around my wrist, and my eyes swung up to meet a devastatingly familiar pair of dark eyes. Theo arched an eyebrow at me, and my body relaxed slightly when I realized he wasn't an intruder.

He was dressed in another pair of black slacks, a gray Henley shirt hugging his torso like a second skin. His hair was disheveled, like he'd spent the last hour running his hands through it.

Why did he have to be frustratingly beautiful?

"*Dámelo*," he prompted, tilting his head to the side before his gaze dipped to the hand holding the knife, my mind finally catching on that the tip of my blade was nudging against his chest. He placed his hand on top of mine, and I quickly released my hold on it.

He put the knife down on top of the counter and

turned to face me again. After a moment, concern bloomed on his features.

He reached for my other wrist, but I yanked my arm away. He grabbed it again, holding it firmly against his chest, tugging me closer to him. His breath ghosted over my face and my breathing halted, my gaze solely focused on his Adam's apple bobbing.

Tilting my chin up, I saw him lift my hand to his face to get a closer look. His jaw clenched, his nostrils flaring. "You're hurt," he stated.

My eyes widened as I looked down at my hand. Shit, I fucking cut myself and it was bleeding profusely, slowly soaking the front of his shirt, a few drops dribbling on the wooden floors.

Of course this would happen to me.

I tugged against his hold. "I'm fine."

He shook his head, huffing out a heavy sigh, a small smirk tugging at the corner of his lips. "Oh, I'm sure you are."

Still holding my hand in his, he grabbed a clean rag and put pressure on the cut as he tugged me to him, leading us into the narrow bathroom. It definitely wasn't made for two people, like the rest of this house apparently.

He pushed me against the counter, looming over me to reach behind my head and open the cabinet above the sink. He then pulled out a clear plastic bottle and brought my arm to the sink, placing my hand right above it.

"This might sting a little," he warned before bending down and pouring a cold solution to the cut across the center of my palm.

I hissed at the uncomfortable sting. This was why I didn't cook. Apparently, I was able to hold a knife to injure others, but not skillful enough to cut fucking vegetables.

He muttered to himself before glancing back at me. "It's a little deeper than I thought. You're gonna need stitches," he stated.

"No, I do—"

He stood to his full height abruptly, halting my thoughts. Before I got the chance to ask what he was doing, he gently placed my hand on the edge of the sink once again and left the room, leaving the door slightly ajar on his way out.

He came back a few seconds later with a small black bag and a bottle of whiskey in hand. He closed the door behind him and brushed past me, reaching for the toilet's lid. He closed it before gesturing for me to sit on top of it.

Stitches meant needles and I strongly disliked needles. "I'm sure this is unnecessary," I muttered, hoping he would just wrap a bandage on it and call it a day. No need for all these dramatics.

"Sit."

His commanding tone pushed my feet to move and obey. He went down on his knees and opened the black bag, took out the supplies and laid them on the counter.

He then propped himself up on one knee and put my injured hand on his thigh.

He was close, *so close*, his body pressed against mine, our breaths mingling in the enclosed space. Overwhelmed by his proximity, I closed my eyes. The sound of a packet ripping open filled the quiet space. I sucked in a sharp breath, pulling back in anticipation.

He whispered a quiet sorry as I tried to breathe through the burning sensation scorching down my throat. My brain had barely registered his apology when I felt a slight pinch before pain sliced across the center of my palm, shooting straight through my arm. My other hand automatically shot at him, clutching his shoulder, *hard*.

My eyes snapped open and I saw him hunching over, stitching the small wound closed. His eyes glanced at my hand on his shoulder before he zeroed his attention back on me, watching me intently.

"*Angel, no te muevas*," he said, his tone apologetic. The term of endearment coming out so naturally, I didn't think he'd realized he'd said it.

"Drink this," he ordered, handing me the bottle of whiskey. I removed my hand from his shoulder, took it from him, and brought the rim to my lips. I took a swig, the familiar burn temporarily distracting me from the pain.

I groaned and focused my gaze on his face as I watched him work, forcing myself to stop wincing every time he sewed my skin closed.

Minutes stretched to what felt like hours and I tried to concentrate on his stitching, but our faces were inching closer by the second and I could feel his breath sweeping across my skin on each exhale.

I should have been focusing on the needle pushing its way across my skin layers, but the only thing that was swarming my senses was his knee brushing against mine, the feel of his thigh straining under my hand, the warmth of his skin branding me where our bare skin connected.

Intoxicated by his proximity, my mind started wondering, imagining how it would feel if every inch of our skin touched, his strong thighs pinning me down while his hands brandished me with his marks.

I shifted and inhaled sharply, his warm and spicy scent warping my senses.

Ya basta, Sofia.

"Olivia," he whispered painfully as if he were the one who had a needle piercing his skin. Coming out of my thoughts, I lifted my head, our gazes locking.

"I'm done."

He didn't release my hand right away, keeping it resting on his thigh. He continued staring at me while his other hand reached for the loose strand of curl on my face, moving it behind my ear.

Breathe, Sofia.

He began to stand, bringing me up with him, our bodies now flush together, the hard planes of his body resting against my soft ones. My injured hand was trapped between us, and he slowly trailed his other hand down until they rested against my waist, his fingers slightly digging into my hip.

My other hand found his shoulder once again in order to steady myself from his dizzying proximity. He dropped his head, his forehead slightly grazing mine. Before I had a chance to process what was happening, the moment came to an abrupt halt as he pulled back, his features back to stone.

"You should shower," he said pointing to my bloody clothes. Kneeling, he gathered the supplies, throwing away the soiled material. I watched him clean his hands and before he replaced the items into his kit, he cut a piece from the rolled gauze.

Still keeping his distance, he said, "When you're done, wrap this tightly around your hand. If you need help, I'll be in the kitchen, cleaning up."

He looked at me one more time, a yearning look in his eyes before he turned on his heels, opening the bathroom door and leaving me.

I don't know how long I stayed stuck in the same position he left me in, when I finally shook myself out of it and moved to turn the shower on before stepping under the hot spray.

CHAPTER 23
THEO

What the fuck are you doing, Theo? The voice in my head scowled.

Sighing, I walked back into the kitchen. I turned the kitchen faucet on and splashed cold water on my face, running my wet fingers through my hair.

Every time I was alone with her, it was getting harder and harder to keep my distance. I was toeing a dangerous line; one I had no business being near.

She was married and her husband was none other than the person who'd hired me to protect her. I shouldn't, *wouldn't* cross that line.

But...

There were these moments when I was with her that I didn't see Sofia, their images starting to blur together in my mind. I knew it was wrong, and no one could ever replace her, but Olivia made the loss a little more bearable. The constant pain crawling under my skin dulled whenever I was with Olivia.

Shaking my head, I looked around the kitchen, trying to figure out what Olivia was previously cooking.

The huge stewpan with chickpeas, herbs, and meat inside gave it away immediately. I pulled out the small blender and finished up the tomato sauce before straining it into the pot. I refocused my attention on the vegetables she was attempting to mince. Attempting being the key word. I had never seen worse cut vegetables in my life.

Not since my attempt to teach Sofia how to do so.

Pushing that thought aside, I went back to cutting, adding the rest of what was needed into the pot. I closed the lid firmly and let it cook while I stood on the island with my laptop open, sifting through the new information Noah had sent me this morning.

It was roughly an hour later when the sound of a door opening followed by soft footsteps drifted through the cabin, slowly approaching. I paused my typing and turned in their direction right as she stepped into my line of sight.

My mouth immediately went dry. *Fuck me.*

My eyes widened at the sight of her in a T-shirt that seemed familiar, the hem grazing her mid-thigh, leaving my imagination wondering what was underneath. The shock of seeing her in such little clothing cleared long enough to make me realize she was wearing *my* shirt.

The sight of her wearing something that was mine

made my heart twitch, but I couldn't tell if it was out of anger for seeing another woman in it or if it was because I'd secretly wanted to see her in something of mine for a while now.

"What are you wearing?" I blurted out. Heat immediately scorched my face when I realized how stupid my question was. I felt the tip of my ears burning, the flush slowly crawling down my neck.

Asshole. Why did you ask that?

She cocked her head to the side and narrowed her eyes at me, glaring. "Do you know where I can find a glass?" she asked, dismissing my previous question.

I followed along, pretending I never asked it in the first place. I cleared my throat and pointed at it. "Um, yes. The top cabinet on the far left."

She padded barefoot into the kitchen, and her arm brushed against my back as she headed toward it. I tore my gaze away from her but kept watching her from my periphery, pretending I was still focused on the information displayed on my computer screen.

There was something about seeing her like this, bare and stripped down of all her protective layers, where I could feel her guard lower, her defenses at bay. These were the moments when she reminded me of Sofia the most.

Comfortable. Carefree. *Beautiful.*

I was still watching her, this time more openly, when she caught my lingering gaze, breaking the spell I was in.

Shaking myself out of my thoughts, I shut my laptop and walked to the stove, needing to occupy my hands with something, *anything*, to keep me from marching up to her and discovering for myself what she was wearing underneath my shirt.

I was reaching for the wooden spoon to stir the soup, when I heard her frustrated sigh. I glanced over to see what was wrong, finding her standing on her tiptoes, struggling to reach for what she needed. The motion caused her shirt to ride up, exposing more of her bare thigh, gray cotton shorts peeking through, and my mind drifted to the idea of those long legs straining under different circumstances.

Bent over on the island, a pleasurable sigh replacing her current frustrated one as I played with her.

Before she could break anything, I closed the distance between us, stepping right behind her and reaching over her. I grabbed one of the tall glasses and set it on the counter next to her.

Her body tensed at my proximity, her fingers wrapping tightly against the edge of the counter. Logically, I knew I should've stepped away after putting the cup down, but my actions hadn't been ruled by logic for a long time, especially when it involved her.

I wished I knew why this otherwise complete stranger made me feel so much. So overwhelmingly so that I wouldn't even be able to tell you why I did what I did next.

Instead of stepping away, I crowded her, planting my hands on either side of her hips, caging her in against the counter. My heart slammed against my ribs, my gaze focusing on the sliver of bare skin peeking through her hair at the nape of her neck, goose bumps slowly prickling across her skin.

My gaze followed the trail, looking down to see the swell of breasts rising rapidly.

Maybe it was the gravitational pull I felt toward her, drawing me in against my better judgment. Or maybe it was simply because I was desperate to feel closer to anything that reminded me of Sofia.

Her breathing turned heavy as she landed back on her heels with a soft thump. "Thank you," she said quietly, bowing her head down.

I clenched my jaw, willing my body to stay in place instead of erasing the distance between us and pressing my body further into hers.

She was a married woman, my brain clearly knew that, but desire to claim her wrapped around my senses, threatening to take over. There was no point in denying that I felt something for her despite all my efforts not to.

My eyes shut, the intrusive thoughts of her body flushed against mine overwhelming me. My arms strained against the counter as I bent my head down next to her head, breathing in a shaky inhale.

"You're welcome," I said breathlessly against her ear.

She was sporting a new smell and it hit my senses,

wrapping around them and tugging at something buried deep within me. She usually wore the same overpowering fragrance, but this was *different*.

I paused and inhaled deeper. Her skin had the faintest hint of something *familiar*.

I was about to step away and return to cooking, when a sense of déjà vu suddenly washed over me, poking what seemed like a distant memory.

Her smell. Her very distinct warm smell. That soft hidden place behind her ear that used to be my favorite place to kiss.

The blood pumping through my veins stalled and time slowed down, anchoring me into paralysis. I could barely move, transfixed in the memories the scent pushed to the forefront of my mind, creating warped visuals of all the moments I smelled it, touched it, *tasted it.*

My hands went numb from how tight I was holding on to the counter.

Scent was a powerful memory trigger and my mind was on fire with the memories of who this scent belonged to.

Sofia Herrera.

CHAPTER 24
SOFIA

I tried to move away from him, but his hands stood firm on either side of me, trapping me. My breath thickened in my lungs at the feel of his hard body brushing against mine, the oxygen lodging in my throat on its way up.

My heart pumped faster, the blood in my veins humming, his intoxicating presence sending mixed signals between my brain and body in response. I swallowed hard against the lump that formed, trying to ground myself before I faced him.

I spun around, the movement putting a slight distance between us, and my gaze lifted to his face. That's when I saw the change. The previous embarrassment from his earlier perusal was long gone now, a dangerous stillness replacing it.

His expression turned me to stone.

At first, neither of us spoke and we didn't look away from each other. The connection was weighed down, tying us together, just like it had all these years ago when our gazes collided for the first time in a hospital room.

I needed to look away, to distract his attention from focusing on me too closely. I opened my mouth to speak, but he cut me off before I could even get a word out.

"Who are you?" His question came out in a simple and cool tone, a complete contrast to how his body was vibrating with rage. I could even feel the wheels in his head spinning frantically as he studied my face closely.

His words stilled my blood, my body going stiff as my heart dropped into my stomach. I frowned, trying to morph my features into annoyance rather than fear. "What's gotten into you?"

He moved closer, his anger rolling off of him in waves. "I said, who are you?" he demanded, his tone firmer this time.

"You're being ridiculous. You know exactly who I am," I snapped, fending off his interrogation.

I attempted to move again, but he inched forward, closing the remaining distance between us. He shifted his hip forward and pinned me against the counter, leaving me no room to escape.

One of his hands slid slowly up my side and gripped my waist, right below my breast. My eyes widened at his sudden boldness, my mind unable to form a thought.

My pulse turned erratic, pounding in my bloodstream.

Despite the fear of him discovering the real me that threatened to swallow me whole, my nipples tightened. Fear mixing with anticipation zipped through my spine, sending a bolt of electricity straight to my core.

Heat pulsed between my legs at his touch and I fought the desire to rub my thighs together. His grip tightened, and my mind immediately conjured images of what his hands would feel like on my bare skin.

Smoothing. Gripping. *Spanking.*

But his next words cut straight through my reverie.

His eyes scoured my face, indignation flaring behind his irises. "You're not Olivia Morales." His harsh tone echoed in my ears, his statement delivering ice through my veins, pulling me back to reality as it dawned on me that he said it with such certainty.

I needed to get away from him. *Now.*

I scoffed, whipping out my hands to push against his chest, hard enough he stumbled back two steps. "You're being delusional. It's a good thing you're not a detective because your deductive skills are severely lacking. Not that your bodyguarding skills are any better."

I sidestepped him, heading to find an enclosed space where I could lock myself. I barely made it into the hallway when he whipped his hand out, tightly wrapping it around my wrist to keep me from escaping.

I opened my mouth to protest, struggling against his grip, but then he was moving, shoving me against the wall, my front hitting the hard surface. He pressed himself fully against my back, twisting my arm and gripping my other wrist. He locked them together and pinned them above my ass.

The breath whooshed out of my lungs from the force of the movement, my heart thudding furiously against my chest to compensate, the frenzied beat echoing through my rib cage.

Every single nerve ending lit up. A deep, welling panic surged through my gut as his harsh breaths assaulted the side of my head.

"Let go of me," I managed to bite out through clenched teeth. I shifted beneath him, trying to get away, but instead accidentally rubbed against his groin. I tried pulling away from him again, but that only made him tighten his hold on me.

"No." He threaded the fingers of his free hand into my hair, tugging at my roots. I let out a choked gasp, tears pricking my eyes as my vision grew blurry from the force of his grip.

"It wasn't a question," I hissed.

He lowered his head, his chin resting in the crook of my neck as he forced me to lean my head against his shoulder, fitting his cheek flush against mine.

"Who are you?" he gritted out against the side of my mouth.

"You know who I am, Mr. Alvarez. Now, let. Me. Go," I said, punctuating every last word.

He tsked, pushing his hips against me, his breath now

ghosting across my neck. "The changes to your appearance were pretty convincing. I'll give you that much." His fingers tightened in my hair, and he pulled, my neck stretching back further.

A harsh stab of pain radiated over my scalp, sending a shocking pleasure straight between my legs. My knees weakened and a tiny whimper escaped me before I could stop it.

I clenched my jaw, my body warring between the desire to reach for him and knowing I should push him away. My chest tightened and I mustered all the strength I had, thrashing against him.

"Fuck you," I hissed.

As soon as my words registered, he let go of his grip on my wrists and spun me around so quickly, I gasped. My back hit the wall and his hand moved up to wrap around my throat, my pulse pounding so heavily I was sure he could feel it.

He brought his body flush against mine, the hand on my neck holding me captive, preventing me from moving any further. He leaned forward until we were at eye level and my eyes widened, shock freezing my features in place.

Despite the fear thrumming through my veins at being made, I couldn't help but drown in the fact that there was something so euphoric about his proximity, it made me nearly dizzy. My body tingled with need and I forced my hands to my sides, my fists clenching hard so I didn't do something out of line, like touch him.

Because I knew if I did, I wouldn't be able to stop myself.

His jaw ticked as he loomed over me, his face mere centimeters from mine. He pinned me with a heated glare, and his hand squeezed tighter against my windpipe, but not tight enough that I couldn't breathe.

"When I ask you a question, I expect an answer." He seethed in my face. "You don't want to see what happens when I don't get what I want." His voice was low, so low a shiver wrapped around my spine, my lips parting on a harsh breath.

Energy buzzed around us, the dark, ominous threat catching me off guard. The air grew potent, nothing except the sound of our heavy breathing filling the quiet hum.

"Now, tell me. Who are you?" he repeated, his hot breath fanning over my skin.

I turned my head to the side, trying to avoid his lips from making contact with my skin. I sank my teeth into my bottom lip, pulling at it to avoid answering.

His other hand gripped my jaw, turning my head back to face him. His thumb reached out to tug at my bottom lip, releasing the abused skin. Absently, my tongue peeked out and swiped across, coming *so* close to the tip of his finger, desperate for a taste.

My chest heaved at his proximity, my breasts rising and falling at a faster rate. I rolled my lower half, squirming away, trying to dislodge the grip he had against my windpipe, but my effort only gave us a tighter fit.

Tension coiled my body tight, tangling my nerves, and anxiety weaseled in my chest as I tried to gather myself to answer his question.

"Olivia," I finally whispered back, wheezing.

He still had me pinned against the wall, but the pressure around my neck loosened. He removed his hand from my chin, letting it graze down my side until it settled on my hip, causing my breath to stall, goose bumps prickling beneath the fabric of his shirt.

His fingers grabbed my hip and dug into my skin, but not enough to hurt. It felt more as if he needed to ground himself. My hands twitched at my sides, desperate to pull him even closer than he already was, desperate to erase any distance left between our bodies.

His hand skimmed farther down, brushing against the side of my leg before his fingers slipped beneath the hem of the shirt I'd borrowed from him. His fingertips drifted up, this time against the inside of my bare thigh, drawing a slow, *painstaking* path.

My body was so on edge that every little contact, every little touch from him felt heightened. He bent down until his lips brushed against the shell of my ear, his breath ghosting over the bare skin, caressing it.

"I don't believe you," he taunted, his palm rough as he gripped my inner thigh, his fingers digging further into my skin.

My breathing came out in small puffs of air, his punitive touch filling me with a mix of pleasure and pain. I was *so* wet, embarrassingly so. I pushed away that fact, trying to reel my body back in from the ache building as I struggled to figure out how to get him away, because he was getting dangerously close, too close for comfort.

My head fell back against the wall with a thud and I tried shifting my focus to anything else besides the feel of his rough hands on my skin.

Shit, shit, shit. Get yourself together, Sofia. Stupid betraying body, stop this. Right now.

A shiver ran along my spine as the back of his knuckles feathered farther up my inner thigh, his fingers inching closer to where I desperately needed him. My heart thundered as I waited on bated breath, but instead he unexpectedly paused to play with the hem of my cotton sleep shorts.

My fingers dug into the wall behind me, gripping it forcefully, hoping it would temper the urge to reach for him. I had to take back control of this battle, *needed* to shift the narrative before he uncovered too much.

My attention dropped back to Theo and I met his gaze with as much conviction as I could muster, letting my desire for him take over before I switched roles and played the outraged wife.

His hand kept gripping my inner thigh possessively when I unclenched my fists from my sides and wrapped my fingers around his, gliding them slowly along my inner thigh until they were resting right *there*. Right where he could find out the effect he had on me.

His body stiffened, and his breath faltered when I stopped dangerously close, his knuckles brushing against my bare cunt. My eyes gauged his face for a reaction as I loosened my grip, hoping he would continue of his own volition.

He swallowed, his throat rippling with a bob. His chest was completely still as he looked down at my hand, and for a moment, I wondered if he was even breathing.

His low gaze flicked up, pausing at my lips before his eyes collided with mine, the fire in them I knew so well lighting my soul on fire. We just stared at each other for a beat and I couldn't breathe even if I wanted to, my lids fluttering.

I finally sucked in a lungful of air, lifting my hips and pushing my exposed center closer to his hand. His hand quickly moved up from my throat, gripping my jaw so tight my teeth cut into my cheek, and he stepped even closer.

His jaw was tense, his piercing gaze locking me in place as a warning framed his expression as if to say, *"do not fucking tempt me."*

"You're playing a dangerous game, *mentirosilla."* he warned.

But tempting him was the only way I could maintain my secret.

When I realized he hadn't moved, my hand came up to

his shoulder, my fingers inching to the back of his neck, threading through his hair. My nails scraped over his scalp before my fingers dug into his hair, forcing him closer.

My heart pounded with adrenaline, my blood heating and sending a warming flush all over my body. I tilted my hips more, causing my breasts to brush his chest as I sought more of his touch.

I felt his body hum with indecision, his straining will battling between lust and wanting answers.

He groaned, finally leaning into my touch, and I thought to myself *I got him,* until he leaned down and whispered against my lips. "I don't believe you," he rasped, a taunting smirk lingering behind, his hand retreating until his fingers rested slightly lower.

Anxiety crept under my skin. "You don't trust me," I admitted softly, attempting to gather his sympathy.

Pulling back, he cocked his head to the side, letting out a low laugh. "No, I don't. You haven't given me a reason to."

I opened my mouth to reply, but my words halted on their way out when his thumb gently stroked my inner thigh in a lazy caress, his touch hot against my skin. My grip around his neck turned bruising as I tried keeping myself upright.

My legs absently fell open, inviting him, wanting to give him better access. He drove his knee between my spreading legs, pinning my back flush against the wall. My pussy throbbed, the flickering pulse beating against his thigh, wetness seeping past the small barrier of the flimsy shorts I had on.

Fuck.

Although I was slightly embarrassed at the thought that he could feel the warmth, I pressed up my toes, our noses grazing. My stomach tightened at how close we were, but I pushed it aside. "I don't care," I whispered. "Your job isn't to believe me. It's to do what you're told."

His mouth parted, his onyx eyes raging like storms as his fingers twitched against my face. I figured he'd finally let me go, but instead of releasing me, he continued trailing small circles over my skin.

I dropped back down on my heels, my fingers tugging at his short curled strands in an attempt to stop him because my resolve to push him away was slowly tapering and I didn't know how long I could keep resisting him.

He rubbed his thigh between my legs, creating a delicious friction, and I bit my lip to stifle the moan threatening to escape. His hand left my chin, his fingers skimming down my neck and shoulder before he removed it. He rested his palm against the wall above my head before slumping his head onto the wall, right next to mine.

He then turned his head slightly inward, his hot breath skating across my cheek and ear. His lips grazed my earlobe, sending me into a full-body shudder. Sweat beaded on my forehead, but I refused to back down from his challenge.

He trailed his thumb farther up my inner leg to land right where his thigh met my core, where my arousal had soaked through my shorts and onto his pants.

He smeared it across the fabric before bringing that same finger against my lips, the tangy scent of my arousal hazing my senses. He brushed his forehead against the side of my head until it rested against mine. His gaze searched for mine, our breath intertwining.

"You *look* like her," he rasped.

His statement was barely above a whisper, but the loaded words registered enough to rob me of my breath. I should really step away now. No good would come out of letting him continue his train of thoughts, but the intoxicating scent suffocating the air had frozen me in a trance, rendering me unable to move.

His hand curved around my back, gliding up the length of my spine, my body bowing to his will. His palm wrapped around my shoulder, pausing to finger the neckline of the white cotton shirt, *his* white cotton shirt.

He glanced down as he laid his hand flat against my chest, below my left collarbone, right where the beat of my heart pounded.

"You *feel* like her."

A strangled gasp escaped my parted lips and our gazes clashed. The calmness in his voice was unnerving, a stark contrast to the heat radiating off his chest and his hard length pressing against me.

Keeping his hand over the swell of my breast, he then trailed his nose down the side of my face, burying his head into the crook of my neck before he inhaled deeply, breathing me in.

He hummed. "You *smell* like her," he growled against my skin.

I inhaled sharply, shaking my head. "I—"

His soft lips skimming across my neck cut me off. His tongue snaked out, flattening against my skin before he gave a long lick from the side of my neck to the soft spot behind the ear, his tongue flicking up at the end.

A low groan ripped out of his chest and he buried it against my skin.

"And you fucking *taste* like her."

A wave of lust spiraled in my nerve endings and my teeth rolled over my bottom lip, biting down in an attempt to temper the moan that wanted to escape past my lips.

I was caught somewhere between craving the feel of his mouth on me, wanting to cave and finally give in, while also needing to keep up this charade of playing Olivia because I knew once the line was crossed, there was no going back.

That's how it always was between us. That's why it took months before we both finally gave in to our desires and let ourselves feel that memorable night.

He gripped the nape of my neck, pulling me to him until our lips brushed. He gently tugged my lip free with his teeth before whispering against my lips a word I hadn't heard in a long time.

"*¿Mi alma?*" he questioned, his whisper pained.

The use of my nickname had my hibernating heart sparking with recognition. Hearing it coming out of his lips in a hefty breath sent a shiver racing up my spine, the hair at the back of my neck prickling.

I couldn't hide it anymore. I tried to figure out where I'd messed up, racking my brain on what I'd done to tip him off. I had been *so* careful with every single one of my actions.

But none of that mattered anymore.

He knows.

I barely had time to process what was happening when I felt myself nodding in response before he yanked me to him, his lips crushing against mine.

CHAPTER 25
SOFIA

I hesitated for a fraction of a second, keeping my lips shut until I finally gave in, my mouth opening on a moan, letting him inside.

His lips molded to mine and my fingers weaved into his hair, tangling and tugging at the roots, while his cupped my face possessively, trying to get as close as possible, each of us fighting for dominance.

My eyelids fluttered shut as his tongue slipped against mine, his hands tilting my head to deepen the kiss, wracking a whimper out of me. I let myself get lost in him, my body becoming pliant in his arms, his knee between my legs the only thing holding me up.

Our kiss crackled with aggression and lust, all the years lost relieving themselves in this single act. He kissed as if this was our first and last time. He kissed me like he wanted to consume me. Like he'd been deprived for too long and my taste was his only cure.

I leaned into his branding touch when suddenly, he stopped. My eyes snapped open to find him pulling away to look me in the eye, his warm palms still cupping my face. He drew in a deep breath, conflict roaming in his gaze.

"Why did you leave me?" he murmured, his thumb lazily caressing my cheek.

I let my gaze wander over his face before settling on a partial truth.

"I had to."

His thumb paused its back and forth motion at my confession.

Sometimes the best lies are wrapped around a core of truth.

Despite my failure to convince him I was Olivia Morales, I couldn't drag him into this. I didn't leave him all those years ago, only for him to end up in the crossfire. I would never be able to forgive myself if I got him killed because of my own vendetta.

One moment, his hands were on me and the next, he was across the hall, running his fingers through his curls. The sudden loss of his warmth sent a slight twinge of fear through my middle.

"You had to? What does that even mean?" He scoffed, his voice gaining a slight edge as he shook his head, a forced laugh leaving him.

There was a pause and his jaw twitched when I stayed quiet.

"You fucking *left* me, Sofia."

A swell of emotions surged in my chest. Losing him was a price I had been willing to pay, but I wasn't so sure anymore that it had been the right choice. I'd never expected to see him so torn up over it.

"Was it because of me? Because of what happened that night?"

"No," I immediately said, unable to bear the thought of him thinking I regretted us.

I shook my head. "You were supposed to forget about me. You were supposed to move on…"

"How could I ever forget anything about you, *mi alma*?" he rasped out, his features contorting into a pained expression.

He started to move, turning away from me and the conversation, but I wasn't letting him go. I had once before, but I wasn't going to do it again tonight. Not after witnessing what abandoning him seven years ago did, when I now knew how much my actions had affected him.

I let my defenses down and went after him, grabbing his arm.

"*Mi cielito*," I whispered and he stiffened, halting in his tracks.

He spun around and I reached for him, craning my neck as I cupped his face, the stubble scratching the palm of my hands. My heart battered furiously against my chest, the racing beat sending it teetering on the edge of a cliff, afraid he was about to reject my touch.

He flinched but didn't push me away. I blew out a small breath of relief.

"Don't you dare think that me leaving was *ever* your fault. You were the only reason I wanted to stay, but I had to leave. I had to do it. For me."

"Why didn't you..." He trailed off when I slid my fingers up his jaw, tugging the curls at the back of his neck.

I lifted on the tips of my toes while dragging him down until his forehead rested against mine. "I never left *because* of you. I left *for* you."

His breathing grew heavier and his eyes drifted closed in a long, slow blink. Before he got another word out, I ghosted a kiss over his parted lips.

He shuddered in my arms and while his eyes were still closed, I pushed the overthinking part of my brain to the side and gently captured his lips with mine, allowing myself to feel.

To just let go and *feel*.

He hadn't reciprocated yet, so I pressed my mouth harder against his, molding my body against his. My kiss started as tentative, my roaring pulse pounding in my bloodstream.

Theo remained unmoving for a beat, but that was all the hesitation he gave before his palm came up to rest softly on my cheek and his mouth started moving over mine.

It started off slow, as if he wanted to take his time reacquainting himself with my taste, but that tempo quickly dissolved into a desperate one. His other hand cupped the back of my neck, angling my head to his liking before he deepened the kiss, sweeping his tongue inside and deftly stroking it against mine.

We poured ourselves into the kiss. The clash of our tongues and teeth was possessive, rough.

Unapologetic.

With one hand still holding me by the neck, he dug the other into my hip, pushing me until my back hit the wall again, his groin now flushed with mine.

His hand slipped beneath the hem of my shirt, trailing it up my side, grazing right under my breast. His breath hitched, a small smile forming on his lips when he discovered I wasn't wearing a bra underneath.

"I've always loved the way you feel in my hands," he muttered against my mouth.

He kept his ministrations light, my breasts growing heavy from his touch. I squirmed beneath the feel of him pressed up against me, my fingers curling in his hair as he roughly cupped one, trapping my nipple with his finger and thumb, then gently twisting.

"And I've always loved the way you make *me* feel," I breathed out.

He twisted my nipple, harder this time, the sensation

right against the edge of being painful. I rose up on my tiptoes, arching into his touch. The intensifying burning ache shot straight to my core, a heady lust spreading throughout my veins, blurring my vision.

He trailed rough, hungry kisses all the way across my jawline, his stubble scraping along the way, leaving burning trails in their wake before he returned his attention to my lips.

Grunting into my mouth, he rocked into me, the thick length of his erection pressing against my core. I rolled my hips against his, the friction of his pants on my bare legs sending sparks up them.

God, that feels good.

I let myself drown in him, savor his delicious, yet callous manhandling. I let myself revel in something I'd wanted for a long time.

Him.

His hand slid out of my shirt, moving up my front to meet the other one at my neckline.

"I *need* to see you."

His words had barely registered when he yanked hard, a deep, guttural noise erupting from his throat. The fabric disintegrated in his hands, ripping under his force. It tore right down the middle, exposing my full and heavy breasts, and he didn't stop until the front of the shirt was completely ruined.

"*Fuck me*," he bit out, his gaze trailing down my front in appreciation.

I gasped, my body trembling. Cool air brushed across my bare skin, and goose bumps prickled all over. I threw my hands down to cover myself, but he grunted in disapproval.

His fists clenched around the bunched material and he brought his gaze back up. He was staring straight at me, with harsh breaths and lust dilating his dark eyes.

"Put your hands down, or they'll be restrained," he demanded.

I didn't immediately obey, contemplating the idea of being bound, and he arched a brow at my hesitation. He moved a hand to his belt, stepping closer in warning until I finally did as he said, lowering them at my sides.

The torn fabric fell down my arms and onto the floor, leaving me in nothing but the flimsy cotton shorts. The corners of his lips turned up at my obedience and that smile alone had more wetness pooling between my legs.

"Good, *mi alma*," he whispered.

A weird sense of disappointment washed over me when he removed his hand from his belt, a regret that I didn't push him further filling me. His gaze dropped to my breast and he lifted a hand, running his knuckles over the top of my breasts, forcing the fleeting thought away.

"These look delectable."

My chest heaved under the hot glare of his stare. He pressed a kiss to my lips before moving away and dragging his mouth down my neck, his teeth nibbling and sucking on the skin.

The thought of him marking me, claiming ownership of my body sent a hot spear through my middle. My back arched in response, *wanting* and *aching* for more.

Theo's warm breath skated over my chest and I looked down at him through hooded eyes as he roughly cupped my breasts between his hands. He bent down to wrap his mouth around a puckered nipple and sucked fiercely on it. His tongue swirled around it before his teeth bit down on it.

Hard.

I sucked in a gasp, a whimper escaping my parted lips. My pussy clenched tight and my hands flew up to grab his hair, tugging at the roots to wrench him away, his onslaught on my oversensitive nipples beginning to be too much to handle.

He released my nipple with a pop and lifted his head to glare at me, the look on his face sending a thrill down my spine.

"Don't you dare stop me. Now, put your hands back down," he ordered.

I obeyed and he resumed his assault before repeating the same delectable torture on the other.

I was slowly getting used to the sensation, when his other hand trailed down my side, making its way between my clenched thighs.

"Spread your legs wider for me," he commanded against the abused flesh of my breast, his hot breath tickling my skin, and I shuddered.

"Sofia, don't make me repeat myself," he added when I forgot to comply since I was too focused on the stimulation he was causing in my body.

My heart picked up, my breathing coming out a little quicker at the sound of his commanding voice. His display of dominance called to a deep part within me. I'd had to make decisions for myself for as long as I could remember, so following his commands felt like a reprieve.

But defiance was weaved deep in my nature.

"What if I don't want to?"

I heard the sound before the sting registered. I gasped and my thighs trembled. I looked down, only to realize he'd slapped me right *there* over the thin fabric of my shorts.

"I already told you, I don't like repeating myself."

He delivered another slap, catching me off guard again as he bit down hard on my nipple. I yelped and a strangled sound left my lips, my legs falling open of their own accord.

"That's it, *mi alma*. Look at you being such an obedient girl."

He rested his forehead against mine and our gazes clashed right as his fingers slipped inside the front of my small sleep shorts, finding my pussy bare and ready for him.

He palmed it, then cupped me with a quiet groan. "*Fuck me*. No panties either... She's gonna kill me," he muttered to himself.

And then he was touching me, carving a maddeningly slow path between my folds, spreading my arousal all over my pussy. Everything around us faded, my attention solely focused on his touch, my gaze conveying the desperation I couldn't conceal anymore.

He let out a whimper as he teased my entrance.

"So fucking wet for me," he said, dotting slow kisses down my temple toward my ear.

He kept brushing his fingers over my clit, but never long enough, making me writhe in desperation for more. I was about to protest, the anticipation getting to be too much, but the words died on my tongue when he finally pressed down on my clit.

"Oh God," I whimpered in frustration when he didn't move. I needed it, needed him. *Now.*

"Yes, *mi alma?*" His voice was full of amusement.

The answer was on the tip of my tongue, but I didn't want to give him the satisfaction of being able to demand everything out of me. Besides, I preferred seeing him riled up.

The curiosity of seeing what he would do if I disobeyed took over. I reached down and gripped him hard through his slacks, my palm rubbing against him.

"Fucking hell," he hissed.

"Two can play at that game, Mr. Alvarez," I taunted him.

"Then let's see who wins." He grabbed my hands and pinned them to the wall right above my head.

He leaned down and spoke against my ear.

"I'm going to fuck you so hard you won't remember your name. So *fucking* hard you won't be able to move for the next week without thinking of me. I'll just keep filling that tight little cunt of yours until it's overflowing. Then, I'll send you right back to that little husband of yours, used and abused, with my cum still dripping down your thighs."

I was panting solely from the lewd picture he was painting for me.

"But first..." He sucked hard on my neck right as he easily thrust a hot, thick finger into my begging pussy, teasing before he added another one.

Holy shit.

"Theo," I moaned, my forehead pressing against his shoulder as I pushed back against his fingers.

"Keep saying my name like *that* and I might give you more."

He eased his fingers out before twisting them back in, painfully slow. Once I was fully seated on his hand, he curled his fingers within me, hitting a delicious spot that had my pussy clamping down.

My eyes closed at how well he seemed to know my body, better than I apparently ever did. It had never been like this, not by my own hands, or by anyone other than him.

Tension coiled within my core and he pulled his fingers all the way out before plunging them back in, this time reaching even deeper than the last. I cried out, squirming at the building pressure.

"Feel that, *mi alma?* Feel how fucking wet you are for me? " He husked across my ear. He nibbled on my earlobe as he continued fucking me with his fingers. The heel of his palm rubbed against my swollen clit.

I'm so close.

"Your pussy is doing such a great job, sucking my fingers in. I'll have to work harder to fully break you in, won't I?"

I was *right there*, right about to tumble over the edge, when Theo snatched his fingers back, releasing a sigh.

What the fuck?

My eyes shot open, and I brought them up to meet his, watching a deviant smirk splayed on the edges of his lips.

"The sad thing is, disobedient girls don't get to come, *mi alma*. They get punished."

I opened my mouth to protest, when he smeared something damp against my lips. I shifted my gaze down to find the fingers that were just inside me resting against my bottom lip.

"Save your excuses," he rasped, pressing his fingers against the seam of my lips that were coated with what I now realized was my own arousal.

He chuckled darkly. "At least your cunt doesn't lie. Now suck. I want my fingers clean."

I gasped at his words and he forced his fingers, up to his knuckle, through my parted lips, pressing roughly against my tongue. I whimpered, my tongue wrapping around them as I sucked myself off his skin.

"That's my girl. You're being so good for me."

His face turned feral as he gradually pulled his fingers out of my mouth.

He slipped his finger under the elastic of the loose sleep shorts, tugging. Once they pooled at my feet, I stepped out of them.

I was now completely naked in front of him while he was still fully clothed, but I didn't care. All I could do was stare deep at the dark brown eyes so tightly fixated on me.

He then cupped my pussy, effortlessly plunging his two fingers again, the embarrassing sound of how soaked I was bearing witness to what his words did to me.

"Theo..."

"Yes, Sofia?" His grip on my wrist loosened as he pulled his fingers out again. He held my gaze with a half-lidded stare, and I ground out a moan at the sight of him pushing his fingers into his mouth, his lush lips wrapping around them as he coated his tongue with my wetness.

"Hmm. What a fucking treat you are."

And then, he came for me. He plunged his tongue into my mouth and I sucked on it, *hard*, my arousal coating the inside of my mouth again, this time tasting even better.

His groan was guttural.

I kissed him back with the same fierceness, and he dragged the hands above my head back down to drape them around his neck. He buried his fists into my hair and

I tightened my hold on him, pressing his body flush against mine.

He nibbled on my bottom lip before sucking it and letting it go with a pop. His eyes were on me and he looked as depraved as I felt.

"Can you taste it, *mi alma?*" he whispered between kisses. "That this cunt and these lips are mine? That *you* are fucking mine? I don't care whose ring you have on your finger because you'll always be mine."

He put a small distance between our bodies and grabbed my wrist, pulling me forward. He placed my hand on his chest, then slid my palm down his upper body until it rested over his strained slacks.

"Unbuckle my belt," he demanded with a low voice as he tucked a fallen lock of my hair behind my ear.

Chills ran down my spine at the contrast between his gravelly tone and his soft gesture.

I did as told, my gaze still holding his. The sound of a belt opening rippled in the air as I loosened it, his pants now hanging low on his hips.

I felt his eyes roaming all over my naked body, and when he stepped in closer, I flinched, stepping back, my back resting against the wall.

"Do you know what seven years of waiting for you feels like?" he asked, his voice now deeper and harsher.

I lightly shook my head, my eyes wide in anticipation of what he would do next.

"I looked for you everywhere, despite the bureau

telling me to stop searching. I almost got fired because I couldn't let go. I drowned myself in my work, drove myself to madness because I couldn't get you out of my head. The hurting never stopped, wondering every day why you would leave." He paused. "Only to find you years later married to another man."

His words sliced through me, regret washing over me. His dark eyes searched mine, and despite the harshness of his tone, all I could see was everything past the anger, down to the pain he was concealing.

He stared at me, breathing fast. "I waited for you, *longed* for you," he whispered softly, exhaustion and resignation coating his voice.

I hurt him, *badly*, and there was only one thing I could do: apologize.

"I'm sorry," I said, dropping my eyes.

He stayed silent for a beat, and I glanced up, his hard brown eyes already on me. His jaw clenched as he seemed to struggle with what to do next, a battle of will warring inside of him.

He finally hissed, yanking out the belt from the loops and folding it in half in one hand, apprehension striking down my body at his next words.

"I don't need to hear your sorrys. I want you to show me."

I frowned up at him and he stepped aside, nodding toward the bedroom. I wasn't afraid of Theo. I trusted him, and I would do anything to have him back, even if it was just for one night.

I shuffled past him and headed to the room, glancing over my shoulder to see him following behind, belt in hand. Unease swept through me once I walked inside and he shut the door behind him, the tense silence between us growing exponentially.

Theo's eyes roamed over my body as he snapped the leather on his palm, the sound reverberating against the walls, and he walked up closer, only a small space now separating us.

My mouth parted and his thumb came down to trace along its edges.

"Turn around and lie down on your stomach," he ordered, his voice low and husky, tinged with warning.

I dragged my gaze up, pausing at the hard bulge straining against his slacks and up to meet his eyes. I quieted the millions of questions bouncing in my head and did as told, lying face down on the side of the bed, pressing my palms flat into the comforter next to my head.

"Look at my pussy dripping for me," he praised, and I dug my face into the comforter to muffle my whimper.

I was bent over and at his mercy, which, in theory, should have been frightening since I hated being under anyone's control, but I didn't want him to stop.

If anything, it was the complete opposite.

I want more.

I was burning up, squirming under the intensity of his stare. Under the burden of silence, I lifted my head and was about to turn around to look at him, but his palm wrapped around the back of my neck, pressing my face into the bed.

"Don't move unless I say so."

My body ached with need as his hand left my neck. He skimmed a finger down the length of my spine, down the crease of my ass, and traced a feather touch down my cunt.

He'd been so meticulous in his teasing, giving me tiny fragments of pleasure, but stopping right before they blasted off.

"Theo, *please*," I begged as he continued his delicious torture, retracing his path, muttering something under his breath in Spanish that I couldn't decipher from under the lusty haze I was in.

The tension in my core tightened, every nerve ending in my body begging for release. I tried pushing against the tip of his finger that was circling my opening, just wanting to chase what my body was craving, when a crack resounded throughout the bedroom.

Fuck.

A sharp sting radiated across the back of my upper thighs. "Theo," I cried out in surprise and in pain, my back arching as I buried my face into the mattress, whimpering.

"That's it, *mi alma*, let me hear you scream my name."

His palm smoothed over where he'd just hit, and as I

was trying to catch my bearings, he delivered another slap to the exact same spot, which was quickly followed by him rubbing over the already tender skin.

I muffled my cry into the plush comforter, my body tensing, anticipating the next blow.

"You look exquisite with my marks on you, *mi alma*," he praised.

I waited for it, but he didn't spank me again, disappointment surprisingly taking over me.

There was a pause before I felt him drop to his knees.

I wanted to ask what he was doing, but it became clear when he grabbed my ass in his hands and dug his fingers in, spreading me wider. I sucked in a shaky inhale from how mortified I was for being *so* exposed.

My teeth slammed into my lips and the taste of copper flooded my mouth. He leaned in and hovered, as if he was waiting to see what I'd do.

When I didn't move, he pressed closer against me and did something I would have never expected.

He inhaled, *deeply*.

"So responsive," he murmured against my wet cunt. "I've barely touched you and your cunt is quivering."

I gasped so hard, my lungs nearly collapsed from the sudden change in pressure. Then, without warning, his mouth clamped on my clit, flattening his tongue over it.

Licking. Sucking. Flicking.

His tongue worked me, sending me into a frenzy against his mouth with every perfectly placed lick. His hands gripped the inside of my thigh, keeping me pressed flush to his face.

A growl escaped him and I ground against him. His teeth nipped at my clit in warning, but I didn't care.

"The—" My spine bowed, my mouth opening on a strangled gasp.

He plunged his tongue inside me forcefully and I panted, my heart pounding.

"*Please,*" I choked out as he continued fucking me with it.

I was so wet I could feel my arousal pooling between my thighs. I was teetering on the edge of an orgasm, but instead of diving deeper, everything abruptly stopped.

"The first time you'll come will be on my cock. Then you can come down my throat while riding my mouth."

CHAPTER 26
THEO

"P lease," she cried out, the sound of her begging a melodious harmony to my ears.

My Sofia. Begging me for more.

Closing my eyes, my palm rubbed against my painfully hard cock, imagining all the things I was now able to do to her. I still couldn't wrap my head around her being here. In front of me. Naked and wanting, to do with as I pleased.

I looked for her for years, and it drove me to the brink of madness thinking I had taken it too far that night for wanting her more than I should've.

I was hired to protect her, not fall in love with her.

But she'd been mine the moment I'd laid eyes on her. She still was even seven years later. Even with her being married to someone else.

She broke my heart all those years ago, and having her

back in my arms was slowly mending it back together, piece by piece.

And fuck did I want more.

More of this. More of us. More of *her*.

I'd been barely able to breathe when I finally had an uninterrupted view of her. I raked my eyes over her body, making plans to savor her. That smooth tanned skin. Those plump breasts, dark nipples just desperate to be sucked on. Those curves and that plump, bare pussy begging to be feasted on.

She was fucking beautiful. And *fuck me*, that smell.

It was intoxicating. *She* was intoxicating. I was barely holding it together.

Just the thought of sinking into her dripping cunt made my cock twitch and my balls draw even tighter.

I slowly got back up, my hands caressing her reddened skin, smoothing the area. I wrapped an arm around her soft stomach as my free hand skimmed up her spine until my fingers tangled through her curled strands, fisting her hair.

Tightening my hold, I pulled on her strands, her back bowing as I brought her up, my front coming flush to her back. My dick jutted hard against the seam of my zipper, desperately waiting to be freed and sink home.

I rested my chin in the crook of her neck and forced her to lean against my shoulder.

"Te ves tan jodidamente hermosa cuando me suplicas," I said, bringing the hand on her stomach down, my ring

finger sliding along the seam of her pussy, dipping in just a little, teasing her hole again.

"Please, Theo, let me come," she whimpered, pushing against my finger, the three inked dots disappearing between her trembling legs.

Soon enough I'll find a way to mark her.

I pushed the tip of my finger into her for a moment before removing it. Her hands came up behind her, her fingers grabbing the side of my thighs, yielding me aggressively into her.

"Theo, I swear if you don't—"

I couldn't wait any longer. I needed to be inside her.

Body thrumming with hunger, I loosened the grip on her hair to spin her, cutting her warning off. My hands slid down the back of her thighs to pick her up and her legs instinctively wrapped around my waist, rocking her hips into me in a shallow thrust.

Hoisting her onto the bed, I laid her back on it, wanting to explore her. My fingers dug into her thighs, forcing them as wide as they'd go so I could look at her.

My eyes didn't know where to look first. My gaze traveled down, tracing the shape of her body. The faint scar on her left side confirmed she was my Sofia. My hands slid over her waist, and I reveled in how good she felt under my palms.

"Fuck, you're perfect. Look at how your glistening cunt is weeping for me." My cock was straining so hard against the seam of my pants, I was on the verge of losing it.

Her breathing quickened, and she squirmed under my perusal.

"Trust me?" I asked her.

"Yes."

Her immediate response was a shot of electricity straight to my heart, firing it to pump harder, blooming under my rib cage.

I placed a kiss to her lips before reaching for the belt I'd dropped on the bed earlier.

"Hands," I ordered and she complied, lifting them toward me.

I brought her hands to my mouth, pressed a delicate kiss to her injured hand, and made sure the wrapped gauze was secured. I lifted my gaze back to her and waited for a beat, in case she'd changed her mind. I then started wrapping the leather around her wrists.

I prepared myself for her to stop me, but she didn't. She just kept staring at me, studying my movements intently, watching me pull the belt tight—handcuffing her.

Once secured, I took a step back and tugged the shirt I was wearing over my head, then tossed it to the side. Her gaze lingered on my body as I slid my pants off, my boxers following shortly after.

Her eyes widened once my cock sprang free, her piercing gaze locked firmly on it. Her mouth parted, her tongue darting out over her lips, and my imagination distracted me with images of how good those would look wrapped around my cock.

"Eyes are up here, Sofia."

She was about to throw a snarky comment at me when I marched toward her, her breathing accelerating with each step closer.

Climbing onto the bed, I sat on top of her, straddling her, my thighs cupping hers on either side. I brought her bound hands over her head and leaned my lips to her ear. Taking a lobe into my mouth, I sucked on it.

"Keep them there," I whispered in her ear before pulling away. She winced slightly as the coarse leather dug into her skin.

She quirked a brow. "Are you going to fuck me now?"

I chuckled and moved to sit back on the heels of my feet. "Patience, Sofia."

"Oh, fuck you, Theo." She huffed and squirmed under me.

"Lie still, Sofia. I'll fuck you soon enough."

I traced my fingers over the soft bruises my teeth left earlier on her breasts, the evidence of who she belonged to now clear.

"Look at how easily your skin takes my marks. You belong to me, Sofia. And I'm going to take back what's mine."

I tugged on her nipples, twisting them between my thumb and forefinger. She threw her head back, drawing in a breath as she tried to wiggle out of my hold.

"Do you understand?"

Biting her lip, she nodded. The corner of my lips curved as I pinched her nipples harder, my cock jumping against her stomach.

"Like it when I play rough, *mi alma*?" I grazed my hands down her sides as I got on my stomach, positioning myself so my face was right between her thighs.

"Yes, Theo, just *pleaseee*, stop torturing me..." she hissed as I ran my nose along the inside of her thigh.

I peered at her while my breath skidded across her clit. Her eyes rolled shut and she moaned as I traced the tip of my tongue up her seam. She tried to twist away, closing her legs over my head, but I forced them wider apart.

I hauled her legs over my shoulders, lifted her ass, and leaned in. After teasing her puckered hole for a moment, I licked a trail up before penetrating her entrance with my tongue.

I squeezed her inner thighs as I continued my assault and she bucked against my face, pressing her legs so tightly against my head, she was practically suffocating me. But I wasn't going to complain. Dying while eating her would be a mercy.

"That's it, *mi alma*, ride my mouth. I want you to drench my face so that everyone knows I belong between your legs."

I lowered her hips and used one hand to push her down against the mattress as I wrapped my lips around her clit, inserting my fingers from my free hand inside of her.

She writhed beneath me, rolling her hips into my face, her cunt my only source of sustenance, as my tongue lapped her arousal.

"Do you hear that, *mi alma?*" I said, coming up for air, adding two fingers in.

My fingers being swallowed by her cunt was the only sound in the room. The wet suction propelled me into a feral state, and I dived back in like a man starving for his last meal, ravenous for her taste.

I curled my fingers inside of her as I bit down on her swollen clit. Her back arched, her heels digging into my shoulder blades.

"I'm coming. Oh God, Theo, I'm coming..."

"That's it, Sofia. Give it to me." I doubled my efforts until I felt her coming down my throat with a cry, grinding her pussy harder into my mouth, spasming around my fingers.

I hummed against her pussy, her taste flooding my taste buds, my senses consumed by her sweetness. My fingers and tongue were still going until I felt her slump against my face.

"Your pussy tastes even better than I remembered." I groaned.

I looked up at her, my mouth and beard covered in her wetness. The look that greeted me was like a sucker punch to the gut. She was staring at me, her face almost as feral as mine, her breathing hard, pupils dilated with lust.

"Kiss me."

I pulled myself up, my body weight falling to rest on her, and I grabbed the back of her head, crushing my mouth against hers. She kissed me back with equal fierceness, sucking herself off my tongue, sending a growl reverberating in my chest.

I dragged her arms over my head, forming a chain around my neck. I groaned long and deep into her mouth as she tightened her hold on me, pressing her body against mine, my cock nestling against her pussy.

She moaned, grinding against the length of it, stroking me, as if she were trying to jack me off with her cunt. Pulling away slightly, she rested her forehead against mine, her heavy breaths coating my lips.

"My pussy tastes even better in your mouth," she whispered against my mouth.

Holy shit. I nearly came right then and there.

I slanted my lips over hers, giving myself more room to thrust my tongue inside her mouth, kissing her deeper and harder. She started sucking on it, matching the rhythm of her stroking.

"Fuck me," she breathed out, rubbing her clit faster on my cock. My breathing picked up, my hands palming any inch I could find on her body.

I grabbed her ass, then took her hips, moving her back

and forth against my cock, making sure her opening and clit slid up my length.

"Theo, please. I want you to fuck me," she whispered.

I laid her down on her back again, and she was about to complain when I reached behind my head, removing her arms and moving to unbind her.

"I know you want my cock. Trust me, I want to be inside you just as badly. But I want to feel your hands on me while I'm fucking you."

Once freed, I tossed the leather onto the floor next to the bed and brought her reddened wrists to my lips, pressing a light kiss over them.

"Do they hurt?" I asked, running my thumbs over the red marks where the leather had chafed her skin.

She shook her head and bit her lower lip. I tugged on her chin, freeing her lip from her teeth. "No, *mi alma*, your words."

"I'm *fine*. Now, would you stop asking questions and fuck me already?" she said defiantly, palming my ass and digging her nails into the flesh, bringing me closer.

I chuckled and leaned over her body, resting my forehead against hers, our gaze meeting.

"Glad to see you're still in there."

My lungs seized at the expression on her face, and her lips parted against mine. I took her hand and wrapped our joined hands on my cock, rubbing it up and down her seam, collecting her wetness before dragging it back down and aligning myself with her entrance, slightly nudging the head inside.

She sucked in a sharp breath and we both glanced down, watching me slide into her for the first time after all these years, until I stopped halfway.

"Look how good your cunt looks wrapped around my cock," I said, letting out a strangled moan. We both watched as my shaft glistened with her arousal, her pussy gliding on my cock as I pulled out, the tip still resting inside.

"I fucking love watching your pussy suck my cock." I groaned, thrusting back in, a little farther this time.

I had completely forgotten how it felt, fire submerging my body, and I was more than happy to let her consume me.

I bore down on her neck, scoring my teeth into her smooth skin, mustering every ounce of strength within me to not blow when I felt her clamp down on me. Her sopping cunt felt exquisite around my cock.

With one hand clamped on her hip, I pulled out and gripped the head, using it to trace circles around her swollen clit before dragging it back down and plunging back into her, this time almost all the way in.

Our lips collided and she gasped into my mouth, her pussy adjusting around me. Her hands slammed against the bed at my intrusion. Her fingers fisted the sheets tightly, and her cunt mimicked the movement by clamping down on me, sending my body heat into a feverish state.

I hissed, sucking in air through my teeth, and turned my chin up to the ceiling, my control hanging on by a thread. "Ah, Sofia, you're killing me."

"Wh-why?"

My hands roamed circles over her sides as I rolled my hips into her.

"Baby, you feel like heaven and…and…" I was panting hard. My voice was merely a gasp at this point. "God, Sofia, do you know how good you feel? You're choking me."

She was *so* fucking tight, and her wetness seeping out eased me in. She rocked forward, but I pressed a hand over her stomach, stopping her from moving further.

"Sofia, stay the fuck still, or I will take you over my knees and spank you crimson until you learn to listen," I gritted out through clenched teeth.

Goose bumps trickled across her skin as she hissed out a breathy moan. *"Fuck…"*

Sharp arousal lanced my abdomen as she clenched around me again and my cock twitched in response. I dragged my thumb down her hip until it landed on her clit and circled it.

A loud sigh escaped her lips and I pressed my lips against hers, swallowing it.

I felt her cunt quiver around my cock as my thumb

picked up the pace and I continued rolling my hips into her, her hips stirring to match me.

"More," she pleaded, her fingers threading through my hair, bringing my mouth back to hers. "More, Theo, *please.*"

"Anything for you." I growled, pulling my hips back and slamming into her eager pussy until I was fully seated deep inside, my pelvis flush against her groin.

Her back arched, her chest rising to meet mine as a moan escaped her parted lips. She fit so perfectly around me. "You're taking me so good, *mi alma. Hecha solo para mí.*"

I pulled all the way out, then plunged right back into her in one long, hard stroke. Her eyes rolled shut as I pulled out slowly so she could feel every inch of my bare length, pulling out just enough that she could feel the crown of my head teasing her entrance.

"Theo," she cried out, my name falling from her lips the sweetest melody my ears had heard in a long time.

"*Mi alma*, look at me," I demanded in a whisper, panting against her lips.

Our gazes locked in an intoxicating stare, cementing that after tonight, I would never be able to let her go. Not that I ever did.

My eyes never leaving her, I pressed back into her dangerously slowly, our moans tangling together. Her hips met mine as she dragged her fingers to my shoulder, her fingernails digging and piercing the skin.

"Sofia…" I whimpered against her skin.

I grabbed both of her hands and pressed them above her head, lacing her fingers with mine. We kept our eyes open as I slowly inched my way in, reaching a deeper level of intimacy. Our bodies locked together, and we both inhaled, my heart pounding against my ribs at our held breaths.

"Say it," she breathed out.

Although I wanted to tell her I loved her, I couldn't just yet. I had to make sure she was fully mine. So I settled for the closest thing to the truth.

"I missed you like I've never missed anyone in my life," I finally said. "Your turn."

A sigh escaped her lips as I rolled into her. "I missed you too," she confessed.

My heart stuttered as I gazed into her, getting lost inside of her. "Say it again."

"I missed you so much"

My control snapped, and my strokes turned punishing, driving into her rougher, harder, *faster*.

"Sofia, I want to feel you come around me. Can you do that for me, baby?"

"Yes," she said softly.

Bending down, I pulled her bottom lip into my mouth while my hips rolled in and out of her, hitting her clit with each stroke. She began riding me until her pussy tightened around my cock, wrapping us in an intoxicating level of bliss.

Her inner thighs quivered, trembling beneath me. "Theo," she shouted. Our eyes clashed as her orgasm took over. Her breathing was strangled, her body tensing underneath mine. A mumbled cry filled the room as she came.

"You're soaking me," I said through gritted teeth.

I slowed my rhythm, drawing out her pleasure until I felt her body go slack. I unwound our hands and slid a finger over her sensitive clit, rubbing harsh strokes while I was still fully seated inside her.

"Theo, I can't—" she gasped, pleading.

"You can, and you will." I chuckled low and deep, right before delivering a short slap on her pussy.

She cried out, her body jerking as she tried to pull away.

"What did I say about listening, *mi alma*?" I warned, tapping her pussy again.

Gripping her hips roughly, I pulled out almost completely before impaling her in one rough thrust. Digging my fingers into her hips, nails scoring her skin, my hips picked up speed, driving my cock in and out, and it didn't take long until she was coming again.

I forced her to look at me, her eyes blazing as hot as the roaring fire building inside me. She let out a string of moans, sending electricity zipping up my spine.

I bent down, my voice hoarse against her lips. "I love watching you fall apart."

My thrusts grew slow and languid as my back muscles

stiffened, my release desperate to escape. My nose brushed over hers, and my mouth grazed over her lips without ever closing the distance.

My hips jerked, and my stomach muscles clenched as a strangled noise forced its way out of my throat, my release unraveling. We both looked down when I slowly pulled out my glistening cock as I came, a thin white line of fluid following.

Cursing under my breath, I gripped my length and pressed my throbbing head against her center, the rest of my orgasm unloading on her pussy, painting it like she was my Mona Lisa.

My legs were barely able to support my weight, my breathing shallow. I hadn't come in a woman in seven years and I definitely had never come this hard in thirty-seven years.

I felt warm cum leaking out of her and sat back on my knees, situating myself between her legs. Smoothing down her inner thighs, I grabbed her under her knees and hiked them up to her chest.

She moved up on her elbows, following my gaze, watching us leaking out of her. Her cheeks blushed with embarrassment and she tried to fight my grip, moving to close her parted thighs, but I gripped harder, keeping them spread.

"Stop. I want to watch it drip out of you." I groaned against her thigh as my cum dripped out of her perfectly swollen cunt. "I like seeing how filthy I made you," I told her, biting the inside of her soft flesh until she whimpered.

Placing a kiss above her pubic bone, I lay on my stomach. "Besides, it's my job to clean up the messes I make."

Flattening my tongue on the inside of her leg, I licked up the wetness dripping from her and she collapsed on the bed, her eyes fluttering shut.

"You came so sweetly for me earlier, drenching my mouth when I ate that pretty pussy of yours. Does my pretty girl think she can do it again?" I muttered against her leaking pussy.

I looked at my cum and her juices mixed together one last time before diving back in with one word echoing in my mind.

Mine.

CHAPTER 27
SOFIA

My body was still humming when he disappeared between my legs, my knees still pushed against my chest. He ran his tongue along the inside of my thigh, and I collapsed on the bed, arms thrown over my face at the thought of him cleaning *us* from my dripping pussy.

"You came so sweetly for me earlier, drenching my mouth when I ate that pretty pussy of yours. Does my pretty girl think she can do it again?" he asked, his words muttered against me, his heated breath cascading across the sensitive skin.

"Yes," I pleaded breathlessly.

And then he was on me, his mouth ravenous as he caught our releases with his tongue and pushed it back inside. I cried out in pleasure.

My hands shot down to grip his hair, pulling his head as tight as I could to my sex as I grinded down while he licked, sucked, and nibbled on my already swollen clit, his stubble heightening the sensation as I rolled my hips into him.

"I can't get enough of you," he hummed, releasing my clit from his teeth. "But you taste even sweeter when you beg."

He dived back in, and then I was coming, *again*, another orgasm exploding through my body—toes curling, cunt clenching around his tongue, and black swarming my vision. A scream tore out of my chest, the sound waves permeating the air.

"*Oh*, Theo…" I panted.

What is this man doing to me? I've never felt hunger like this.

"Open up, *mi alma*, taste how good we are together."

Confusion cut through me at his command, diluting the blissful fog, and I opened my eyes, only to find him looming over me.

He thumbed my chin, prying my lips open. I stared up at him, waiting. He pressed his thumb into my mouth until he felt the back of my tongue. Tears brimmed in my eyes as I fought the urge to gag.

He leaned forward, coming so close our lips nearly touched, a wicked smile gracing his lips. His eyes glimmered and I waited for him to say something, but he remained silent.

Instead, he opened his mouth and spat a warm liquid into mine. My eyes widened in surprise when a sweet, tangy taste swarmed my senses, a dripping thin filament connecting our mouths as he pulled away.

Our eyes clashed, a dark hunger swarming his irises. "Swallow," he grunted, gently closing my mouth shut. I barely recognized his voice. It was deeper, huskier, drowning in lust.

I whimpered and did as I was told. I was tasting him for the first time and it sent a shudder of pleasure throughout my entire body, a rush of arousal pooling in my core as I gulped it down. His hand rested around my neck, his thumb stroking it as it bobbed.

"Such an obedient angel," he praised, and I bit my lip to hold in another whimper.

He leaned closer and used his teeth to detach it from mine, biting it in return. Then he kissed me, *devoured* me with such fervor, I melted into him with a soft sigh, my arms wrapping around his neck, pulling him closer.

He held the back of my neck, and I returned his kiss, plunging my tongue into his mouth, sucking and stroking against his.

This kiss was different. It wrapped around us, allowing us to pour everything we couldn't put into words into it.

Theo settled next to me and pulled me into him, our limbs tangling in each other. He slightly pulled away, his soft fingers dragging up and down my spine as we caught our breaths, the thrum of our hearts beating in unison.

He gazed down at me, his dark eyes taking me in

with such softness. He looked so at peace and that pulled at a string of my heart, knowing I hadn't told him everything.

Pushing the thought away, I sighed at the feel of his lazy caresses and smiled up lazily at him, my eyes heavy and my body sated.

"You're going to put me to sleep if you keep that up." I snuggled closer to him, nestling my head into his chest, his chin resting on top of my hair.

I barely heard his response as my eyes grew heavier, his hand rubbing slow circles down my back. The last thing I remembered was feeling something heavy being draped over us and no matter how hard I tried to fight it, sleep eventually consumed me, the whispers of an "I love you" plunging me into unconsciousness.

I felt his warmth seep into my skin as I slowly came to. I woke up with a content smile grazing my lips, realizing last night was the best sleep I'd had in a long time.

I blinked my eyes open and stared up at the face that was only two inches away from mine. Theo was still sound asleep, softly snoring.

Sleeping on his stomach, his head was resting on his arm, while his other was splayed across my middle. He looked so at peace that I couldn't help but reach for him, my thumb brushing across his cheek. He slightly stirred, his arm tightening around me, pulling me closer.

His brown curls were messy from my incessant pulling last night. One of his curls fell onto his forehead and my hand moved to brush it back, my thumb smoothing down the slight crease that was forming on his forehead.

He was so fucking beautiful.

I'd never gotten the opportunity to do this, just lie next to him and watch him be. The only time it had been a possibility, I'd left in the middle of the night without saying goodbye.

But now, waking up next to him, watching him sleep, was the only thing I found myself wanting to do for the rest of my life.

It's not time yet, Sofia. And only if he forgives you after everything.

I closed my eyes and took a shaky breath, relishing in this peace for a few more minutes.

Ignoring the pang inside my chest that hated me for pulling myself away from him, I took a deep breath and gently moved his arm off me before rolling out of bed.

My gaze flicked down on the bed and I frowned when I found where I'd slept clean. I touched between my thighs, only to find no traces of last night. It suddenly dawned on me that he'd cleaned me after I fell asleep last night.

Mi cielito.

I tiptoed across the room and grabbed his shirt from

where he'd tossed it last night, then pulled it on. I glanced at him one last time right before I slipped out of the bedroom. Where his expression was peaceful only a moment ago, his brow was now furrowed, the corner of his lips turned down and selfishly it warmed my heart.

I quietly padded to the bathroom across the hall, leaving the door open, and turned on the shower, waiting for it to warm up. I tugged on the seam of his shirt and pulled it over my head.

I looked at myself in the mirror and noticed something had changed. Traces of the girl I used to be stared back at me. Despite my body being sore from last night, my heart was perfectly at ease for the first time in what felt like forever.

Steam filled the bathroom, fogging up the small mirror. I stepped under the spray and closed my eyes as the heated water prickled down my skin.

My thoughts drifted to everything that happened last night. Somewhere in the back of my mind, I knew I should've pulled away. That I should've pushed him away and played the role of the indignant faithful wife who just kissed her bodyguard in a moment of carelessness.

But the passion coursing through us washed the thoughts away, reminding me I'd been his first. As a matter of fact, I'd always been his.

I'd never stopped being his. As much as he'd never stopped being mine.

It had been a while since anything had felt this good,

so as selfish as this might've made me, I was going to relish in this temporary reprieve while I could.

Our heated moments flooded the space around me and before I could stop myself, my hand brushed over my skin, ghosting over a nipple. I inhaled sharply at the sensation and gave in, letting my mind wander, my hand slowly working down the front of my body.

I sensed him the moment he stepped into the bathroom. The glass door slid open and I looked over my shoulder, my body slightly to the side, my hand stopping its path down.

My heart soared at the sight of him. I felt the heat of his eyes as they touched every part of me. My lips. Across my jaw. Over my breasts. Following intently the water sluicing over my body, down to where my fingers slipped over the top of my pussy, lightly grazing my clit.

Goose bumps sprouted along my skin and the moment his gaze found mine again, I was all but panting.

He stepped under the water until his chest was pressed to my back. A tingle surged through me when I applied pressure. He wrapped his arms around my shoulder and I leaned back into him, my head dropping over his chest. He pressed a light kiss on the side of my head.

"Morning, *mi alma*," he whispered against my skin.

He brought his other thick forearm around my waist, trapping me against his growing erection. His hand snaked up to palm my breast as I worked my fingers faster, sending heat flaring through me.

He let out a low groan. "That's it, play with my pussy for me."

A slight moan escaped me as he tugged on one of my nipples, his teeth nipping my earlobe. My muscles cramped and tightened, my body vibrating with the clash of his hand on my body while I played with myself.

Then, I was falling over the edge, my orgasm crashing through me, Theo's name falling from my lips on a shaky exhale.

His lips placed another small kiss on my temple as I turned to face him. I looked down at his erection, biting my tongue as I moved to my knees, but he stopped me.

I frowned, but he curled his finger beneath my chin, raising my eyes back to his. "Seeing you come undone for me was all I needed this morning," he declared, turning me back to settle against him.

I let my head fall back once again, peace rolling through my body.

He squeezed a dollop of shampoo into his hand and began washing my hair, massaging the roots. I let out a deep moan at his ministrations, his nails digging in for a moment before he continued drawing circles along my scalp.

He remembers.

The first few months after the accident had been the hardest. I was barely able to get out of bed, let alone shower. I was always overcome with fatigue as I'd mourned my parents and the life I'd once known.

Theo eventually had stepped in and helped take care of me beyond the scope of what his job required. He'd helped feed me, get me out of bed, and shower. He'd even spent hours online, watching tutorials on how to wash my curls properly since he didn't want to ask me directly.

I looked up at him, brushing my reminiscing away to savor the present. I met his gaze as he worked his hands down the sides of my head, the brush of his fingers against the nape of my neck sending a shiver down my spine.

He rinsed my hair and worked the conditioner into my curls, letting it set as he cleaned the rest of my body. He touched me with such delicacy and took care of me with such devotion that I had to hold my emotions back from spilling out.

This felt right. It always had.

And once he was done, I did the same for him.

"I missed this, missed *us*," he said huskily, taking my face between his palms. He placed a gentle kiss on my lips and they parted with a soft sigh.

I missed us too.

After washing everything off, he turned the shower off and grabbed two towels, bundling me in one and wrapping the other around his waist. He wrapped his arms around my body and just stayed still, his head on top of mine, his eyes closed as we both relished in the feel of each other.

I glanced at the image of us in the mirror until I zeroed in on the hand on top of mine, noticing something on his ring finger that hadn't been there the last time I'd seen him.

I didn't remember him having any tattoos.

"Theo," I said quietly. He hummed, meeting my gaze in the mirror.

I traced my finger over the ink, and his skin broke out in goose bumps under my touch.

"What's this?"

He tensed behind me. "Look closer."

I obliged. It was a tattoo of three black dots, equally distanced, with a vine that wrapped in the back. I turned his palm over to see what it led to, only to find the initials SA next to it.

Wait.

It finally dawned on me what this meant. I turned in his embrace and faced him.

"Theo," I said softly.

He closed his eyes for a moment, his shoulders slumping. "It's always been you. It's only ever been you."

He'd inked me on his skin. Our three squeeze hand signal. The initial of my first name combined with his last name.

A lone tear escaped, trailing down my cheek. He hooked his finger under my chin and his thumb brushed across my cheek to wipe it away. His eyes searched mine as he towered over me. I opened my mouth to say something, but nothing came out.

"I know," he said softly.

I lifted on my toes and brushed my lips against his tentatively. He opened up for me and I wrapped my hand around his neck, tugging him forward.

Without hesitation, he wrapped his arms around me, hauled me off my feet, and pinned me to his chest. His tongue swept into my mouth and everything around us vanished.

My legs wrapped around his waist as he placed me on the bathroom counter. We kissed until we were both left breathless.

He broke the kiss and brought me back to the bedroom, then placed me gently on the bed. He walked over to the dresser and grabbed clothes for both of us.

"Those aren't my clothes," I noted, chuckling.

He grinned, walking back to me. "You look better in mine," he said, removing the towel wrapped around my body and patting me dry. He then pulled down another one of his shirts and helped me into a pair of his boxers.

"How come you have so much stuff here?" I asked, curious as to how he had time to pack so much stuff when I'd barely been able to bring a few things with the time constraint.

"This is my place," he confessed.

"Oh."

He studied me, his eyes roaming over my face before he continued. "I used to come here a lot after you left."

I dragged in a shaky breath, his confession sending a spear to my heart, regret filling me for having put so much distance between us, for robbing us of more moments like this.

But hopefully I'd be able to redeem myself once all of this was over.

He dropped his towel and stepped into a similar outfit to mine. He disappeared for a moment before coming back with my hair products and a plain black T-shirt. He then sat right next to me on the bed and grabbed my hand in his. I placed my head on his shoulder and he placed a kiss on top of my wet hair.

"Sit on the floor," he commanded softly.

He grabbed a pillow from the bed and dropped it on the floor for me to sit on. He started massaging the products through my curls, and I leaned into his touch, groaning.

God, this feels so good. I missed this. Missed us. Missed *him*.

This just felt right. *He* felt right. He always had.

Last night felt liberating, but sooner or later, I'd have to push him away again. I wasn't done with my plans for Victor just yet.

But in these small moments with him, nothing else seemed to matter. Not my need for revenge, not my lies or our circumstances, not even our potential end. It was like being in the middle of a raging storm. Despite all the things swirling around, threatening to consume me, I was safe in the middle with Theo.

Pulling myself out of my thoughts, I remembered we hadn't used any protection last night.

"About last night," I started, "I'm on the pill."

He grabbed the comb and started brushing, detangling my curls. "I know." He paused before revealing, "And I haven't been with anyone else."

I whipped my head around and looked up. "What?"He grabbed my head and turned it back to face forward. He resumed brushing. "You heard me, Sofia. I haven't been with anyone else since you, *mi alma*."

I brought my knees up, hugging them to my chest. Although I'd managed to get an awful lot of migraines or managed to keep Victor's schedule busy enough to have him away most nights, sleeping with him had been inevitable. Despite my heart or body never being into it, I'd wished I hadn't been with anyone else either.

"Why?" I asked softly.

I waited for his answer as he wrapped my hair into the T-shirt, securing it with a satin bonnet on top. Once he was done, I stood up and turned to face him.

I stepped between his legs, draping my arms around his neck. His hands moved up my legs, settling on the backs of my thighs as he pulled me closer, lowering his head to rest it on my stomach.

"It's always only been you," he murmured against my shirt.

The certainty of his confession reached through my

ribcage, sinking into my dormant heart, branding and reviving it.

Fuck, I love this man.

I'd loved him for a long time now, but I couldn't tell him just yet. It would be unfair, especially when I was still keeping so much from him. One day, I'd lay it all down for him and would never stop reminding him every day of how much I cared for him.

I knew he loved me too. I could feel it. But he was holding back, scared to push me away with those precious three words.

I stroked a hand down the side of his face before I cupped his jaw, forcing him to look up at me. I bent down and pressed a kiss to the edge of his jaw. I peppered kisses across it as my fingers sank into his hair.

My hands tugged as I laid a tender kiss on his lips before pressing my mouth more firmly against his, my tongue swiping across the seams, demanding entry.

He groaned against my mouth before opening and colliding his tongue with mine. He moved his hands up to squeeze my ass, then lifted me onto his lap, wrapping his arms around me, pressing our bodies closer.

"I love seeing you in my clothes," he murmured against my lips before working down my throat. He buried his face in my neck. "My heart, my whole body, scream *mine* when I see you wearing them."

His hands slipped under his shirt, sliding up the curve of my back, making it arch beneath his touch. I ground gently against him and he turned into me, pressing a kiss to my bare skin.

A shiver rolled through me as he did it again, this time lower. A moan fell from my lips as my body coiled with desire. Hungry eyes looked up at me as he peeled his shirt away from my body and pressed a soft kiss against my breast.

My hands moved down to grip his shirt. When he lifted his arms, I guided the material over his head, letting it fall behind me.

My hands skimmed across his tanned chest, through the light patch of hair on his chest. I ran my fingers through it and down his carved muscles that were begging to be tasted. He shuddered under the pads of my fingertips.

My eyes searched for his as I worked my hands up to cradle his face and leaned in, pressing my lips to his jaw. "It's always been you."

As soon as my mouth brushed against his, he snapped into action, his tongue slipping into my mouth as he snaked one of his hands up. He gripped the nape of my neck and pulled me closer to delve deeper, and I let myself drown in him.

If I couldn't tell him how I felt, I wanted to use my body to convey what any words would fail to communicate. When it was just us, nothing else existed.

But I knew our time was limited.

He doesn't.

CHAPTER 28

THEO

We spent the next few days slipping back into a routine, one that was very close to the one we used to have. Having her back in my arms and waking up to her every morning after all these years was more than I could have ever asked for.

Reality kept digging into my mind, reminding me that although these past few days had been the best in a long time, it was simply a matter of time before our realities came crashing back.

I still had questions lingering in the back of my mind, questions about why she changed her name and appearance or even why she married Victor of all people. I wanted answers, but at the same time, deep down, I didn't want to know.

What if her answers weren't what I wanted to hear? And most importantly, I simply wanted to bask in whatever time I had with her and not spend it arguing.

I was standing at the island, still trying to find who'd shot at her, when she walked into the kitchen wearing another combo of one of my shirts and boxer briefs. She'd been sporting my clothes since that night and it made my heart skip a beat every time.

I loved watching her wearing something that belonged to me.

She wrapped her hands around my middle and placed a kiss between my shoulder blades. "Come with me."

I laced my fingers with hers over where her hands were resting on my stomach and looked over my shoulder at her. "Where to?"

Instead of giving me an answer, she just grabbed my hand and steered us through the kitchen and out the back door. I followed her lead as she walked toward the lake, stopping midway.

My socked feet grew cold as we walked over the damp soil, small rocks digging into the bottoms of my feet. It was already late, the moonlight streaking across a perfectly still lake.

She turned back and planted a small kiss on my lips. I stifled a groan when her fingernails trailed the nape of my neck.

"Take off your clothes," she demanded. "We're going for a swim."

My eyes bulged. "Baby, it's fucking freezing."

273

She shrugged and her brown eyes met mine as she reached for the front of my jeans, popped the button, and slid the zipper down. My breathing hitched when her fingers brushed against my cock.

She then turned around, leaving me standing there, and walked over to the lake. She paused at the edge, dipping a toe and snapping it back with a shiver. She took a deep breath and just walked fully clothed into the lake, the dark water rippling around her, the now drenched shirt clinging to her body.

I watched her, contemplating whether to get in and join her. She glanced over her shoulder and smiled at me, giving me one of those precious smiles only I was privy to.

And fuck if I wouldn't do anything for that smile.

"Are you going to just stand there and stare at me or are you going to get those pants off and join me?" she taunted, her eyes sparkling with a challenge. She slid her arms away, pushing herself farther into the lake.

"Sofia, don't go too far."

She smirked, pushing herself farther away. "You better come get me then."

I slid my pants down, my socks following, deciding to mimic her and keep my shirt and boxer briefs, hoping they would keep me warm enough. Goose bumps broke out across my skin as I hit the water and dove under, the water submerging me.

I pushed my curls out of my face as I resurfaced. She

stood right in front of me, her dark hair pushed back by the water that soaked it.

"This is fucking cold." I groaned, shivering.

She chuckled as I pulled her to me, her legs wrapping around my waist. She grinned at me, the moonlight shimmering across her face. I pressed a kiss to the corner of her mouth.

She was intoxicating, and I didn't think I could ever get enough of her.

We stayed quiet for a while, bobbing in the water as her hands threaded through my wet hair, her nails scraping every once in a while against the nape of my neck while I rubbed circles on her back.

I stared at her, my eyes roaming over her features. Warmth expanded in my chest, pushing until it felt as if it might burst. Peace was usually described as being in a state of tranquility or quiet.

But she'd always been mine. Like a balm to my heart, she always quieted everything else.

She was my peace. My own salvation. *Mi alma.*

I pulled back slightly. My lips brushed against hers, a featherlight whisper of a kiss. Her body arched into mine, her lips parting on a soft sigh. I rested my forehead onto hers, our gazes colliding, our breaths mingling.

She shuddered when I rocked softly into her. We gently kept moving against each other, our bodies moving in unison, building. She rubbed harder against my length, the thin, wet fabric the only thing separating us, and the friction only increased the pleasure.

"Sofia..." I groaned, the plea coming out on a thick rasp. My hand sneaked up the hem of her shirt, resting on her hip, stroking the skin there as we continued rocking back and forth against one another.

The intense connection stalled the breath in my lungs, and a few minutes later, we came in unison. My lips instantly on hers, swallowing her soft cry.

"I wish we could stay here," she whispered quietly against my lips after coming down off the high, her lids fluttering closed.

My chest squeezed at her confession. "Me too, *mi alma.* Me too." I kissed her forehead and she leaned her head forward, burying it in the crook of my neck.

It was in moments like these, moments that felt so good, so *right*, that it hurt the most. These moments were a constant reminder that this was fleeting, that these perfect moments had a potential end.

She eventually drifted off to sleep and I carried her back inside, cleaning and drying her before changing her into another sleeping shirt.

I lay in bed next to her and watched her sleep for a while. It was probably creepy, but I couldn't look away. Her chest rose and fell on steady breaths, a content expression on her face.

I brushed her hair and wished I had the power to keep us cocooned in this space and moment forever.

But no matter what my heart wanted, it wasn't up to me.

I would fight for her, but I needed her to fight for me as well.

We were lying on the couch, debating on which ice cream flavor was the best, which was obviously cookie dough, when the notification of an email pinged from my computer.

I shifted, unwrapping my arm from Sofia's shoulder, and grabbed my computer from the coffee table.

The email was from Jaxon.

She glanced over my shoulder as we both read it.

It was time to go home.

We lingered, reluctant to break the dreamy haze, as we quietly packed our bags, stolen kisses in between. I felt a pang in my chest as we made our way to the car, a long ride awaiting us.

We didn't speak much during the car ride, my hand clutching hers the whole time. We only stopped once on the way back, long enough to refill the tank and eat.

My mind raced with a million thoughts and worries. I didn't have all the answers to my questions, but all I really wanted was her.

My eyes moved to look at her, only to find she was

asleep. Her head was resting on the headrest, her thick, full lashes fanned out over her cheekbones. I briefly watched her chest rising and falling with every breath she took.

I turned my attention back to the road, one thought plaguing my mind.

I hope she still wants the same.

CHAPTER 29
SOFIA

After days of frenzied planning, the night of the gala was finally here. It had been a week since we got back from the cabin and I'd done everything to stay occupied, making sure Theo and I had no time alone.

Not for his lack of trying. Every day, he would aim to get me alone, but I'd immediately shut him down, apologizing and blaming it on the busy planning.

When in reality, I just didn't trust myself around him, afraid he would chip further at my walls, and have me revealing everything before I had put it all to rest.

I spent the day getting ready, at *my beloved*'s request, since tonight was apparently an important night for his company and it was a requirement that I looked the part. Tonight wasn't even about us, but since I'd been tasked with organizing the benefit, it reflected directly on Victor, and by default his company.

After adding the last touches to my outfit, I headed down.

"Finally." Victor scowled, his lips pursed.

He began ranting about how late we were going to be, but I simply let it fade in the background as I grabbed a shawl, wrapping it around my shoulders, just in case the night got cold.

We stepped outside, and I walked down the front stairs, the sun setting down on the horizon.

Quite the perfect night for revenge.

Theo was waiting by a car, and the moment he felt my presence descending the stairs, every ounce of his attention was directed at me. His stare pressed against my body, leaving a trail of fire erupting in its wake.

Our eyes connected, and every moment we had at the cabin came crashing back, regret instantly filling me, reminding me I was still lying to him.

Soon, Sofia. Soon you'll be able to tell him everything.

I snapped out of my thoughts, averting my gaze, and turned my attention back to Victor. I trailed behind him, moving toward the car Jaxon was waiting by, but Victor stopped me in my tracks.

"You're driving with Mr. Alvarez. We're taking two different cars, just in case."

Victor still feared the *threats* on my life and thought logically it would be safer to drive in separate cars as a distraction in case anyone was following us around.

I wanted to object but knew the decision was final and

there was no valid argument for me to bring up. Besides, if this was the last opportunity I had to spend time with him, even just by being in his presence, before he ended up hating me, I wanted to take advantage of it.

So, I simply nodded and forced my legs to move until I stood right in front of Theo. He moved and gestured for me to go first.

He then slid in next to me in the back seat of the SUV, the driver shutting the door behind him. His delicious scent flooded my senses, intoxicating me in the enclosed space. He was so close, yet felt so out of reach.

I grabbed my phone from my purse to distract myself and kept my gaze focused on it as the driver pulled away from the driveway, making his way to the main road. From my periphery, I saw Theo lean back against his seat, his head turned to look out the window.

My entire body felt the weight of his presence as we sat in complete silence, except for the music lulling out of the speaker. Despite the partition separating us from our driver, Theo wasn't trying to make conversation and I was grateful for it.

My attention was still focused on my screen when I felt heat searing my side. I snuck a sideway peek down, only to find Theo's hand resting against the seat separating us.

My dress's slit bared most of my left leg and his fingertips slowly grazed the exposed skin before he retreated it slightly back.

He was still staring out the window, but I knew him. His body was conveying more. He was seeking reassurance. He wanted to know whether or not what happened at the cabin was real.

I pocketed my phone into the purse resting on my lap, contemplating what to do next. I needed to complete my mission, but I also wanted to remind him that I was his.

The two needs battled in my mind.

Before I could second-guess myself, I glided my hand down the side of my thigh, brushing the leather seat. But just as I was about to link our hands together to squeeze it three times, like we'd always done to make sure the other was all right, the partition abruptly slid down.

"We're almost there," our driver announced.

I quickly removed my hand, cowering. I clutched the purse on my lap to tamp down the impulse to touch him when our driver left the partition down.

My nerves intensified when the gala's venue came into view, but I forced them down, focusing on the end goal.

Tonight, I'd kill Victor Morales and finally lay my parents to rest.

Once parked, Theo climbed out and rounded the car from behind to open my door. He held out his hand for me to take. I paused before placing it in his, his thumb brushing across my knuckles, goose bumps erupting all over my skin.

I quickly pulled my hand away, composing myself as I avoided his gaze and focused on the car behind us, watching Jaxon step out of the car and open the door for Victor.

Victor walked over to my side and slipped his arm around my waist, pulling me flush against his side. "This looks amazing," he whispered in my ear before pressing a slight kiss to my cheek.

I muttered a small thank you, forcing myself not to look at Theo, but I could *feel* the weight of his stare burning a hole in the side of my head. My chest tightened, remorse swelling in my chest, knowing he had to witness the gesture of affection and Victor's hands all over me, even though I'd much rather have him at my side.

Focus, Sofia. Just one more night of pretending.

We walked up the red-carpeted stairs and into the metropolitan building I rented out for tonight's event. The brown-bricked structure had skylights and floor-to-ceiling windows on the top floor. The venue was located in Bemes's harbor district, right across from the port, making it the most convenient location to execute my plan.

We gave our name to the usher, and he quickly stepped to the side, sweeping his arm in front of him, motioning us inside. "Have a nice evening, Mr. and Mrs. Morales."

Inside, the gallery hall served as a ballroom, where the main event took place. Crystal chandeliers were hanging from the massive ceiling, bright lights glaring down on the polished floor, staff carrying gold platters of hors d'oeuvres and champagne flutes.

Theo and Jaxon each took a stance on opposite sides of the room, while Victor zeroed in on some attendees. He brought me along as we went around the room, making small talk and enforcing ties with some of the donors and other society leeches.

It took everything in me not to glaze my eyes over during some of these conversations. Instead, I kept a charming smile on as I pretended to listen, nodding every now and then to seem engaged.

But eventually, the chatter in front of me faded away and my eyes surveyed the room, searching for him again. He'd changed position, now leaning against a wall in the far corner.

Although he was trying to blend into the decor, it was impossible to keep your eyes off him.

Transfixed, I took the rest of him in for the first time tonight. He was wearing a black suit with a black blazer and shirt, encasing his build. His pants were molding his strong thighs that just a few days ago were wrapped around my waist, pinning me down as he made me forget about all of this for a little while.

His gaze met mine, and his jaw ticked, his deep brown eyes aiming to peel back the layers I'd tried hiding from him. I tried to look away, but his gaze was too ensnaring, an invisible thread connecting us, and I couldn't bring myself to break it.

Not until I felt Victor's firm hand around my waist, snapping me out of my daze and bringing me back to the conversation we'd been having with the mayor. Victor had kept me plastered to his side since the moment we'd walked in. Like he was afraid I might vanish.

I need a break.

I stuck by Victor's side until thankfully a distraction presented itself in the form of the mayor's wife, just in time for the start of tonight's auction.

Menos mal.

"Apologies," I said, placing a hand on his chest. "I'm just going to check on everything. I'll be right back," I finished, leaving them to their conversation.

Victor hummed in agreement, giving me a small, dismissing peck on the cheek, barely paying attention to what I just said as he kept his attention on the prestigious guests.

Gliding around the room, I weaved through the small groups, quickly making sure they were enjoying themselves, and made my way toward the large white French doors in the back, in dire need of some fresh air.

I grabbed a few canapés from the catering trays lining the tables on the way before pushing through the doors and walking across the long dark hallway. My red bottom heels clacked against the wooden floors as I headed toward the staircase at the end.

I stood at the bottom of the steps, peering down at myself, wishing I were dressed in a more comfortable attire to do this, but that would have obviously raised suspicions.

The long black dress I was wearing hugged every curve of my body, the squared neck transforming my modest cups into a more luscious pair. The slit baring most of my leg, stopped just shy above my thigh, black heels encasing my feet, giving my small frame a few extra inches.

Holding the side of my dress to prevent it from trailing on the ground, I hauled myself up the five stories. Once at the top, I made a right turn and walked a bit farther.

Large canvases and unused furniture lined the walls, white sheets covering them. The staff had used this part of the building as storage to make room for the event downstairs.

I steered left when I found the set of glass doors I was looking for. I pushed them open, allowing the night air to wash over me, the cool and quiet calming my jittering nerves.

Shake it off, Sofia. You spent years training for this and preparing for tonight.

I took a deep breath and stepped out onto the hidden terrace I'd found when I visited the site a few weeks ago.

I plopped the miniature version of a *briouat* in my mouth to satiate the hunger as I walked across it. I leaned against the steel railing and took in the view, scanning the length of the property's grounds.

Below, the gardens rolled up behind the building and bled into the harbor across the street. Street lamps cast light upon the empty grounds.

The air was filled with the faint music echoing from the ballroom downstairs, blending with the sound of boats coasting away, leaving behind the promise of peace that I'll be able to revel in soon enough.

I wasn't sure how much time had passed when a door swung open, the faint sound of the quartet intensified in the air. Then, a warm presence appeared behind me, his arms suddenly circling around my waist to bring me back against him, the heat of his body wrapping around mine like a blanket, gooseflesh peppering my skin.

My hands tightened against the railing, the cold biting into my palms. I sighed and leaned into him, pressing my body into his. My breathing evened out, my head relaxing against his chest. I placed my hand above his and he threaded his fingers through mine.

My eyes fluttered shut, as I let his woodsy scent consume my senses.

"Sofia," he whispered low.

He slowly slid his left hand down the curve of my waist to rest on my hip. A soft rumble of satisfaction vibrated through my body, settling deep in my core. I focused on the weight of his hands against my body, his knuckles drawing slow circles against my waist.

My need for him was so fierce it left me breathless.

His lips pressed against my temple, peppering soft kisses along the side of my face before he brushed them against the slope of my neck, branding me and sending another wave of goose bumps scattering across my skin.

I pressed further into him, a soft moan leaving my lips and threading through the languid atmosphere.

The tension swirling around us was so overwhelming that it sent an icy bucket of realization down my spine, reminding me I had to put a stop to this.

For now.

I swallowed the lump in my throat and fostered the courage to push him away against my will.

"We can't do this," I whispered so low, I wasn't sure if he'd even heard me.

But the previous current of electricity running between us suddenly evaporated, Theo freezing behind me at my confession. He grabbed my chin and maneuvered me so I was now facing him.

He angled my head up, but my gaze was cast downward. "Sofia, look at me," he urged, gripping my chin tighter.

I looked up at him in the darkness, his eyes dark and shining with confusion under the moonlight, the silver light hitting the angles of his cheeks, the strong lines of his neck straining from the weight of my confession.

"What do you mean by *we can't do this*? Can't do what, Sofia?" he asked, cocking his head to the side, surprised by the sudden change in my demeanor.

His hand left my chin as he reached for me, but I took a step back.

The air left my body as the lies scratched their way

out. "I mean we can't do this." I gestured between our bodies. "Us."

"I'm sorry?" he said, stunned, the weight of my words making him stumble back as if I'd physically pushed him.

"I'm married and I'm not willing to end it yet," I lied, hoping the darkness surrounding us masked my pained expression.

Theo knew me too well. He was too attuned to me so he'd know if I was lying. But I was hoping that maybe in the dark, he wouldn't be able to decipher me as easily as he usually did. I hoped the harshness of my words would hurt him enough to let go.

I'd become a professional liar and never once felt guilty about any lie that helped me get here, but *fuck*, this was hard. I hated myself for doing this to him.

He stood still, in shock from the cruel echo of my words.

"I can't give up on my marriage," I added.

He snapped and stepped forward until my back was firmly pressed against the banister. My hands gripped it, resisting the urge to touch him.

He snaked his hand up my front, pressing his palm above my chest, where my heart rested under my rib cage.

"This is mine. This has always been mine," he declared, every word slow and deliberate as he moved closer, fitting himself against my front.

My heart cracked at his words. I knew my words

wouldn't convince him, so I turned my head away from him when he dipped to kiss me.

He flinched, blinking several times as if I'd slapped him. He finally released me and stepped away quickly, putting distance between us, making me instantly miss his scent enveloping me.

Cold air swept over me, replacing the previous warmth he'd seared against my skin, and I wrapped my arms around my middle, trying to keep it at bay.

The previous warmth in his eyes dissolved into a burning rage, my words finally solidifying in his mind, the realization of my lies seeming to click. His gaze hardened, and his jaw clenched, my betrayal hitting him square in the chest, splitting it open for me to watch it bleed.

"You're serious," he said after a beat. I kept my eyes on his chest, refusing to meet his cold gaze. "You're choosing him over me, is that it? I saw you looking rather comfortable with him tonight. Is he what you want?" His voice dripped with venom.

No, I wanted to yell at him. *You're what I want, but I can't have you. Not just yet.*

I wanted to confess, wanted to stop him from walking away. I wanted to take back everything I'd just said, but I couldn't.

So I settled for the easiest way out. Silence.

Theo shook his head, his expression turning stoic before his gaze drifted to the skyline behind us, huffing out a sardonic laugh. He pressed his lips together and nodded, seeming to have accepted my decision.

I could feel his heart closing over the wounds I'd caused, the repercussion of it turning malignant in my blood. "Fine, Sofia. If that's what you want," he finally said.

Tears burned behind my eyes at his detached tone. I watched him take off as he slammed the glass doors shut behind him, disappearing from view.

I stood there, shivering as I fought the urge to go after him and explain everything. I wanted to run after him and beg for forgiveness, expose my lies because seeing the gutted expression on his face hurt me more than I could've imagined.

But I had to remind myself what tonight was for.

Despite having the man I'd always wanted right within my reach, I had dead parents and a debt of vengeance to collect. I hadn't come this far not to collect my retribution.

Shaking it off, I headed back inside. After making sure no one else was on the floor, I stalked toward the loosened vent where everything I needed to subdue Victor had been sitting since my visit last week.

I noticed the camera flickering. I dismissed it, knowing the cameras that covered this side of the building had been interfered with, showing a replica of footage from last night.

The other cameras weren't tampered with since I needed them to show the people who'd shown up tonight.

But since this side of the building would be restricted to guests, it wouldn't raise suspicions.

Moving the old mirror set in front of it, I wiggled the unscrewed vent's door, removing it from its place and setting it beside me. I then grabbed the small duffle bag that sat inside. Unzipping it, I reached inside of it and picked up my thigh holster, securing it and strapping on my Beretta to my right leg for easier access.

My hand reached back inside to grab my last piece of equipment when my fingers brushed against the edges of a tucked piece of the last tangible memory I owned.

I slipped the photo free from the hidden pocket, the smell of a home lost wafting through my nose. The edges were frayed, the colors smudged in the bottom corners. But the family smiling back at me was still the same, trapped in time as if that unforgettable night had never happened.

This had been *Baba*'s last birthday we'd celebrated all together before I'd left a few days later for college.

I looked up, holding back the tears that were threatening to spill out. Bringing my gaze back down, I caught my reflection, hovering over the snapshot in my hand. My eyes flickered across the picture, comparing the young woman there to the one staring back at me.

She looked carefree. Happy. But *she* hadn't witnessed her parents being brutally murdered. *She* hadn't experienced emptiness, what it felt to have no home, nothing anchoring her.

You have Theo. Had Theo.

The person I was with him wanted to wake up, wanted to revolt and stretch under my skin, but Victor had created this new version that was hungry for retribution.

I had to push any thoughts of Theo aside because what I was about to do left no room for emotions. My revenge needed to be devoid of emotions. Any feelings could mess up my plans and that was something I couldn't afford.

I checked the time before dropping a quick text message to Victor, inviting him to join me in the gardens for some alone time, knowing he would jump at the opportunity and make sure Jaxon stayed behind.

Grabbing the rest of what I needed, I hurried to the end of the hallway, past the exit door, and found the hidden staircase leading straight to where Victor would be meeting me.

My spine stiffened with every step I took, anticipation squeezing my middle as I approached my target.

Time for your sentencing, Victor Morales.

CHAPTER 30
SOFIA

"**Y**ou're here," I said sweetly as I walked toward *my husband*, wrapping my arms around his middle.

Victor turned around in my embrace and pressed a soft kiss to my lips. "*Mi amor*," he drawled.

I suppressed my disgust and plastered a smile on my lips.

"What are we doing here?" he asked, a sly smirk on his face.

I kept my tone flirtatious as I grabbed the lapels of his suit, bringing him closer. "I thought we could have some fun."

He looked above my shoulder, his attention on the building behind me. "We can't just leave."

I batted my lashes, tugging at his tie with one hand, raking my nails from the other down his shirt, stopping at his belt. "It'll just be for a little while. I promise."

He groaned, a shudder of pleasure rippling through his body as I cupped him above his trousers. My skin crawled as his reaction, bile rising up my throat.

"Fine. But we have to be quick," he finally agreed.

Like this man knew how to be anything else but quick. I shook my head internally, focusing my attention back on him.

"Not here," I said, leading him by his tie as I guided him to the container port.

"Where are we going?"

I pointed to the cameras. "Away from curious eyes."

"Smart," he said smugly, smirking down at me as he followed my lead.

Once we were close enough, I stopped in my tracks and turned to face him. Victor's expression darkened as he closed the gap between us. Wrapping his disgusting fingers around my throat, he walked me backward, slamming me against one of the containers.

"Always tempting me," he rasped, licking his lips, glancing down at my body.

My stomach heaved and I whipped my head to the side to block out his repulsive sight, my hands coming up to rest against his arms.

It's almost over, Sofia.

He focused his attention on my now exposed throat, trailing sloppy kisses down the side of my face before burying his face in the crook of my neck, nipping and sucking the skin there.

His hands started skimming down my sides, and I tensed once his fingers reached my bare skin. Humming to himself, he slowly drew it up along the side of my exposed leg, but I grabbed his hand and placed it on my ass instead, distracting him.

His grip tightened against my backside and he grunted, thrusting his body against mine. I planted my hands against the cold metal behind me and waited. Time stretched and every second felt like hours.

While he busied himself on my neck again, I reached for the syringe tucked in my dress, strapped against my thigh next to my Beretta. I readied the needle and grabbed the back of his head, pushing him further into the crook of my neck, angling him exactly how I needed him.

I took a deep breath and aimed for the side of his exposed neck. The needle pinched it before breaking the surface of his skin, the white liquid embedding itself through his veins.

He took a step back, bringing a hand to his neck, and a smile graced my lips. This time it was genuine and not a rehearsed one. He attempted to storm in my direction but failed, falling to his knees.

"Olivia?" he asked, pausing as he noticed the slight slur in his voice.

"What have you done?" His slur was getting worse and he noticed, his face contorting into an angry expression.

The sedative finally took full effect, and his body swung back as he slumped to the ground, his head smacking against the ground in a loud thunk. I walked up closer and stood above him as he lost consciousness, becoming limp and pliable to my will.

I'd injected him with enough sedative to knock him out long enough for me to move his body and get him ready.

I grabbed his phone from inside his suit pocket and typed out a quick text to Jaxon, sending him and Theo home. Gravel crunched beneath my heels as I walked to the edge of the water, my toes touching the lip of the concrete block.

Once the message was delivered, I threw the phone into the water, watching it slowly sink to the bottom.

I glanced down toward the dock, watching a vessel pull into the port. Bemes's port wasn't vast by any means, but it was big enough for suppliers to use.

Since my husband had every worker here sitting inside his pocket, it had been easy to ask them to turn their heads the other way tonight, keeping this section of the terminal empty.

I headed for a storage container next to one of the warehouses and grabbed a dark tarp from inside, bringing it back to where Victor's body was splayed. I unfolded the tarp and hoisted his body on top, then kneeled beside his body to check his pulse.

I loomed over him for a second, watching for any movement, but when nothing happened, I folded the plastic over his body and reached down to remove my heels, then threw them on top of him.

I quickly surveyed the premises, making sure there was still no one around before I grabbed his body and dragged him through the rows, making my way to where his judgment awaited.

Let your trials begin, Victor Morales.

CHAPTER 31
THEO

I adjusted my suit, trying to ease the anger that had been racking my body since I left her alone on the balcony. I headed back to the main floor, where I assumed my previous position as the mayor's voice flooded the room, announcing the last few items to be bid on. I kept my eyes on the French doors, waiting for her to follow behind shortly after and rejoin the guests.

When we'd walked in earlier, I'd been supposed to scan the throng of people, working my way through every evening gown and expensive suit, assessing for any threats, but my gaze kept landing back on her because no matter how packed a room was, she was always the one to capture my attention.

As soon as she'd left Victor's side and made her way out of the main room, I'd seen the perfect opportunity to have a moment with her, to finally have her all to myself after days of not being able to.

I'd made sure Jaxon was covering Victor before I had taken after her. I'd walked around, trying to find the staircase that led to the secret balcony on the far corner of the property, knowing she would have known about it and needed a quiet space to escape since she'd never been a fan of loud and crowded rooms.

When I'd finally found its door and stepped outside, she'd been facing away, her lone figure leaning against the railing. I'd stopped a few feet away, letting my gaze rake down her body, finally taking the time to soak her in.

The breeze had played with the fabric of the black gown draping her body, ruffling the skirt and sending the fabric clinging to the mouthwatering outlines of her perfect body.

She was always exquisite, and this dress simply highlighted that even more.

The dimmed golden lights had gleamed against her warm, tanned skin, and her hair tied in a low bun, some of the curls escaping it, framed her face while others kissed the delicate slope of her neck.

I'd followed the groove of her bare spine down to where her dress swept right above the curve of her ass. My breath stuttered, my heart pounding fast.

Only one word came to mind.

Devastating.

Nothing could've stopped me from walking up to her,

my fingers desperate to touch her. After all these years, I just wanted to finally claim her as mine. Fuck the consequences.

But then, she'd broken my heart. Again.

I racked my brain, trying to understand the sudden change in her demeanor. We seemed to be on the same page just a few days ago. But whoever I left on that balcony wasn't my Sofia. Whoever that person was, she was a completely different person, one I didn't recognize.

I never expected her to push me away, to fucking choose him over me. She hadn't said those words exactly, but her silence was all the answer I needed.

Message received. Loud and fucking clear.

She'd been quiet and distant since we came back from the cabin, but I'd attributed it to the endless preparations that had been required for tonight's event and her husband being clingier than usual.

Morales stuck to her side almost every second of the day, leaving a possessive fire constantly pulsing through my veins every time I saw his fucking hands on her.

I found myself having to muster all the restraint I could find not to kill him for thinking he had the right to touch her. I knew it was irrational since she was still his wife, but titles meant nothing. She was mine in every way that mattered.

The only time I'd had the opportunity to get her away was last week when she'd had to come here, to make sure everything would be set and ready for tonight's gala.

I'd tried to follow her inside and find a way to give us a private moment. But instead, she'd insisted on me staying put inside the car and driving straight home once she was done, apologizing and claiming she had a million more things to do.

I tried to hold onto my anger, but I was failing miserably, regretting leaving her all alone upstairs. I snapped out of my thoughts and looked around the room.

Something was off. Sofia was nowhere to be seen. I couldn't see her, couldn't *feel* her presence in the room.

I quickly swiped my gaze around to find Victor in case she was back at his side, but he was also absent.

I left the room once again, climbing the stairs two by two to make sure she was still on the balcony, but when I peered through the glass door, she was no longer there. I looked around, searching each room on the floor to no avail.

What the fuck?

My heart dropped, panic surging through me as I burst through the glass door, deciding to look around one last time before heading back downstairs and alerting Jaxon.

Leaning up against the railing, I scanned the length of the property, letting my eyes rove over every inch visible. I was about to head back inside when I saw a silhouette appear out of the corner of my eye.

The harbor.

I narrowed my eyes, hovering to get a closer look before it disappeared.

I couldn't tell whether I was imagining it, but a figure dressed in a black dress, the skirt billowing behind them, was dragging something wrapped in some sort of gray tarp.

Sofia?

I would recognize her anywhere, but what was she doing at the container port?

And what on earth was she hauling around?

Right as she steered behind a corner, the tarp lifted slightly, revealing what was concealed.

But it wasn't a something. It was a *someone*.

CHAPTER 32
SOFIA

I stayed tucked in the darkened corner of the room while I patiently waited for him to wake up, which should be any minute now.

The inside of the cargo was empty, except for the desk lining one side and the single chair sitting in the middle, my subject bound to it. My instruments lay on top of the table, lined and ready to be used for his hearing. A low lamp shed light across the surface, illuminating the rest of the room in a soft yellow glow.

His arms were strapped to the arms of the chair with rope, his legs bound in a similar fashion.

Morales slowly roused from his unconscious state. He tried to move, lightly stirring against the metal chair he was anchored to, only to realize he was completely restrained.

He struggled, this time harder, against the bindings

that were holding his arms and legs wide, leaving him spread out and immobile for me to play with. He jerked again against the rope, a muffled noise resonating against the hood that covered his head.

The clear plastic tarp crinkled beneath my heels as I walked to the table, selecting an option. I leaned against the edge and crossed my legs, flipping the serrated knife back and forth.

"Who's there?" he shouted, filling the quiet room, the echoes of his muffled wailing answering him back.

Fucking pathetic.

I bet he hadn't imagined his night ending this way. He'd agreed to meet his wife for a fun time, only to end up bound under completely different circumstances.

Not knowing his own wife was the one behind it. A smile curved my lips, knowing he was finally getting what he deserved.

Knife in hand, I stopped when I was directly in front of him, looming over his body. Satisfaction was already building in my stomach at the fear that emanated from his body.

"*¡Puta madre!* Where the *fuck* am I? Show your face, *pinche pendejo*," he roared, struggling.

I quickly silenced him by bringing the knife to rest against his pulse point, softly pressing the tip against his bared skin. I'd removed his jacket and shirt before binding him, only leaving on his dark gray slacks and his crisp white undershirt that would soon be painted crimson.

His body immediately tensed at the sharp feel. I couldn't feel his pulse turning erratic, but I could imagine how rapidly it was now beating from how fast his chest was heaving as I pressed further against his skin without ever breaking the surface.

I dragged the tip of the knife down, along his jugular, gliding it across the length of his body. He grew even more stiff, his throat bobbing down when I grazed over his dick, finally settling the blade over his thigh.

He tried to kick me, which only urged me to slam the blade into his thigh, enjoying the sound of his flesh tearing from the force, relishing in the ringing of his muffled screams.

"Let me out, you son of a bitch! Do you even know who I *am*?" he barked, the chair rattling beneath him as he continued struggling in vain. I watched in fascination as his blood dripped onto the tarp, becoming the first strokes of my masterpiece.

I stood up straight. "Shut up," I hissed.

Bloodied knife in hand, I rounded him and stood at his back. I grabbed the fabric on top of the hood that was over his head and pulled it off, striding back to face him.

I tossed the fabric onto the table as he shook his head, slowly peeling his eyes open, letting his vision adjust, and gradually taking in where he was.

Then, I stepped forward into the stream of light.

He was still taking in his surroundings when his eyes

finally focused on me. They widened and I watched a myriad of emotions flicker across his face.

Confusion bled into recognition before transforming into relief, only to quickly spiral into surprise.

"O-Olivia?" he questioned, startled by my presence.

"Well, hello, dear husband. Fancy seeing you here," I greeted him, my tone humorous.

"*Mi amor*, wh-what's going on?" Victor asked, still trying to put two and two together, trying to determine whether his brain was playing tricks on him.

His brows furrowed and he craned his neck, scanning the room for more people. "Let my wife go," he said to whoever he thought was behind me, only to be met with silence.

He brought his attention back to me, and I let out a dry laugh. "It's just me, *mi amor*," I answered, spitting out the endearment like it was wrapped in venom.

His brows pinched in confusion. "What do you mean, it's just you? Who's forcing you to do this?"

A smile spread wider across my face when his expression faltered, the realization of who was standing in front of him, a knife coated with his blood in hand. His eyes grew wide in surprise when I brought it up, running my finger against the sharpened edge, the slick feel of his blood sending a thrill of satisfaction humming through my veins.

His jaw muscles clenched as a mix of fury and betrayal swept across his face. *Perfecto*.

I stalked back toward him. Pinching the side of my dress, I placed the excess fabric out of my way, behind me, and squatted down. My elbows rested against my knees, the blade hanging between my legs.

A twisted sneer curled my lips and I stared up at the man responsible for my life taking such a drastic turn. "You don't recognize me, do you?" I asked mockingly, cocking my head to the side.

His gaze shifted and I could see he was preparing to attack, now that I was in a more vulnerable position. Because that's the only way this piece of trash knew how to fight.

When you were at a disadvantage.

"What kind of games are you playing?" he asked, glaring at me.

Pushing to my feet, I marched around him, running the tip of the blade along the planes of his body, his blood leaving a trail behind, sinking into the fabric it met.

"I was nineteen the last time you saw me. But I'm all grown up now, so let me refresh your memory," I said, now facing him.

Stepping back, I brought my empty hand up, pretending to be holding a gun as I winked at him.

"Sleep tight, Herrera," I taunted him before pulling on the imaginary trigger.

His eyes roamed over my face, the three words finally triggering recognition to wash over his features, a sense of understanding downing on him.

His face paled drastically, as if he'd just seen a ghost. I guessed that's what I was for him, since I was supposed to be dead and not alive and well, holding his life in the palm of my hands.

"That's... *impossible*," he whispered, watching me in complete disbelief. "It can't be. I killed you. You're supposed to be dead."

I shrugged my shoulders. "Well, I survived."

His shock slowly faded and morphed into pure disdain.

"I guess your aim just wasn't that great after all." I chuckled, shaking my head. "Such a rookie mistake not to check if your target's still breathing before leaving them to bleed dry."

I stepped closer, dragging the knife across his temple. "Guess that's what happens when you get too comfortable letting other people do your dirty work. When it was your turn to get your hands dirty, you couldn't even follow through. Like many other things actually."

Hatred burned over his features as his rage took over. He looked murderous as he launched himself at me, but he didn't get very far, the bindings keeping him put.

He pursed his lips and spat. "*¡Asquerosa!*" he said through gritted teeth.

Wet saliva sprayed across my cheek and dripped down my face. I used the back of my hand to wipe it, then smeared it on his pants.

"Ah, ah, ah," I tsked. "Now, where are your manners?"

I flashed him a dark smile, and before he registered the movement, I rammed my knife into his other thigh, matching the other side. I twisted it once before ripping it away.

He whined in agony, pressing his lips together to contain his scream.

He finally stopped whining when the slow creak of the container's door opening filled the room, a sliver of moonlight filtering through, shimmering against the blood pooling under Morales.

The door shut soundly behind the person who made all of this possible. I didn't bother to turn around to know it was her, her familiar scent drifting to me.

"It's nice of you to finally join us," I said as she stayed hidden in the shadows, her low chuckle echoing against the walls.

"*Please*, help me," Victor whined, believing someone might be able to help him, might have come to his rescue.

Little did he know that she would be the last person to answer his pleading call.

Ignoring his plea, I stepped up closer and used the edge of the blade to tip Morales's chin up. He stared up at me, insults collecting at the tip of his tongue.

"Isn't this the prettiest view?" I said, reaching for the back of his head and wrenching his perfectly coiffed hair, exposing his neck.

I slid the knife in just a tad bit farther down, right along his jaw until I met with resistance. A sense of gratification filled me as I watched percolating sweat drip down the side of his face, his body trembling.

The blade sank into his skin and a drop of blood slid down the slope of his neck. "Look at you bleeding so well, and me being the cause of it."

He growled in defiance. "What do you want? You want money?"

Letting out a dark chuckle, I shook my head, withdrawing the blade from under his jaw. "What I want is answers. I couldn't care less about your filthy money."

I paused. "Not that you have any left."

He frowned. "Excuse me?"

I gave him a sheepish smile. "Your accounts are empty, dear husband. The schools in our neighboring districts are *very* grateful for your generous donations."

He let my words sink in before his eyes narrowed, his gaze filling with a new wave of rage.

"You wouldn't *dare*."

Shaking my head, I laughed to myself. "Oh, *mi amor*, of course I would."

He opened his mouth to spit other insults at me, but the back of my hand connected with the side of his face before he could.

"Now, what makes you think it's okay to insult a woman?" I glanced over my shoulder, winking at my guest. "I think he needs another lesson, *no*?"

He followed my gaze, frustration clear on his features since he was unable to discern who I was talking to.

"I'll have to agree," they finally said.

Shock froze over his features, the familiarity of the voice washing over him as she stood next to me and finally revealed herself. His body stiffened, his mouth hanging open.

He whispered her name, disbelief coating his voice. "Elena?"

He closed his eyes, shaking forcefully, his head trying to dismantle the ghost he was convinced he was seeing. "It can't be you. It's impossible."

His eyes flickered back and forth between both of us.

"Surprise!" She let out a small chuckle. "Happy to see me, *esposo?*"

CHAPTER 33

SOFIA - FIFTEEN MONTHS EARLIER

I made my way past the edge of Bemes, heading straight for Adrar. Once in their neighborhood, I parked my car where no one would pay much attention to it. Turning the ignition off, I unlocked my tablet and pulled up the security footage from Morales's summer house.

As expected, two guards were outside on the porch playing cards while his wife was in the living room, sitting on the couch, book in hand.

I glanced at the time. There were still several hours before nightfall, so I patiently waited for the dashboard clock to tick over into the new day.

It was five past midnight when Valentina's call rang through the car.

I stuck my Bluetooth in my ear and slipped out of my

car, tablet in hand. I placed it on the roof while I grabbed my tools from the trunk.

"Valentina," I greeted her.

"Two guards are stationed in the kitchen. No other movement on the premises. Elena's fast asleep in the bedroom."

"You have a clear shot?"

"Yes."

"Take it."

I watched the footage in time to see the two men fall over each other, without a sound or a fuss.

"Targets eliminated," she said through the intercom.

"You've got the body?"

"Yes, it'll be set up in the living room before you get there."

I paused, anticipation of finally being able to get this started coursing through my veins.

"Thank you."

She hummed before cutting our communication. Strapping my Glock against my thigh, I shouldered my backpack and made my way down the beach, running the short distance between my car and the house.

I had met Elena Morales three months ago in a public bathroom of the country club she frequented weekly for a luncheon with the wives of her husband's circle. As soon as she left to use the restroom, I followed behind and made sure no one would be coming in.

After locking the door, I waited inside one of the stalls until she came out.

Thinking she was alone, she stared at the mirror for a moment and her mask dropped, sorrow filling her expression. Her makeup had slightly rubbed off, highlighting the secret she'd been hiding.

She'd reached inside her purse for her makeup bag, bringing out what she needed to conceal it, which was when I had come out of my hiding place and offered her an opportunity.

It could have gone against me, but she only hesitated for a few seconds before accepting eagerly.

Gun in hand, I sneaked in through the back entrance, the alarm already disarmed by Valentina when she came in before I got here to stage the cadaver that had been tampered with Elena's DNA onto the couch in the living room.

I marched into the kitchen and spotted the two men slumped on the floor, a hole decorating each of their foreheads.

I bent down, checking their pulses to confirm they were dead. Not that I doubted Valentina, but one can never be too sure. I was living proof of that.

I doused both the kitchen and the living room, the stench of death lingering in the air rapidly mixing with the woody sweet scent.

I reached behind and took out the awaiting box of matches from my backpack. Striking one, I held it in front of me, watching the flames engulf the strip of wood, a bitter puff of smoke snaking up toward the ceiling.

I let it slip through my fingers, the flame raging once it hit the floor. I left the kitchen and stalked down the corridor, my black boots thumping against the wooden hallway, splashes of gas forming in my wake.

I pulled out three more matches, striking them all at once. Adrenaline coursed through me at the sting and *pop* of the flame coming to life.

I dropped them behind me as I made my way up the stairs, a path of gasoline trailing me.

With accelerant dousing the place, I had less than five minutes before the fire consumed the rest of the residence. I halted mid-way up the stairs, throwing the empty gasoline can past the banister and taking the rest of the stairs two by two.

I veered left once I was on the top floor, running to her bedroom, the heat of the fire close on my trail, coming straight for me. I burst the door open and Elena bolted upright at the sound of the door crashing against the wall.

"Sofia?" she asked, perplexed. Her eyes widened as she looked past my shoulders.

"The house is on fire," she shouted, alarmed as she pointed to the smoke billowing into the room.

I marched to her bed, threw the covers off, and hauled her to her feet. "I'm aware. I'm the one who set it on fire."

She stumbled to a stop. "What?"

Elena was aware I was coming to get her but didn't

know the details of my escape plan. The less she knew, the better. I didn't trust her enough yet to reveal every-thing to her, just in case she slipped and told her husband.

I highly doubted it, but one thing I'd learned over the years was to never trust too easily. Sometimes the people you trusted the most ended up being those who betrayed you the worst.

I quirked a brow at her. "Listen, we can have a conver-sation later, but as you can see, if I don't get you out right now, we'll join the remains of this house."

I ran to her closet and pulled out a pair of joggers and a sweater. I turned to face her again, throwing the clothes at her. "Put these on."

She stayed still for a moment.

"Hurry, we don't have time," I urged her.

She was finishing getting dressed when a flare of orange roared up through the doorway, rapidly spitting sparks and gnawing anything in its path.

Fuck. I thought I had a bit more time.

The walls flickered with red and amber shadows, my nostrils filling with a sharp and pungent odor. I tried to take a deep breath, but my lungs burned from the sting of the smoke.

Knowing I wouldn't be able to make it to the initial exit I'd planned on using, I looked around the room until I found a solution. Pulling Elena behind me, I dived for the window across the room. The smoke seared my eyes as I struggled to pry it open for a bit, the fire a ticking time bomb.

Come on, don't do this to me now.

Finally, a sharp wind battered its way inside, a sucking sound bouncing against the walls. I only had a few seconds before the fresh air would fuel the fire. I shoved Elena through the opening, screaming for her to jump.

She hesitated and I looked behind, seeing the flames retreating. *Double fuck.*

I hauled myself through the opening and grabbed Elena's body, twisting us in the air as we plunged down. My bones screamed in pain as my shoulder crashed against the lawn.

I curled into myself as the backdraft blasted the house, the sky above us exploding into shades of oranges and red, shattering glass raining down on us. Flames ripped through the window, curling against the house's façade.

I looked to my right to find Elena's body unmoving.

"Elena," I croaked, pushing to my hands and knees, scrambling to her.

I reached for her body and shook her urgently. "Elena," I shouted again when she finally peeled her eyes open, coughing forcefully.

She drew a shallow, shuddering breath, turning her attention to me. "Sofia," she wheezed.

In the distance, I heard the sirens approaching. We couldn't be found here.

I hauled her to her feet. "Run to the beach," I explained.

She glared at me. "What about you?"

"I'll be right behind. Go," I urged her.

I watched her run across the yard and the deck. As soon as her feet hit the dunes of sand, I grabbed the grenade from my bag and threw it through the open window we'd just jumped out of.

I didn't wait to see if it landed as I rushed to the beach, Valentina's boat weaving through the ocean, slowly coming into view. I was almost at the end of the small boardwalk to the beach when it detonated, harshly throwing me forward, my front landing in the sand.

I peered up, seeing Elena pausing and swinging back to search for me. I hauled myself back up and ran to her. The sounds of sirens blazed from the front of the house, the authorities and firefighters arriving.

We both made it to the water's edge, the tide gripping at our legs. Water splashed over my boots, clinging to my black jeans, and we leapt over the waves, swimming a little farther out to meet Valentina.

A ring buoy was thrown my way and I maneuvered behind Elena, pushing toward it. Valentina pulled the cord before dragging Elena into the boat and I followed right after.

I pulled my Glock from its holster and released the clip, letting it hit the ground with a muted thud, the rest of my equipment following right behind. Valentina offered us warming blankets before moving back to the front of the boat and driving us away.

Elena and I stood side by side, waves rippling beneath the boat. I placed my elbows on the silver railing, staring out. I watched the flames consume the property, the dark smoke billowing in the air.

Fire was a powerful tool. It always disintegrated everything in its path and I relished the small victory it provided me.

Step one was completed.

Most of the time, people would think someone out for revenge would want to lash back violently, but witnessing your nemesis living in pain, suffering a loss, would be so much more rewarding.

Death would come eventually, but he needed to be alive to reap the rewards of his crimes.

Be prepared, Victor Morales.

I glanced toward Elena and watched years of sorrow slowly evaporate. She watched as her past caved in on itself like a skeleton.

The remains of her old life were now a stepping stone for new beginnings.

Her freedom and my revenge.

CHAPTER 34
SOFIA

He glared at Elena, a murderous look in his gaze as he rapidly spewed insults at her.

My expression soured. "Watch your mouth, asshole."

I stepped between his spread legs, and my fingers surged forward, nails digging into his chin to bring his attention back to me. "And don't you dare look at her. You lost that right a long time ago."

"What the fuck do you think you'll be able to do? You're both just pathetic women." He continued to berate us despite his vulnerable position.

Men. I scoffed to myself.

I raised my fist and punched him across the face, my ring creating a tear on his upper lip.

"*Pu—*"

I cut him off, jamming my fist into his face again. He gasped on air.

Elena chuckled at my side and Morales turned his attention to her again, so I used the tip of my blade to drive his attention back to me.

I cocked an eyebrow. "Do I have to repeat myself?"

He roared in response, spitting the blood that had gathered in his mouth, the drops landing on my fingers.

With a sigh, I cleaned the blood off my fingers with the blade and pried his mouth open. He sucked in a sharp breath.

"Open," I ordered.

He cursed, refusing, but I used the small window of opportunity to bring the flat of the knife over his tongue, swiping his blood against his tongue.

"Swallow," I said, gripping his cheeks tight to keep them closed. He jolted against my grip, but his throat finally bobbed when he saw Elena aiming her gun at him.

I stepped back and crossed my arms over my chest. "Now that we've washed down your inappropriate manners, tell me why you killed my parents."

Thoughts of that night crept into the moment, making me remember the first time I'd laid eyes on this man.

I CREPT DOWN THE STAIRS, *making sure not to wake anyone, since Baba had a press conference in the morning to announce a new legislation. Me and Mama were supposed to go on a girls' retreat, but she felt bad leaving Baba behind.*

I barely made it to the last stair when I froze in place, as I stared down the barrel of a gun, a vicious sneer on the other end. From the corner of my eye, I could see Mama and Baba bound and slumped on the floor.

The scream died in my throat when the barrel of the gun slammed against the side of my temple.

I was jolted out of the memory, the sound of Morales's laugh grating against my ears.

I looked back at where he was sitting, his laugh baring his blood-tainted teeth. "Why would I do that? You're gonna kill me an—"

He didn't get the chance to finish his sentence when his laugh was replaced by a piercing scream, the sound soothing against my eardrum. I turned my attention toward Elena, only to see her silencer aimed at his knee, smoke billowing from the muzzle.

I knew I loved her.

I nodded in her direction, silently asking if she was okay, and she replied with a shy grin. Valentina had been training her, but shooting a target wasn't the same as shooting a living being.

"Jesus, *fuck*," he screeched.

I stared back at him. "Yeah, he's not gonna be much help," I snarked. "I'm gonna ask you one last time. Why?"

Spittle flew from his mouth as he grunted, choking to get air in.

"Your father had been messing with the cartel and my

business for years. He kept changing the laws, making it difficult for us to deal. We tried bribing him, but he wouldn't budge," he confessed, sounding almost bored.

"Too much of a saint," he spat.

Pain seared down my middle at his revelation. For the past eight years, my life had been leading to this moment. I'd survived and searched for answers but could never figure why anyone would come after my family.

I lost my life simply because my father was a disruption in their little endeavors, and they needed the obstacle out.

"You and your mother were supposed to be out that night. You two were just a mere inconvenient collateral. I never liked loose ends, so I put a bullet between your bitch of a mother's eyes and then emptied the last bullet on you," he finished, a smug grin on his face.

Blood started pounding furiously in my ears.

Inconvenient collateral.

Loose ends.

My nostrils flared, an onslaught of white heat zipping down my spine.

I walked away from him and dropped my knife onto the plastic tarp. I pulled my gun from the holster strapped to my thigh and stood straight.

"Victor Morales, you took everything I had, everything I loved. It's been a pleasure destroying all you've built."

I clicked the safety off, pointing the barrel up at him. The shocked expression on his face combined with the coolness of the barrel under my fingers provided a satisfaction I couldn't explain.

With this gun, I would be able to wash away everything I no longer wished to feel—pain, grief, loneliness, the nightmares that kept haunting my dreams.

The time has come for your end, Victor Morales.

With my right arm extended, I asked. "Any parting wishes?"

A slow grin crept across my face and before he was able to answer, I muttered the last words he'd said to me when he thought he'd gotten rid of me.

"Sleep tight, Morales."

My fingers curled against the trigger, tightening. I shot without flinching, emptying the chamber.

It took three bullets to alter my life, but I only needed one to end it all.

The ringing sound bounced against the walls as a fresh bullet hole appeared between his eyes. His head slumped as dark blood gushed from the wound, staining Morales's stunned face before pooling down the covered concrete floor.

The stench of blood quickly filled the air, burning the hairs of my nostrils. I felt wetness drip on my face and wiped my cheek.

I brought my hand in front of me, noticing a mixture of blood and brain matter coating my fingers. A wave of nausea rolled through me, but I bit down on my tongue and swallowed the bile that surged in my throat

A sense of solace washed over me, the peace I'd been seeking seeping into every inch of my skin. Although his death wouldn't wash away my grief, there was relief in knowing I'd obtained the answers I'd been looking for.

I'd finally be able to rest, to bring my parents a justice they never were granted.

Elena and I stood side by side, staring down at the dead body.

I wasn't much of a hugger, but something within me sprang and I turned to her, embracing her tight. "This is over. You're free."

I released her and walked away from his body, my footsteps halting in front of the table on the side. I grabbed what I needed and walked back over to her.

"She's coming to pick you up and take you wherever you want," I explained, handing her a backpack with her new passport and some cash so she could finally live her life in peace.

"Did you have to shoot him between the eyes?" Valentina asked in my ear, chuckling.

For the past few months, I'd been taking a cut for every vessel and container coming in and out of the city on my husband's behalf, and his business partners were about to find out he'd double-crossed them, only to find Morales already dead.

"It's the Barreras' signature. The police won't question it and close the investigation since they have them in their pocket," I replied.

Valentina was a hacking genius and ex-sniper I'd met through the dark web when I was digging into Morales's life. She worked for The Collector, a vigilante who lent a helping hand to those in need, whether it was to clear a debt or to seek retribution in exchange for a favor. If we didn't deliver, he'd come to collect his debt.

Valentina was actually the one behind the brunch shooting. The shooting that allowed me to spend the best week of my life.

Theo.

I had to return to the party before he noticed I was gone.

"Could you send someone to clean this mess up and stage it to look like a hit from the Moroccans? I have a party to return to."

I heard her muttering to someone in the background before she let me know that someone would be on their way.

With those parting words, I strapped my smoking gun back in the holster attached to my thigh and we made our way out of the cargo container. Nothing prepared me for what I found waiting for me outside.

That's when I came face-to-face with him.

CHAPTER 35

THEO

My phone had buzzed with a new text.
I'd grabbed it from my pocket and my eyes had flicked down at the screen.

> Victor Morales: Have the rest of the night off. My wife and I will be having a late night. Have Omar drive you back if need be and you can leave the keys for the other car with the valet.

A warning instinct had tugged at my senses.

Something is definitely off.

I'd only hesitated briefly before I left the balcony. Using the back exit to avoid any suspicions, I'd headed for the port to find her. To find out what she was up to. For a while, I'd walked across the lot, checking between container stacks for any signs.

It had been surprisingly quiet. Albeit it was a Sunday

night, I'd expected a few workers to be here. But no one had been in sight.

I'd slowed down when I heard the sound of a gun cocking ripping through the air. I'd carefully followed the sound, keeping my footsteps silent against the gravel.

I'd scanned the premises until I noticed one of the cargo container's doors had been slightly ajar. I'd approached it carefully, drawing my gun up.

I'd glanced through the opening, preparing to intervene once I'd seen Morales bound in the middle of the room, a small pool of blood staining the floor beneath him.

But a shadow moved and its voice ripped through the silence. I'd frowned, recognition tugging at the memories of how familiar the voice was. Eventually, it'd stepped out from the shadow, its profile coming into view.

Nothing could've ever prepared me for what I found.

What the fuck?

My vision had shifted, the reality in front of me becoming slightly blurry, disbelief coating my view.

I'd shaken my head, blinking rapidly, trying to dispel the image in front of me, thinking that my mind had been playing tricks on me. I'd waited for the sight in front of me to dissolve into something different, but it never shifted.

I'd stood still as my heart had dropped, sinking to the bottom of my chest. My gun had gone slack against my thigh as I wondered if I'd stepped into some alternate universe.

But I'd never woken up from whatever twisted dream I'd slumbered into.

"Sleep tight, Morales."

Her voice had pierced the fog and unveiled the next scene as I'd watched her become someone completely different.

The weight of those three simple words finally sank in, assaulting my mind.

"You left," I'd said.

"I had to."

My pulse had pounded at the memory.

A muted pop had rung through the room, the smell of metallic discharge and blood drifting into the night, reaching my nostrils.

My heart had pounded heavily against my chest, as I'd grappled with the onslaught of information washing over me in tidal waves.

My shock slowly had morphed into anger, only to settle on hurt. The bitter taste of her lies had exploded in my mouth and I'd swallowed harshly against them, until they'd coated my insides.

Part of me had expected her to come out and deny what I'd just seen, but I'd only watched her walk out in complete disbelief.

My blood seized in my veins, all the oxygen leaving my

lungs painfully. My ears thumped loudly, the drumming of my over-beating heart echoing in my head.

My hands gripped forcefully the handle of my gun, betrayal coursing through my bitter veins. My chest grew heavier as the truth slowly crept in. The expression on her face told me all I needed to know. I studied her and watched regret etched in every line on her face.

"Sofia?" I questioned with a rasp, unable to say more as a knot formed in my throat.

As I stared at her, I wondered if anything she told me had ever been true.

CHAPTER 36
SOFIA

I froze, a bolt of dread lashing through me, waves of guilt drowning me once my eyes met his. That same guilt that had been weighing on me ever since that night I left him seven years ago.

His eyes widened, arms limp at his sides. His mouth parted, my name falling from his lips on a breath like a question. "Sofia?" His voice broke, the devastation on his face pummeling at my chest, the breath previously lodged forcefully leaving my lungs.

It hurt to look at him, to see the damage my lies had done to him. But unfortunately, this was a price I knew I might have to pay one day.

My mouth parted, a soundless plea escaping as I took a step forward, but he stepped back before I could reach for him. He looked away, betrayal shaping the edges of his features.

His eyes bounced from Elena to me and he pulled at his hair, turning away from us. He shook his head repeatedly, murmuring "this can't be happening," while pacing back and forth.

Tires screeched over gravel and we all instantly drew our weapons, pointing them toward the source. We all watched as a black SUV rolled into view, the person we'd been waiting for sitting in the driver's seat.

Both Elena and I lowered our weapons, holstering them, and Theo followed suit when he realized I was no longer aiming at our newcomer.

Valentina rolled down her window, the wind whipping her auburn hair, as she called after Elena.

"Coming," Elena shouted before turning her attention back to me.

"*Gracias por todo*, Sofia. I would've never been able to do this if it wasn't for you." She wrapped me in a warm embrace, squeezing me tighter at the end, reminding me of my mother's bear hugs.

Her gaze flicked back to the man behind me as she cupped my cheek. "It was nice meeting you, Theo. Take care of her, will you?"

Without waiting for his answer, she walked away, her gaze locking with mine over her shoulder one last time before she rounded the hood and climbed into the passenger's side.

The sound of tires faded away as the SUV disappeared from our view and between the multicolored cargo containers. When I finally turned my attention back to him, my heart cracked at the sight of the betrayal painting his deep brown eyes.

"Were you ever going to tell me?" he finally asked, his voice low and quiet.

My eyes darted to his fists, watching him clench and unclench them repeatedly, his knuckles turning white.

"Theo, I can explain," I began.

His eyes darted from my face to my hands before meeting my gaze again. For a split second, a flicker of concern flashed through his expression when he noticed the traces of what I just did marring my hands and face, but that quickly vanished, replaced by distrust.

He huffed out a laugh. "Explain what, Sofia?"

My eyes focused on the tense line of his shoulders, the slight tremor in his hands before he turned away from me. I watched him take a deep breath before he spoke again.

"Everything was fucking a lie," he muttered.

"Not everything," I whispered.

He whipped around, facing me again. Anger rapidly consumed him and radiated off him in tidal waves, submerging me in their path.

"You lied to me." There was a pause before he went on. "Again," he finished, his tone harsher this time.

My gut clenched at his tone.

Shaking my head, I pushed against the lump forming in my throat and took a step closer, reaching out to grab his hand. "Let me ex—"

I'd barely touched him before he pulled it away, as if I'd burned him. His arms shot up, effectively cutting me off as he backed away from me again.

"Do not touch me," he gritted out, his jaw twitching from how tightly he was grinding his teeth.

I pressed my lips together, watching him through watery eyes. I squeezed my eyes shut, dropping my head, a hot tear escaping and flowing down my cheek, the saltiness flooding my taste buds.

I swallowed down the rest of my upcoming tears, breathing through my nose as I tried to gather myself because he deserved an explanation. I slowly opened my eyes again and looked at him, my eyes begging him to forgive me.

"Please," my voice cracked. "Please, *mi cielito*, let me explain."

His eyes darkened and he snapped forward, his hand pushing against my chest until my back hit the cargo container where Victor's body was rotting, the cold seeping through the thin fabric of my dress.

Caging me in, he forced my legs open with his knee, his right hand landing right beside my head, sending a loud thud resonating around us. He leaned over me, bringing his face closer, barely leaving an inch separating us.

"Don't. You've lost the right to call me that."

Trying to stay calm, I brought my palm up to rest against his forearm, but he shook me off and grabbed my wrists in his left hand, trapping my hands between our flushed bodies.

His chest rose rapidly as he spoke. "Stop touching me."

"I'm sorry."

He gave me an incredulous look, his breathing uneven. Dipping his head closer, he removed his hand from the wall, bringing it to coast down my body until it reached the opening of the slit on my dress.

He snaked his hand up inside my thigh. A deep groan reverberated from his chest when his fingers brushed against the strap on the inside of my thigh as he took my gun out of its holster.

"Theo," I whimpered, trying to fight against his hold on my wrists, but my resistance only made him tighten it, provoking a snarl out of him.

"What is it, *mi alma*, are you going to feed me more lies?" His words were cold, a chill slithering down my spine.

The distrust and anger layering his voice sent a sharp pain piercing through my chest, but I pushed it aside, knowing there was truth to his statement.

I'd lied to him seven years ago and continued to do so even after he'd uncovered who I was.

He ran the warm barrel along the inside of my leg, dragging it up at a torturous pace, goose bumps sprouting in its wake. My heart rate sped up, fear thrumming in my veins.

"I didn't want to drag you into this mess," I confessed, my voice strained.

My arms still pinned between our bodies, he leaned in further, bringing his lips closer. "You always have excuses," he whispered, his warm breath ghosting over my lips.

His fierce eyes were locked firmly on mine as he traced the lining of my dress's slit, stopping at its juncture. Pulling the fabric to the side with my gun, he revealed what was underneath.

Me. *Bare.*

The cold air hitting my center sent a shiver racking through my body. Curiosity washed over his features and his gaze dropped to look for the cause. I kept my gaze on his face as I watched his restraint slowly slip.

After a beat, he finally looked up and spoke against my lips.

"Hmm, look what we have here," he murmured, pressing a feather kiss to the corner of my mouth.

I felt my gun ghosting the soft skin of my thigh, inching closer, and I shuddered at the touch. My fingers started going numb from the grip he had around my wrists, so I tried shifting slightly to relieve some of the pressure.

"Such a fighter you are, *mi alma*. It's sweet that you think you're going to get away with it this easily," he taunted me.

My lies had been to protect him, but that didn't change how much I hated that I'd lied to him for so long. I hated that I put us in a situation where he debated whether or not he could even trust me.

I needed to make him understand. I needed him to *forgive* me because I didn't spend the last few years without him, only to lose him all over again.

I can't let that happen. I won't.

My heart pounded furiously in my chest as I realized there was only one way to show him how I felt.

Any resistance I had slowly seeped from my body and I relaxed in his hold, becoming pliable to his treatment, relinquishing control for the first time in years.

As soon as he felt the shift, he pressed his body tighter against mine, his breath skating across my cheek as he continued to maneuver the gun closer to my center. My teeth sank hard into my lower lip as I tried to suppress a moan.

His eyes dropped, following the movement.

He chuckled darkly, pressing the still warm muzzle directly against my throbbing clit.

"What is it, Ms. Herrera, you no longer have any fight in you?"

I hummed, a shocking desire zipping down my spine at the foreign sensation of a weapon *there*. Arching my back slightly, I lifted further into his touch, my pulse rampant in my ears, excitement and fear pounding through in equal measures.

He moved again, trailing my gun down, sliding the warm muzzle easily down my pussy with how wet I was.

"*Que hermosa mentirosa*. Look at you being so responsive," he praised, stroking me at an excruciatingly slow pace.

I swallowed down a moan as my head flew back, thumping against the steel, resounding echoes resonating against the walls on the other side. I was barely able to form any thoughts, all responses stuck in my throat.

My nails dug *hard* into his palm, and my eyes squeezed shut at the overwhelming sensations. I quieted my mind and allowed my body to take over.

He continued rubbing the barrel back and forth against my pussy, sliding through my lips, collecting the wetness I knew was seeping from my cunt. I arched further, grinding against it, hoping he'd take the gentle invitation and give me what I wanted, what I needed.

A moan that was desperate to escape lodged its way out when suddenly, I felt *nothing*.

Bewildered, I opened my eyes, only to be met with the sight of Theo bringing the dripping gun up.

He was inspecting it, the port's lighting reflecting against the wet barrel, eliciting an approving sound from Theo's lips.

"You like this, don't you, *mi alma*?" he breathed out, a mischievous look on his features.

"Does it turn you on that I'm using the same gun you used on him on your pussy? When *your husband's* body is still warm on the other side."

Bringing the barrel to his mouth, he smeared the

wetness against his bottom lip and I watched as his tongue snaked out, watched him lick *me* off his lips. My eyes widened at the gesture, need sliding thickly down my core.

A deep moan rolled out as soon as my taste coated his tongue. He tilted his head, his eyes roaming over my face.

"*Dios, amo tu sabor en mi boca,*" he murmured, and I whimpered at his words.

"Theo," I pleaded, my nails most likely breaking his skin, my explanations long-forgotten under the fog of lust he was creating, his name the only word I managed to get out.

He lowered the gun closer to my entrance, dipping his head down until his lips were again just a whisper shy from mine.

"What is it, Sofia? I know you can use your words, *mentirosilla.*"

His tongue lashed out and licked across my bottom lip. "Or do you just like using them to spew lies?"

I gasped at his harsh words, and my tongue swiped against the seam of my lips where he'd previously licked, letting our mixed taste flood my taste buds, the remnants of my arousal overpowering everything else.

He clenched his teeth. A deep growl rumbled from deep within his chest. He finally released my wrists, a tingle running through my fingertips as the blood rushed back.

He pressed the now cool barrel against my core with

more pressure this time, his free hand landing on my hip with a punishing grip.

"You're about to take my punishment *again* like the good girl you are, since apparently you didn't learn your lesson the first time around," he ordered.

My back arched in response, my arms flinging around his neck, clinging as he started working my hips against the railing.

The tip of his tongue snaked out, licking a trail up the column of my neck to my ear, his facial hair grazing my scorched skin.

His teeth gently nipped the sensitive skin beneath my ear, a wracking shudder passing through my body at the thought of him giving me more of his markings.

My nipples tightened against the silk of my dress, catching his attention. He lowered his face to bite down on one, sucking it through the fabric.

"You've deprived me of these for too long. My mouth has been aching for days to worship them again, coming every night just at the vision of your body writhing beneath my licks and nips."

He alternated his relentless sucking, wetting the fabric as he guided me back and forth, the friction from the railing against my slippery skin drawing out both pleasure and pain.

My knees grew weak from his ministrations, his thigh between my legs the only thing keeping me upright. My teeth sank harder into my lip at the image my mind conveyed of him alone in bed, coming solely at the idea of his mouth being on my body.

I only realized I'd split flesh when a tang of copper hit my taste buds, a strangled noise slipping through at the taste. He raised his head at the sound, then slipped his tongue out to lick a drop that was trailing down my chin.

This must be what insanity felt like because I was grinding against a weapon, but I couldn't bring myself to care enough to stop him.

I just want to feel. Want him to consume me.

Another noise escaped me and I squeezed my eyes closed, my movements turning more frantic. He slid his palm down my hip and over my butt, gripping my ass to slow my movements.

I then heard a sudden thud, realizing he just dropped my gun to the ground when the previous weight against my cunt disappeared.

"If you're gonna come, it'll be on something that's mine. Not something you've used on him. Now, be a good girl and open wider for me, *mi alma*," he ordered between heavy breaths, nudging me with his knee.

An unintelligible noise escaped me at his praise, sending my thighs falling farther apart.

"You drive me fucking insane, Sofia, you know that?" Suddenly, he pushed two fingers inside me, barely giving me room to adjust before he added another one.

I sucked in a sharp breath, letting my head fall forward. Shoving my face into his neck, I muffled my moan. He removed his hand from my ass to grip my chin, lifting it so I was now looking at him.

"Don't you dare deprive me of your sweet sounds." His fingers inside me picked up their pace, each thrust deeper than the last. "Give them to me, *mi alma*, I want to hear you."

I moaned loudly, pleasure washing over me in intense waves.

"I spent seven years looking for you. You've marked my body, my soul. And when I finally found you, you decided to run from me again," he growled, pulling out his fingers completely before sinking them back in again.

I could clearly hear the suctioning sounds as he continued fucking me relentlessly with his fingers, prolonging my pleasure, embarrassment flushing my entire body in response to the loud slurping noises.

"What if your plan didn't work, Sofia? What if you got injured or worse, got yourself *fucking killed?*" He let go of my chin, his palm slapping against the steel wall behind me.

I had barely come down from my high when he angled his fingers in a way that sent my eyes rolling to the back of my head, a moan slipping free past my lips, my hands tugging the curled pieces at the nape of his neck.

"What would I have been supposed to do if that had happened?"

His vulnerable tone hit me square in the chest and I

brought my gaze to his, noticing wetness gleaming on his cheeks.

Fuck, what have I done?

I moved my hands from his neck to cup his face and leaned forward, sending his fingers shifting inside me.

I pressed a light kiss to his lips. "*Lo siento mucho, mi cielito.* I didn't want to lose you if my plan took a wrong turn. I couldn't risk losing you," I whispered, my heart lodging in my chest, emotions clogging up my throat.

He softened a little at my words, his forehead dropping to mine, his pumps slowing as he inspected my face, attempting to see if I was telling him the truth.

Whatever was etched on my face seemed to fuel him. Muttering a curse, he slipped a third finger inside, stretching me even wider, the pricks of pain quickly transforming into pleasure.

I opened my mouth and Theo dipped down, capturing my pleasurable sigh with his.

He grabbed my thigh, hiking my leg around his hip, my heel digging into his ass. We stared deep into each other's eyes as he sent his fingers sliding farther in, fucking me in quick, hard strokes. His thumb landed on my clit simultaneously, drawing desperate circles.

My hands shot out from my sides to cradle the back of his head. I snaked my fingers through his curled strands and tugged.

I drew in a shallow breath as another orgasm steadily

climbed. I clenched around his fingers, and his mouth parted on a breathy *fuck*, his erection nudging me.

We moved against each other while he devoured my mouth as if he were trying to brand himself with my taste. Sparks flew through my veins, leaving a buzzing wake all over my body.

"More, Theo. I need more."

"I know, *mi alma*. I know," he groaned in my ear, nipping my earlobe before kissing me again.

I latched onto his bottom lip, sucking on it before I bit down *hard*. My hands reached for the front of his slacks, dragging his zipper down and slipping a hand inside. I gripped him tight and he jolted in my palm.

I slowly stroked him from the base all the way up to his tip, feeling pre-cum oozing from it. I swiped my thumb over it and used it as a lubricant on the way back down.

His jaw flexed in response, his nostrils flaring. His hunger was palpable, clearly letting me know he wanted more.

"Stop playing and take me out," he whimpered, the sound drowning against my neck.

God, I love that sound.

"Don't tell me what to do." I moved my hand up his length for a few more strokes, moaning at the feeling of him in my palm.

I needed him inside of me. *Now.*

I freed his cock and tapped it over his thumb that was still stroking my clit.

He jolted at the contact, gripping my thigh harder. "Easy, Sofia. You're gonna make me come."

"Then put it inside of me," I said, squeezing his dick as I ground harder against his hand.

I was right at the edge when he slid his fingers out, pushing my hand away.

He grabbed the base of his dick, giving it a single stroke, swiping my arousal along himself. I shot a frustrated glance at him, but before I could protest, he slammed into me.

"Oh my *God*." I gasped, closing my eyes, the pressure of him inside sending me into an intoxicating bliss.

His mouth was back on mine, devouring me before he pulled all the way to the tip and lingered, breaking our kiss, my eyes snapping open.

"Do *not* rob me of seeing you come. Now, keep your eyes on me and give me another one," he commanded, and I nodded, breathing heavily.

He dropped a small kiss to my lips and slid back in. His hand moved to hike the leg wrapped around his waist farther up, pushing it until my knee was against my chest, and the pressure grew to an almost unbearable level until he plunged deeper into my pussy, hitting a spot I didn't even know existed.

"*Fuck me*," he groaned from the tight fit.

My standing leg shook as he continued sinking his

cock inside of me. We kept our gazes locked as he drove into me. "That's it, *mi alma*, come for me again."

My toes curled, and my hips bucked against him as my pleasure reached a new high.

"Theo, I'm so close..." I begged, my heart thundering.

"Then let go, *mi alma*."

The weight of his body on mine combined with the way he was looking at me was too much to handle. I dropped my forehead to his, and we both inhaled sharply. My orgasm took over, and my cunt spasmed so tight around him, I almost blacked out.

"Yeah, Sofia, just like that... that's my girl," he said, rocking into me while peppering my jaw with rough kisses, his teeth nipping at the skin, prolonging my release.

The only thing that brought me back was his warm cum painting my cunt. Breathless, I didn't move, not that I would have been able to anyway. He loosened his grip, my leg resting again at his hip.

I felt warm cum trickle down my thigh and glanced down, his eyes following my gaze.

Still inside, his cock jumped, and Theo's eyes glittered with mischievous thoughts, a growl escaping his lips as he nipped my bottom lip.

"Told you one day I'd send you back to him with my cum still dripping out of you."

I gave him a nudge, chuckling at his misplaced joke, but he cupped both sides of my face, and I brought mine over his. He leaned down, kissing me softly before pulling back, his brows bunched together.

"Theo, what's wrong?" I asked, looking into his eyes, concern filling my chest at his fearful expression.

"Promise me you'll never leave me again."

I leaned into the palms of his hands and promised not to leave him.

But when I woke up the next morning to an empty, rumpled bed, he'd been the one who'd left me.

CHAPTER 37
THEO

I lay still on my couch, gaze set on the ceiling, watching intently as the blades from the fan whirled around.

I'd been doing this every night for the past three days, my mind replaying every single moment we had together, never giving me a break. I unraveled every memory we'd shared, trying to stare at them from different angles. I sat awake at night, trying to figure out if there was any truth to anything she'd told me.

How could I trust her moving forward when I felt like everything we ever had was founded on a lie?

My mind drifted back to the night of Victor's murder.

Jaxon had had his wife pick him up from the venue, while I'd told Omar that I'd get home on my own, letting him spend the rest of his weekend with his family. Once the coast had been clear, Sofia and I had driven back to the Morales residence.

After showering, washing away any traces of her crimes, we'd both gotten into bed and since I couldn't fall asleep, I'd spent the whole night watching her, reminding myself of the person I loved.

But the more I'd stared at her, the more the betrayal from her endless lies and games had settled in, my heart agonizing as the seconds passed. Instead of the peace she'd always brought me, I'd felt a weight settling on my chest, depriving me of air, until it eventually became suffocating.

I'd needed to get out of there, needed to process everything, so before she even woke up, I'd been long gone.

I wasn't sure if I'd made the right decision, but everything hurt.

Everything about her had been different that night. It'd felt like the world had tilted on its axis and I'd stumbled into a parallel version of my life.

From the way she'd carried herself, the way she'd talked, to the way she'd pulled that trigger with no hesitation. Everything about her had seemed different and I hadn't been able to recognize her anymore.

But what really hurt the most was that she hadn't thought she could trust me. That she hadn't trusted me enough to help her or even just be there for her.

Her mistrust splayed my heart open, bringing out something I'd buried deep.

I'd always felt like no one could possibly love me, that I wasn't deserving of love. But then, she came along. She made me feel like there was a possibility of being loved, that *I* was deserving of love.

Now, she was making me doubt that. Had she ever really loved me if she couldn't trust me with her demons?

She never even told me she loved me, my brain mocked me.

My brain was waging war. A part of me clung to the fact that she'd left me and lied, but a larger, louder part of me, the man in love with her, drowned in a well of guilt that only seemed to deepen.

I made her promise not to leave me again, and yet I did exactly that to her.

I loved her despite the feelings of betrayal she'd implanted in my heart, but I didn't know if I could trust her.

I thought I could put it past me and forgive her, but I needed time away. It would be unfair to her to start our future with any resentment on my end.

And right now, I didn't know where I stood.

A loud ringtone jolted me from my thoughts, but I let it ring. My mother had been calling me nonstop ever since I'd relieved myself of my bodyguard duties. I'd ignored her repeated phone calls, knowing she'd be able to decipher what was wrong immediately, and I wasn't up for any interrogation.

My phone rang again and I scrubbed my hands over my face, sitting up on the couch to pick up. Noah's name lit the screen, the blue light illuminating the dark space.

Why did he always have to call so late at night?

Groaning, I picked up the phone and lay against the back of the couch. "Yes?"

"Why aren't you answering?" Noah muttered.

"Noah," I warned.

"Open up." *Click.* Confused, I looked at my phone screen. *What the fuck?*

A knock resounded in the room and I glanced toward my front door, finding his face peering in through one of the large windows in the living room.

Muttering a curse, I dropped my phone on the couch and headed toward the front door, then swung it open.

"What is it with you and late-night visits?"

He glanced down at my clothes and then into my place. "You look like shit."

I'd been wearing the same outfit for the last few days, barely able to shower and eat, sulking on my couch all day.

Although he had a valid point, I chose to ignore his dig. "Get to your point." I grunted.

He shoved past me, marched to the couch, plopped down on it, and propped a foot against his knee.

"Victor Morales is dead," he finally said.

"I know." The door shut behind me as I passed behind him, heading for the kitchen.

Grabbing us beers from the fridge, I popped them open against the counter, then tossed the caps into the recycling bin before walking back into the living room.

"Why aren't you with his wife?" he asked.

I swallowed around the thick knot that'd formed in my throat at the mention of Sofia.

"Contract's over," I lied, handing him a bottle before taking a seat on the chair across from him.

I took a large gulp, the cold liquid making its way down my throat.

Noah hummed before taking a sip from his own. He was silent for a few minutes as he just watched me, analyzing me.

I rolled my neck, uncomfortable under his scrutiny, waiting for him to continue.

Instead, I decided to break the silence. I'd overheard Sofia mention their name briefly that night, but despite my searches, their connection with Victor Morales was still a mystery.

"Have you ever heard of the name Barrera?" I asked.

He startled at my question. "No. Why are you asking?"

"Just something I overheard."

"Now tell me what happened between you and Olivia Morales?"

My brows drew down in confusion at his dismissal. I squinted my eyes, questioning whether I should push it or not. After another long silence, I'd settled on the latter, deciding to put the questioning on the back burner for now.

"I'll give you a guess," I grumbled, taking another sip.

"She's Sofia."

I placed my bottle on the wooden surface, staring down at the table. I ran my fingers through my hair, the cavity in my chest closing in, twisting my heart at the mention of her name.

"She is." I scoffed.

"And?" he prompted.

I looked up at him, meeting his gaze. "And nothing. She lied," I said, not hiding the irritation in my voice anymore.

"You should talk to her."

I shook my head. "I can't."

"Yes, you can." He sighed, getting up and making his way to the door.

He lingered, his hand clutching onto the door as he looked over where I was sitting.

"Listen, I might not be the best at giving advice in that department, but if there's one thing I know, it's that you shouldn't let whatever happened take her away from you again."

He flicked his gaze away, as if lost in thoughts before shaking himself out of wherever he went. "You'll just end up regretting it," he said quietly.

The door closed behind him with a soft click, his last words echoing around the empty space.

I made my way back to the couch and lay on it once again, resuming my previous position before he'd interrupted.

For the next few hours, I mulled over his words, realizing he was right.

The ink etched on my skin was the last thing I saw before I drifted to sleep.

It'd been two weeks. Two weeks of not seeing her. Two weeks of not speaking to her. Two weeks of not having her in my arms.

I'd tried drowning myself in work, picking up more clients than I could handle at a time, trying anything that would keep my mind off the fact that I missed her. But nothing seemed to work. Nothing seemed to replace the hurt and confusion she'd caused.

Everywhere I looked, reminders of her infiltrated my mind. She occupied every space.

To add to it, I drove by her place every day, waiting, *hoping*, to catch a glimpse of her with unfortunately no luck.

I know, *pathetic*.

It would be so easy to just get out of my car and be with her. To slide back into what we once were, to have her in my arms. But how much worse would it be if she walked away again.

My mind and heart were at an impasse. On one hand, my heart *wanted* to march inside and get her back, while my mind wanted to preserve my heart from breaking all over again.

She'd always been mine, but did she see me as hers?

In reality, it wasn't that I didn't believe in what we shared at the cabin. She'd finally felt like mine again, but I didn't know whether I could trust it.

If I was honest with myself, I was scared to trust her. She'd left me once. What would stop her from doing it again?

I'd convinced myself that if I could distract myself by being mad at her, the pain that came from longing for her would dissipate enough for me to work through it. I'd made a half-hearted attempt to hold onto my anger since it made it easier not to feel the hurt quite as deeply, but it was slowly bleeding away every day.

A few days after my conversation with Noah, I'd finally called my mother back, apologizing for missing her calls. She'd started asking about Sofia, but I'd just kept brushing off her questions. I could sense she'd wanted to push, but diving into that conversation would only add fuel to the fire.

Turning the ignition off, I walked out of my car and up the driveway, glancing up at the property I'd built. I'd bought the place a few years prior and spent months remodeling it until it was perfect.

Until it was exactly how I remembered *she* wanted it.

All these years, I'd found solace in living in something that reminded me of her, but now it was just pure torture.

I unlocked the door and walked inside, meeting a deafening silence. I desperately needed to get out of this place, just for a little while.

The next morning, I was on the road, driving to the only place that helped me heal in the past.

Despite the trust I had in her being tarnished, my love for her was still there. I hoped that after a stay at the cabin, I'd finally get her back.

CHAPTER 38

SOFIA

Forty-eight hours after I'd killed *my husband*, I'd showed up at the station hysterical, demanding they find him. They'd taken down my statement and after confirming my airtight alibi, they'd begun their search for him.

Less than twenty-four hours later, they'd found his body rotting at the docks. The ME had released Victor's body quite quickly after the police closed their investigation.

No one really had questioned what happened that night. They'd seen the dried bloodied hole decorating Morales's forehead and simply connected the dots, blaming rivalry for his murder.

After his funeral last week, I'd arranged his affairs, dismissing his staff with enough money to last them until they got back on their feet. Selling the house had been a bit more complicated since it had been tied to his company, but his partners eventually declared bankruptcy once they'd found out that he'd been dealing in some shady business all these years, running their accounts dry.

It'd been exactly two weeks since I last saw Theo. Just two weeks and it felt like years already, every minute apart chipping away at my sore heart.

Ever since I'd woken up to an empty bed the next morning, I'd been reeling with how to approach Theo. I was still trying to figure out how to explain everything.

How I could begin to fix what *I* had broken when I wasn't even sure if I still had all the pieces to mend it in the first place?

Truthfully, I'd been cowering away in the house because I was afraid of his rejection. It wasn't like I could blame him, not after I left and lied to him repeatedly.

But I wanted him. I just didn't know how to win him back.

It was still early in the morning when I slid the glass doors in the kitchen open. Cold wrapped around me, a shiver running across my body as I made my way across the yard.

I pushed the door of the pool house open and stepped inside, his distinctive scent hitting me, invading my senses.

The hollowness that had formed in my chest that morning when I'd woken up alone resurfaced. The dull ache I'd tried pushing away was growing and expanding over me.

I glanced around his former space, the remnants of his presence still lingering in the air. I walked over to his bed, lowering myself to the mattress, and grasped at the sheets that still faintly smelled like him.

It felt like soon enough, his presence would completely vanish, and I didn't know if that was for the best. I clung to the sheets harder, a tear escaping, tracing a burning path down as I closed my eyes.

I'd given him space because if there was any chance of an *us*, I needed to know that when Theo looked at me, he would see *me* and not the years of lies I'd put us through.

I'd wanted to give him more space, but I was done doing that. I didn't want to wait any longer. I wanted the opportunity to apologize, tell him how sorry I was for everything.

I left the pool house and pulled my robe tighter against my chest as I jogged across the lawn, quickly closing the patio door behind me to avoid any more of the frigid air following me inside.

I swiped my keys off the counter and climbed into my car.

After a quick search for his address, I'd driven by his

place, but the driveway had been empty. After waiting outside for an hour with no sign of movement inside, I came straight here. I'd memorized the address after we came here a few weeks ago and decided to give it a try.

The thought of being here without him weighed against my chest, but I pushed it aside, knocking on the wooden door. I stood there, on his family's doorstep, hoping they knew where he was.

"Olivia?" she greeted me, surprise etching her features.

"Umm... it's actually Sofia," I confessed, giving her a weak smile.

Anxiety filled my veins as the seconds passed, her expression unreadable.

"Come in, *cariño*," she finally said, breaking the silence that had been surrounding us.

His mother opened the door wider, motioning for me to come inside. The door clicked shut behind me as warmth wrapped around my cold body, the smell of bread baking filling the air.

I followed her into the living room and plopped down next to her on the cream couch, staring anywhere else but at her.

I fidgeted, playing with my hands as I glanced around the room, my gaze landing on a picture with all of them.

They all looked so happy, so *normal*. My heart squeezed at the memory of a similar picture I had safely tucked in my wallet. Maybe one day I'd have that.

Have that with him, my heart hoped.

"Sofia." The use of my real name jolted me out of my thoughts, and I twisted to the side to face her.

"Is," she hesitated, concerned. "Is everything okay? Are you okay?" she finally asked.

I looked up, her question taking me by surprise. It had been a long time since someone had asked me if I was okay.

"Yes." I sighed, feeling guilty that she was concerned about me when I was the one who broke her son's heart.

"I'm looking for Theo," I mumbled under my breath. "I went to his house, but he wasn't there, so I thought he might be here."

"I'm sorry. I haven't seen my son in two weeks. We talked on the phone briefly last week and I could tell something was wrong, but I didn't want to push him. My son has a stubborn tendency to shut down when he's hurt. I've learned the hard way to let him come to me on his own."

My throat tightened, guilt filling at the thought that I was the cause behind why she hadn't seen her son in a while.

This was all because of me. All because I'd kept secrets from him, pushed him away.

I looked down, focusing on my hands to try and keep my tears at bay. "He's mad at me. Honestly, I can't blame him," I whispered, my voice slightly breaking at the end, my eyes glistening with unshed tears.

She cupped my cheek with one hand, her gesture filled

with affection that I'd missed, reminding me of when my mother would comfort me.

"Ah, *cariño*, if there's one thing I'm sure of, it's that my son could never hate you."

The term of endearment pushed a tear to escape, her thumb coating with the salty mixture. Before I could stop it, another tear fell, and another. She swiped her fingers over my cheek, brushing them away.

"I don't know what happened between you two, but I know my son loves you. I saw it the first time you came here with him. He couldn't keep his eyes off you. And I can see that you love him just as much."

Eleonora's statement resonated deep inside my rib cage, igniting hope within my soul.

Maybe, just maybe, there was still hope. Maybe I hadn't lost him completely.

I swallowed the knot in my throat as more tears slipped down and nodded weakly. Her arms wrapped around me, and I mimicked her gesture shortly after.

I still wasn't used to being hugged, but this felt good. We sat there, fixed in an embrace. I closed my eyes and for a brief moment pretended she was my mother, holding me to her while giving me advice on how to go after the man I'd spent years loving.

My face was pressed against her chest as the illusion slowly faded away.

I finally cleared my throat, pulling away from her embrace. "Do you know where I could find him?"

"There's only one place I know my son would go if he was trying to escape."

The cabin.

She tucked a loose curl behind my ear, softly tugging at my chin for me to look at her.

Our gazes collided, hers full of regret as she confessed. "My husband died from a heart attack when my youngest son Santi was born. I was a mess. I barely could care for myself, let alone two kids and a newborn."

She paused, her eyes filling with tears. "Theo took over, taking care of us and helping me through my grief."

She wiped at her gleaming cheeks. "I wasn't myself and would lash out very easily. He shouldn't have had to shoulder the responsibility so young, and I regret my actions every day because it pushed my son to retreat within himself."

She paused again and I wrapped my hands around her, hoping it would bring an ounce of comfort. "My beautiful Theo hasn't felt love very often in his life and feels undeserving of it. I try to write my wrongs every day, reminding him how much he's loved. But when you spend years feeling unloved, it starts to sink in deep and embed itself in your heart."

And me leaving him and lying only reinforced that notion. *Fuck.*

I hugged Eleonora one last time before heading to my car. Once inside, I plugged my phone into the system and dialed Valentina's number. On the third ring, she finally answered.

"I'm busy," she said, her sigh bleeding through the line, her typing loud in the background.

I huffed at her response, adjusting the heat in the car. "I need you to find an address for me."

Valentina's typing stopped, and I heard her taking me off speaker, connecting me to what I assumed was her earpiece. "Can't find it on your own?"

Silence filled the line, and she chuckled, amused by my discomfort. "Let me guess, you're looking for your bodyguard."

My insides tensed, not liking that she automatically knew who this was about. "My *ex*-bodyguard. He stopped working for me two weeks ago," I murmured.

"So what do you need me for?" she asked, and I could feel her smirking.

Swallowing, I confessed. "I don't have my equipment, so I need you to look into the bureau's database and find any properties owned by a Theodore Alvarez. Or anything linked to his family."

"Let me see what I can do," she replied and before I could say anything else, she ended the call.

A few minutes later, my burner pinged with two addresses, one of them being his place, which I'd already visited earlier.

I gripped the steering and closed my eyes, blowing out

a slow breath before peeling my eyes open and ignoring the anxiety surfacing.

I entered the address in my GPS and pulled out of the driveway.

We'd waited seven years to be us and I wouldn't waste another second. I knew he probably didn't trust me anymore, but I would make him listen to me.

It's time for him to hear the full story.

CHAPTER 39

SOFIA

A few hours in, I pulled off the highway near Azilah, stopping quickly for gas before jumping back onto the road. Since the gray skies made it hard to tell how much time had passed, I peered at the display, noticing I was almost there.

I drove another hour on wooded two-lane roads before I slowed the SUV, merging into a single-lane road. I kept driving up the narrow entry until I found the small hill he'd driven up the last time we were here.

The rain had finally let up, only drops from the over-hanging pines splashing on the windshield as I navigated deeper into the forest, the tires catching deep grooves every once in a while.

It wasn't until a few minutes later that the trees finally thinned, revealing the small clearing where the cabin stood.

As I drove closer, I noticed that someone was here, grabbing bags from their trunk.

My heart soared at the sight of him. My Theo.

He quickly dropped the bags back into the trunk, retrieving his gun from the holster at his side and aiming it right at my car pulling into the small driveway.

I slowed my car down to a stop behind his truck. Turning the keys up, I cut the engine off and got out of the car, hands held high. His gun was still drawn up when his eyes crashed against mine.

My chest ached with a warmth so intense, it seared through me from the inside out.

I took the time to study him, my eyes roaming over his face, taking in the slight changes. I hadn't seen him like this in a long time, not since I'd watched over him the days following my *disappearance*.

His under-eye circles were enhanced, and a thicker stubble adorned his jaw, his tousled hair slightly longer.

Fuck, I missed him.

Those dark brown eyes assessed me from head to toe before colliding with my own again and he lowered his Glock, his defenses lowering once he registered it was only me.

His body was locked tight, but no emotion flashed on his expression, preventing me from getting a read on how he felt about me being there.

I'd pictured this moment repeatedly in my head on the

way over, but now that Theo was standing in front of me, I could barely utter a word.

The last time I'd seen him, he'd left the next morning. I'd stayed in bed all day, my mind running through endless scenarios. Although I'd been so angry at him at first, it had slowly dissipated throughout the day, settling into hurt, but I didn't blame him for leaving.

I would have done the same if I had been in his position, especially after learning about his childhood.

I'd wanted to apologize, to run after him and tell him my side, ask for his forgiveness, but I'd known I had to wait.

The air was charged between us, filled with so much that had been unsaid. So much that I hoped he would let me say, but the apology I'd rehearsed in my head on the way here was long-forgotten.

So instead, I took a deep breath, regaining my composure. I opened my mouth to speak, but he cut me off before I could say anything.

"Leave," he said gruffly, looking away before turning his back to me.

Well, that answered my question.

The forest seemed to be *so* quiet apart from my thundering heart before rain started to drizzle, forming a faint mist around us.

My heart kicked into overdrive as he closed his trunk, leaving his groceries behind. He stepped away from me and my chest squeezed tight, my ribs threatening to strangle my lungs. He took another step and panic seized me.

I shook my head, my mouth opening on a ragged breath as I approached him again.

"No," I said firmly.

He spun to face me, his dark eyes studying me. A few raindrops had collected across his skin, his rain-speckled lashes now curved low, sitting dark and heavy against his tanned cheeks.

He let out a breath. "Sofia, I don't have time for this."

He started to turn away again, but I stopped him by grabbing his arm. I didn't drive all the way here to have him turn me away.

"Make time."

His brow furrowed and his jaw tensed as he crossed his arms above his chest. "What do you want?"

A knot rose in my throat and I closed my eyes, letting his voice sink in after days of not hearing it.

"You," I whispered, my voice hoarse, peeling my eyes open. "*Te deseo*, Theo."

He reared back, his breath hitching at my words as if I'd struck him. It was hard seeing him so tired from our separation, but seeing him react like that to my words hurt even more.

A fire erupted inside me, burning brighter, fueling my next words. Theo had always doubted whether I'd loved him or not, if he was worthy of love, and instead of showing how worthy he was, how perfectly he was made for me, I'd gone and let him believe the same brutal lie he'd been telling himself all these years.

That I'd left because of him.

My heart hammered harder against my chest, the echo thumping in my ears. I took another deep breath and cut off whatever he was about to respond.

"I fucked up."

His eyes blazed with anger. I held up a hand, silently asking him to let me continue, needing to get the words out before I lost my nerve.

"You think I left because I didn't want you, but I left because I fell in love with you. Because I couldn't bring you down with me. Because I love you so much that I couldn't bear anything happening to you. I couldn't see your heart burn with mine on my way to seek retribution for my parents."

Theo stared at me, his eyes flicking back and forth between mine as my words slowly sank in. I didn't think he expected me to confess *that*.

"I needed to do it for me. *For them.*" My throat tightened, the words barely audible.

I looked up again, meeting his eyes once more. "I knew that if I told you, you would have said fuck it and followed me, destroying everything alongside me. But I couldn't ask you to sacrifice your career for me. Sacrifice yourself for me."

His expression turned ravaged. "Who gave you the right to make that decision for me?"

"Theo," I breathed. I moved to say more, but my words died in my throat when he spoke again.

"No, Sofia," he yelled. "I loved you. I was so in love with you, and you left. You're the love of my life and after everything, you just left. I couldn't *breathe* without you. Couldn't sleep without you. I *waited* for you, *searched* for you for *years*."

"You have to forgive me," I pleaded, but he refused to meet my eyes, his jaw clenching as he stared into the distance.

"I missed you every day. I kept looking for you. My mind kept reaching for you. My heart soared at the thought of you, grasping at any memories I had of *you*," he cried out, his face twisting with agony.

He ran his hand up through his hair, pulling at the strands, and glanced around. "Fuck, my *fucking soul* kept reaching for you, but whenever I was reeled back into reality, you were never there. I just kept losing you over and over again. The ghost of your presence haunting me day and night."

His jaw clenched as he stepped away. "I don't know if I can trust you," he confessed, ashamed. "I want you so much, *mi alma*, but I don't know if I can trust you not to leave me."

The nickname he gave me all those years ago flew from his tongue and speared through my middle. I sucked in a shaky breath, and tears sprang in my eyes, my chest squeezing so tight it felt like it was snapping my heart in half under his confession.

I stood there for a moment longer, closing my eyes and forcing myself to take a deep breath. I swallowed my tears down, refusing to let them fall until I got out everything I wanted to say.

I opened my eyes, pushed my shoulders back, and walked closer, pressing my body to his. I lifted my hands to his face and rested my palms against the sides of his face, framing it.

He closed his eyes at the contact.

"I'm so sorry, *mi cielito*," I said thickly. "I need you to give me another chance, to give us another chance."

Our eyes connected and my heart thundered against my rib cage, mustering the courage to finally utter the words I'd known about a long time ago.

"*Te amo tanto, mi cielito*," I finally confessed, my vision blurring from unshed tears.

I felt his body tremble against mine in response. He tried to look away, but I reached for his chin, bringing his gaze back to mine.

I waited for him to say something, *anything*.

But he didn't, his Adam's apple bobbing.

My eyes drifted to his full lips, and before he could say another word, I pressed a tentative kiss to the corner of his lips, pulling back right after.

"Sofia." My name came out on a broken whisper. His

hands flexed up, and the impulse to reach out for me halted, dropping them back to his sides.

"I—"

His words cut off when I leaned on my tiptoes again, now planting a soft kiss on his lips, waiting for a response. When he didn't return it, I ran my tongue against the seam of his lips, demanding entry.

A groan rolled through his chest and I slightly pulled back, whispering against his lips.

"Theo, please forgive me?" I asked, agony ripping through my heart.

My chest tightened at his silence. Theo opened his mouth to speak but paused, clamping it shut again, his jaw flexing from the motion.

The sky clouded over our heads and claps of thunder rumbled in the distance. The previously slow raindrops fell harder, the storm getting louder as sheets of rain started falling, instantly soaking us in their wake.

I kissed him again, my fingers curving around the nape of his neck, holding him closer. He took a shuddering breath, sagging into me.

Thunder boomed again, a flash of light illuminating the darkening forest for a fraction of a second behind him as he pulled away.

I looked up at him, his dark wet hair falling in front of his eyes. The longer I stared at him, the more my emotions became heightened by the silence around us, only the pelting rain and our harsh breaths breaking the silence.

My stomach flipped, the fear of losing him creeping in, mixing with the pain already present. I wasn't willing to lose him all over again.

All I had left was to pray that the rain would wash away my lies and allow us to have a clean slate.

CHAPTER 40
THEO

It was taking everything in me not to return her kiss, to drown myself in her and pull her lips into mine. My emotions were waging an internal battle within myself. The want to let her back in fiercely competing with the fear she'd leave me again.

"Theo?" she questioned, her bottom lip trembling at my silence, tears falling down her cheek and slipping through my fingers.

She looked up at me through her lashes. "Let me remind you that I'm yours. That I've always been yours."

My eyes searched hers as I towered over her, the vulnerability and remorse clear in her expression. Reaching out, I gently cupped her face and bent down, swiping her tears away.

"Please don't cry, *mi alma*. I'm sorry for failing you. I'm sorry for not coming to you sooner. I was devastated when you left, but I was more angry at myself for not being there when you needed me."

She closed her eyes, leaning into my touch.

"*Mi cielito…*" her words trailed off as I brushed my lips against hers, a whispered touch that ignited a fire in my veins.

"Promise me something?"

"Anything."

"No more leaving."

Her tears fell harder as her hands came up to rest above mine. "No more leaving."

When I arrived a few minutes before she did, I had already started to regret coming and was about to pack to go to her when she showed up, completely derailing my plans.

I still couldn't believe she came for me. For most of my life, I'd felt undeserving of the kind of love she offered me

I kissed her. I kissed her because I had to. I kissed her because I wanted to. Because I *needed* to come home.

She parted her mouth on a soft sigh, her hands clutching my wet shirt as she melted into me.

My hands were still cupping her jaw as our lips tangled with each other. My hands then moved down, and I wrapped one around her lower back, pulling her tighter against me, while the other found its place at the side of her neck.

I groaned as my tongue delved into her mouth, kissing her harder. My thumb instinctively drew circles against her pulse point, assuring myself that she was real. That she was really here.

A tiny whimper broke from her chest from what felt like relief, her body arching into me, our bodies starved for each other.

I pulled back to breathe and laid my forehead against hers, memorizing this moment in any way, shape, or form that I could, needing to hear those words again to make sure I wasn't dreaming the first time she'd said them.

"Say it again," I said against her lips, my voice deep and strained.

As the words *te amo* came out, I locked my gaze with hers and whispered the words I'd been dying to tell since I first laid eyes on her seven years ago.

"*Te amo, Sofia. Siempre te he amado.* I first fell in love with you when we fought over who was the better cook and I've loved you ever since."

I wrapped my arms around her and hauled her off her feet, pinning her to my chest, the wet fabric of our shirts clinging together.

Her legs wrapped around my waist, locking us together as I walked to the door, rummaging through my pockets for the keys to unlock it.

She buried her head in the crook of my neck, nipping and licking at the skin there as I attempted to work the keys in. I muttered under my breath for the door to unlock and sighed in relief when I heard the click.

Finally.

I shut the door behind me with my foot and stepped out of my shoes, reaching behind my back for hers. I then carried her straight to the bedroom, not bothering with how cold the place was.

A problem for later.

I slanted my mouth over hers, my tongue delving deeper to tangle with hers, her body surrendering to mine as a delectable moan left her lips.

I sat on the edge of the bed as she straddled me. My hands pulled at the hem of her soaked shirt, dragging it up until it was whipped off her head and sailing across the room, landing on the floor with a wet thump.

My mouth latched onto her neck, kissing and nipping while her hands reached down to pull my own shirt off. The heat of her skin pressed into mine as her hands roamed my skin, tracing up my arms and over my shoulders and chest.

My hands splayed over her spine as I brought her closer to move my mouth to the swell of her breast. My fingers latched onto the back of her laced bra, working it free. I cupped my hands under her breasts, bringing them to my mouth and sucking.

"Oh, *God.*"

I gently bit down on a nipple and she mewled under my ministrations, her hips grinding against my erection, begging for friction.

"I want to hear my name, Sofia." I growled against her skin as I brought my attention to the other side.

"Theo," she breathed.

"That's it, *mi alma*. I'm the one you call for when you feel this good."

And then we were in a frenzy, competing in a desperate race to discard the remaining clothes off our bodies. She lifted her hips as I wrenched open the button of her pants, yanking the zipper down and dragging the denim down her legs. Stripping her jeans and socks off left her in nothing but matching lace underwear.

I ripped them off with a quick tug, then tossed them aside. Then, I claimed her mouth once more, standing up to lay her on the bed. I pulled away for a second to finish undressing, my cock springing free, aching for her.

I dragged my thumb between her drenched cunt before bringing it to my lips and sucking down on it.

I hummed. *Fuck, I missed her taste.*

"I'll eat you later, but I need to be inside you now."

"Yes," she begged, her hands reaching for me as I hovered over her. I reached between us, dragging the tip of my cock against her clit, and it sent a shudder through her body.

I lined myself with her entrance, slipping inside just barely, a shameless whimper ripping from my throat before I thrust all the way in.

Her back arched and she cried into my mouth.

"You always feel so good." I groaned against her lips.

She clung to my shoulders as my hands clutched her waist, my fingers digging into her as I pulled out and pumped my hips, harder this time before doing it again. I rocked into her faster, *more needy*, over and over again.

I grabbed her leg and pulled it above my shoulder, angling my hips so my groin could rub against her clit as I continued to fuck her.

I slowed my pace, withdrawing until only the tip was still inside her before thrusting my hips once, eliciting a sharp gasp from her swollen lips.

I brought my mouth down to hover over hers. "Can you feel me, *mi alma?*" I whispered, gliding my hand down her leg.

She angled her head, nipping at my lips. "Yes, I feel you."

I hummed. "Who owns this pussy, Sofia?"

I rolled my hips into her, and she shuddered against me, a slew of whimpers falling from her lips.

"You," she gasped.

My eyes traced down, watching our bodies together, my cock sinking into her tight cunt.

She was a fucking masterpiece no artist could ever do justice to.

I loved this woman. And she loved me.

My vision blurred from the acute grip she had on my cock, the pleasure igniting in my body, my soul overwhelmed with a feeling of pure happiness. Just like it was every time I was in her presence whether that was just being with her or inside her.

"I'm close, Theo," she cried out.

My control slipped and I let myself drive harder and faster into her, my head falling back, eyes rolling. A groan escaped from the feel of her perfect cunt wrapped around me.

I dropped my chin, looking down at her. "You were made for me. Your pussy was created for my pleasure and my pleasure alone. Isn't that right, Sofia?"

"Theo." She inhaled sharply, her head falling back, her eyes shutting.

My hands slid up, my fingers grabbing the skin between her hip and thigh, pinching.

"Eyes on me, Sofia," I ordered.

I slid my mouth to her ear, satisfaction filling me at the way she shivered beneath me.

"And I asked you a question." I bit on her earlobe.

"Yes, Theo. Just as you were made for me."

Sweat coated our skin. Her screams entwining with my own moans battled with the noises deriving from our flesh slapping against each other. The crescendo of our pleasures echoed throughout the cabin.

I switched between kissing and nipping her lips, hovering close above them, making sure I swallowed every noise she produced.

"You take it so fucking good, baby." I praised. "That's it, be my good girl and come for me."

Her eyes joined mine in an unwavering grip as she clutched hard against me, my forehead collapsing to hers as she neared the edge, ready to leap.

My thumb landed on her clit, rubbing it faster, desperately chasing her toward it.

Her eyes rolled back and she broke, a scream releasing from her throat, and I followed right behind her.

"*Fuck.*" I buried the sound in her neck, my orgasm rocking through me and stealing my breath as ropes of cum filled her.

We both came down at the same time shortly after, breathless, my head still swimming from the waves of emotions.

I kissed her forehead. "I love you, Sofia Maria Herrera."

She kissed me. "I know," she whispered. "I love you, Theodore Anas Alvarez."

I grinned at her use of my full name.

This had to be what utter bliss felt like and I felt so privileged to bask in it with her. The feeling seeped inside my chest, cracking open from how much I was addicted to her.

I wrapped her legs around my waist, still deep inside her as I forced myself up and into the bathroom.

We had sex again in the shower before I cleaned us and tucked us back into bed.

I slept peacefully for the first time in weeks and when I woke up the next morning, she was still there.

I never thought I would find happiness, but then she came into my life, showing me that we all deserved to be loved.

EPILOGUE

SOFIA - THREE YEARS LATER

It was Theo's and my second year anniversary today. Two years filled with more love and happiness than I could have ever asked for. After losing my parents, I'd never thought I'd be able to have a family, to *feel* again.

After coming home from the cabin, we'd wasted no time and I'd moved in with him.

And then, a few weeks later, he'd proposed, and we'd gotten married in a private ceremony by the beach with his close family present.

He'd wanted to invite Noah, but he'd been away on an assignment, unable to attend. I'd thought of inviting Elena since she'd been like a mother figure to me while we'd worked together, but I wasn't comfortable risking her new identity.

It had been a difficult day, with not having my parents with me, not having my dad to give me away, but I knew they were watching over me, at peace that I'd found my person.

Besides, Theo had made sure to include them in our ceremony. He'd left two of the front seats, those where my parents would have been, empty, my mother's favorite flowers wrapped around them.

He never ceased to amaze me.

Theo knew how important having my parents with me that day was and he'd given me the opportunity to have a piece of them with me. He'd made our day even more special.

I could hear him in the kitchen already, dishes rattling as he cooked. He'd tried to teach me time and time again, but I was still as helpless as I was when he'd first attempted.

Besides, I loved watching him at work in the kitchen. There was something about watching my husband cook that just always did it for me.

I made my way out of our bedroom and strolled down the hallway, my mouth already watering at the scent of frying dough. I stepped into the open kitchen, only to find my husband hovering over the stove, two steaming small glasses of tea on the counter next to him.

The image of him shirtless, wearing only a pair of black boxer briefs sent a low fire blooming in my core. They molded his strong thighs and backside, the waistband clinging to the definition of his hips.

That is all mine.

I walked over to him, wrapping my arms around his middle as I placed a kiss between his shoulder blades.

"Hi," I said against his back, snuggling my face into him.

I briefly closed my eyes, breathing in his heady scent, wanting it to cling to me like a second skin. I loved waking up to his scent on my skin. It felt like having him with me at all times, even when we were apart.

"Morning, pretty girl."

He glanced over his shoulder, a small smile tugging at the corner of his mouth. He bent his head down and I rose up on my toes for him to place a small kiss to my lips.

"What are you cooking?" I asked and as if on cue, my stomach growled.

He lifted his arm so I could snuggle up at his side. "Your favorite," he said, smiling in my hair before pressing a kiss at the side of my head.

I looked down to see him flipping the *msemen* in the pan, a stack already piled on the side of the counter.

"Need any help?" I asked, knowing he'd turn my offer down.

He chuckled. "Baby, we both know the answer to that." He delivered a small slap to my ass. "Go sit your pretty ass down while I finish this."

I playfully smacked his arm and grabbed one of the cups, making my way behind the island that was covered in flour, a few small balls of dough sitting on top.

I plopped down on one of the high chairs. "Does this have *shiba?*"

Laughter erupted in the room. "Not after the last time you spent thirty minutes lecturing me that it ruined the taste for you."

I should be annoyed, but his laughter sent a flurry of warmth through my body. "It's not funny. You hadn't told me and I had been so excited to have some tea, only to discover you'd added some."

"Will never make that mistake again. I promise." He chuckled, returning to his task.

I took a sip and watched him move through the kitchen with command and grace, something I definitely would never be able to do. My skills were more valuable in other areas.

He stalked over to the pantry, grabbed the honey and butter and put a small amount into a bowl before placing it in the microwave to heat up.

He then made his way to the counter. His forearms flexed as he flattened and spread the dough, preparing more squared pieces.

"You look good in the kitchen, husband." I never got over being able to call him that.

His gaze drifted up as he folded a piece. "And you look better bent over that counter, *wife.*"

His eyes darkened and memories of when I'd come home last night after a day at the teaching center flooded my mind. I'd barely made it inside the kitchen where he'd been cooking dinner, when he stopped what he was doing to bend me over, making me come more times that I could remember.

I chuckled nervously, blushing at his words. Even after three years together, he still had the same effect on me.

I spun the chair I was sitting on around, facing away from him, looking around the space. *Our space.*

While I'd been in protective custody with him, he'd always encouraged me to think about my future and what I'd want from it, where I'd want to be.

One day, we'd spent the entire night just talking and I'd absent-mindedly described my perfect home.

Only to discover years later that he'd built it for me, something I'd only noticed the day I'd moved in.

We parked in front of a two-story house, with a Mediterranean exterior. He got out of the car while I admired the place, waiting for him to open the door before getting out myself.

He didn't like when I opened my own doors, so I obliged whenever we were together.

"Why are you being so quiet?" I asked as he reached for my hand, the car door clicking shut behind me. I'd been here briefly the last time, but I'd been too preoccupied with watching him to take in his house.

"Tell me what you see," he said, gesturing toward the house.

I studied the house more closely. Large windows, cream

stucco walls, a red clay tile roof, the wooden door, the blue-grayish accents.

I described the house for him and looked up at him, confused. "I don't understand."

He came closer behind me, wrapped his arms around my waist, and I rested my head on his chest.

He cleared his throat. "Look closer."

It finally dawned on me when he spoke again. "It was going to be ours. Well, it can still be if you agree to move in with me."

THE SOUND of the microwave dinging jolted me out of my thoughts. My gaze drifted back to Theo as he took the bowl with the melted ingredients out and opened one of the drawers. He grabbed a spoon to stir and combined them together.

"I love you, you know?"

"I know, *mi alma*." He glanced up at me, giving me a smile that only I was privy to.

The genuine openness and joy in Theo's expression still tugged at this part of me that I didn't know existed before I met him. After losing my parents, I never thought I'd have the opportunity to love again. To be happy again.

My happiness intensified when I remembered the gift I'd hidden in our closet that I would give to him later.

As I looked at him at work in the kitchen, I hoped he didn't mind the last secret I was currently keeping.

"I love you too," he said as he rounded the kitchen

island, a plate filled with the flatbreads drowning with honey and butter, exactly how I liked them. He placed the plate on the counter and stepped between my legs, towering over me.

His hands skimmed up my thighs until they rested against my hips. He pulled me closer and tilted my chin with his forefinger, placing a gentle kiss to my lips.

"Happy anniversary, Mrs. Alvarez."

"Happy anniversary, Mr. Alvarez."

He took the seat next to me, our legs intertwined as we ate and talked about his new case. This normalcy with him felt beyond perfect.

I can't wait for the little family we've created, I thought to myself as I rubbed my belly.

EPILOGUE
THEO - 6 MONTHS LATER

A crack of thunder pierced through the silence, and I blinked sleepily as lightning flashed through the room.

I looked down at Sofia next to me. She was curled on her side, tucked into me, her back plastered against my front as one of my arms rested around her waist.

The rain battered against the windowpanes and I felt Sofia breathing so peacefully next to me, still sound asleep, her dark curls swept over the top of her pink silk pillow.

My fingers skated over her belly, an indescribable happiness washing over me. It had been a little over six months since she'd surprised me on our anniversary, announcing that she was pregnant with our first child.

My chest tightened every time I looked at her growing

a life we'd created together. I'd always been in awe of her and found her more mesmerizing by the day.

I closed my eyes, overwhelmed by how lucky I was. I could barely wrap my head around all of this being real. We'd been married for almost three years and calling all of this mine was still pure bliss every time I realized it.

Mine.

My wife.

The house *I* built for *us*.

Our family.

After we found out she was pregnant, we finally went back to where she'd grown up and laid her parents to rest. It was the first time she'd seen her parents' graves. She hadn't had the ability before since we'd put her in protective custody right away and once she'd left, going back to Bal El Mansour would have been too risky.

We had a small funeral with just the two of us. She'd sat on the grass, staring at her parents' headstone the whole day, talking to them. Since I'd been here before to ask for their daughter's hand, I stood a few feet back, giving her the space I knew she'd need while still being not too far if ever she needed me.

The sun had been slowly setting down when she'd gotten up and we'd driven back to our hotel. The day had finally set in a few hours later when we'd been in bed and I'd spent the rest of it holding her as she'd cried and sobbed into my chest, sad over what was and what could've been.

It hadn't been easy for her, and even though I'd done anything I could to help her through her grief, I'd known the what-ifs would be something that would still flicker in the back of her mind.

It wasn't easy knowing that sometimes there was nothing I could do, but she always told me that me being there was more than enough and I just had to believe her.

A few months after Morales's death became old news, she started working at the center she'd volunteered at during their marriage. I knew it made her happy to be there for them because I could see the joy on her face every day when she came home.

Some days came with their obstacles, but for the most part, the last few years with her by my side had been the greatest years of my life.

She stirred next to me, pulling me out of my thoughts. Her body slid against mine, the white T-shirt she was wearing riding up, revealing her to me.

The room was dark except for the moonlight making the rain shimmer on our bedroom walls, showcasing the outline of her bare ass.

I squeezed her hip as she ground against my growing erection and my name escaped her lips on a moan, eliciting a deep desire in my chest.

Even after all these years, the want to possess her, to mark her, to *claim* her never tamed down. I still couldn't stop reaching for her when she was close, and I looked forward to crawling back into bed at night, knowing I would get to sleep and wake up next to her for another day.

I still wanted her now just as much as I'd wanted her ten years ago.

"Theo," she breathed out on a soft sigh, rolling against me again.

"Mmm," I said against the crown of her head, but she didn't answer.

She was still asleep and was probably having one of her dreams. She'd been having them more often these last few weeks, and I wasn't complaining.

My mouth latched onto the nape of her neck, kissing it softly as I glided my hand under the front of her shirt, up her stomach, and through the valley between her breasts.

I cupped them alternatively, my fingers toying with her nipples. I knew they'd been more sensitive recently, so I traded between squeezing and pinching them.

"Oh," she moaned and moved against my erection that was wedged between her ass cheeks, gliding up and down searching for more.

My hand trailed back down the planes of her stomach toward her drenched pussy, the tips of my fingers teasing her clit despite knowing she was already ready to take my cock.

I collected the wetness from her weeping cunt on my fingers and propped myself on my elbow, rubbing her arousal over my cock.

I grabbed her knee, opening her up by lifting her leg

and resting it over mine. I then grabbed my cock with my other hand and nudged her entrance.

"More," she whispered, her eyes still closed.

Slowly, I stroked my way inside, rolling my hips.

She shuddered against me, whimpers falling from her lips. Then I sank home, my eyes pinching shut from how good she felt. I rolled into her with a shallow thrust, nipping on her earlobe before sucking it between my lips.

I bit back a groan when her pussy clenched around my length, her pulse thrumming against her neck.

"So fucking good, *mi alma*," I whispered against her ear.

She finally peeled her eyes open, tensing for a second before relaxing, molding the curve of her ass deeper into me.

"Theo," she pleaded breathlessly, her voice hoarse from waking up. I withdrew all the way out before I thrust back deep inside her, pulling out a husky moan from her throat.

I snuck a hand back into her shirt, continuing my previous ministrations. My other hand made its way over her head to grab her hand resting there, holding it in front of her against the bed, our fingers linking, the similar tattoo etching both of our ring fingers peeking through.

She'd surprised me with it on the day of our wedding as I slid her ring in place, noticing the black inscriptions that hadn't been there previously. She'd had the three dots with my initials engraved on the other side, just as I had hers on mine.

I pumped and pumped my hips, the sound of my groin slapping against her ass filling the room, joining her sleep-addled moans, spurring me on. I slanted my hips, most likely hitting that spot inside of her she loved since her legs squeezed tighter together, making the sensation of being inside her that much better.

Her head tilted back and I caught her lips, kissing her. My tongue dove against hers, the sensation consuming me. I rolled my hips in a slow tempo, pleasure pooling down my spine as my fingers went from one breast to the other, giving them the attention they were craving.

"You consume me," I whispered into her ear.

I pinched her nipple and a cry rolled past her lips, her head kicking back as she came all over my cock.

I groaned into her neck, then bit where it met her shoulder as my thrusts grew faster and more relentless, the previous tempo I'd set long-forgotten as the pleasure that had previously settled at the base of my spine swelled.

My hips slapped against hers, the noise of me sliding in and out wet and sloppy. With one last solid thrust, a hoarse sound ripped out of my throat as I came, holding her to me.

I twitched inside her, ropes of cum filling her sweet pussy. She reached for my head, bringing my lips to hers and swallowing my groans.

With a gasp, I pulled my mouth away, using our joined

hands and my free hand to latch around her chest. Drawn into my frame, the warmth of her body seeped into my skin.

We stayed quiet for a moment, our harsh breaths filling the room. She settled her head under my chin and let out a deep sigh as I kissed the top of her head, the scent of warm vanilla and coconut swarming my senses.

I cupped her breast once again, my lips lingering at the space below her ear, which happened to be my favorite since her reaction to it was almost always immediate.

She tipped her head back, searching for my mouth. I found her lips and my tongue met hers, tasting, savoring her.

As the minutes dragged on, I hardened inside her again, and she instinctively drove back toward my hips, driving me deeper into her cum-filled cunt.

"I love you," I said against her mouth.

"I love you more, *mi cielito.*"

I ripped my mouth away as I pulled out of her, my cock protesting loudly.

"I want you on top of me," I urged her as I ran my palm up her leg before palming one of her cheeks. "Now."

She turned to face me and raised herself up, sliding a leg over my body, straddling me. She lifted her shirt over her head, revealing the hard little mound where our son or daughter sat.

Coming down, she hovered over me, her mischievous eyes colliding with mine.

She reached back, aligning my tip against her, her wet cunt still weeping with my cum.

She hovered above my cock and I was becoming impatient. I tried lifting my hips up, but she stopped me, pushing her hand down my stomach.

"Mr. Alvarez," she teased, nibbling my jaw, "you want your wife to ride you?"

I groaned in response, rolling my hips up into her. Her fingers trailed down my chest, and she dragged her nails lightly down my stomach, my skin coming alive under her touch.

"Please, Mrs. Alvarez. I need you," I whimpered against her mouth.

My moan got lost in her mouth as she sank onto me slowly. I sucked on her bottom lip as I grabbed her hips, urging her on.

She removed my hands from her, plastering them next to my head as she rocked back, sheathing herself completely onto me. My head kicked back in ecstasy.

She placed one of her hands on my chest as she rocked back and forth and soon, I started thrusting my hips up, kissing her mouth hard.

We were still making out when she came harder this time, and I joined right behind her, letting out a hoarse groan as I came again. She collapsed on me, both of us breathing harder.

My arms were wrapped around her back, her breasts plastered against my sweaty chest.

"I fucking love you, Sofia Alvarez," I murmured above her head.

"I know," she said, chuckling.

There were many things I loved about my wife, but her laugh was definitely up there.

I lifted her head off my chest, give her a quick kiss, and smiled against her lips.

One of my palms slid down the length of her spine, ending at the small of her back. I gently pulled her up and flopped her onto her back, then headed to the bathroom, where I grabbed a small cloth and wet it with warm water.

After cleaning us both, I tucked her back under the covers, and she snuggled against me.

My lips trailed down Sofia's spine and she let out a sleepy moan that had me sighing, a small smile tugging at my lips. I still couldn't believe this was my life, that I got to have the love of my life tucked into my arms.

She'd turned my life from something I was living to something worth living for.

THANK YOU FOR READING!

Enjoy *Nemesis*? Please consider taking a second to leave a review!

Book 2 in the Vendetta Series is coming soon.

Come chat about what you read! Join SeRaya's Warriors Facebook group: facebook.com/groups/serayaswarriors

JOIN SERAYA'S WARRIORS!

Authorseraya.com

Here's where you can chat all things SeRaya and get access to first looks, exclusive giveaways, and the best place to connect with me!

Instagram: instagram.com/authorseraya
Tiktok: tiktok.com/@authorseraya
Facebook Group: facebook.com/serayaswarriors
Pinterest: pinterest.com/authorseraya
Goodreads: goodreads.com/author/show/27810782.
SeRaya

ACKNOWLEDGMENTS

I can't believe I get to write this. I've always dreamed of being able to do it, but never thought in a million year that I'd say *fuck it* and just do it. You wrote a book and actually put it out there. You did it. I'm proud of you for finally putting yourself first and doing something for you. I love you.

To my friends, you know who you are. I'm eternally grateful for every single one of you. You've supported me and became a family that I never thought I'd have. The love and encouragement you have given throughout the time we've known each other is something that I will never forget. Thank you for being there every step of the way, for being my ride or dies and some of the best people I've ever known.

To my second half, my sister, I love you. I would have never thought that I'd meet a complete stranger and they'd become one of the most important people in my life. You literally keep me sane and I'm grateful every day to not only call you a friend, but to call you family. I love you so much sweet girl.

To my book special edition-partner in crime, I love

you. You are one of the best people I've ever met and I'm so grateful that the universe put us on the same path because I can't imagine my life without you in it.

To my pretty girl, you already know how much I love you and how grateful I am for your endless support. Thank you for always being there for me and bringing my book to life in music.

To Jess. I have so much to say but thank you for always answering when I call and letting me bounce my fifteen thousand ideas while I try to plot and add world-building at the last minute. I love you.

Baby girl. You already know. We don't do emotional, but I'm fucking grateful to have you in my life. I love you.

My sissy. Thank you for always being there for me and always pushing me to believe more in myself. Billboards we're coming xx

To Cat. I'm so grateful to have met you and thank you for bringing my baby to life with this gorgeous fucking cover. I can't wait to create more magic with you.

To my editor and proofreader, Emily: thank you for making my words shine and making this story the best it could be.

And last but not least, to you the reader. Thank you for taking a chance on my stories. The love you have shown me is beyond anything I would have ever imagined. None of this would have been possible without you lovelies and I cannot wait to see where we go next!

ABOUT THE AUTHOR

SeRaya is an author of romance books that are both dark and steamy, aiming to write stories that will give you the best of both worlds. She has a weakness for morally grey characters and happy endings. While darkness is what she loves most, she's a hopeless romantic at heart (but will deny it if you ask). Besides being cozied up with a good romance book, she enjoys rewatching her favorite tv shows and discovering new food places. She's happily single (because never settle for less), but busy with her many book boyfriends.

Made in United States
North Haven, CT
27 April 2023

35951169R00250